the
author's
table

My Name is John Singer

An Extraordinary Historical Romance

LISA G. SAMIA

proudly presented by

DESTINY WHISPERS PUBLISHING, LLC

TUCSON, ARIZONA

WWW.DESTINYNOVELS.COM

Author Copyright © 2016 by Destiny Whispers Publishing, LLC
LISA G. SAMIA, Author
MY NAME IS JOHN SINGER / Destiny Whispers Publishing, LLC
Copyright © DESTINY WHISPERS PUBLISHING, LLC / April 26, 2016
Special Historical Release First Edition / April 26, 2016

ISBN-13 # 978-1-953504-06-0
ISBN-10 # 1-943504-06-7

Executive Editor: Leslie D. Stuart /.DestinyRose-Reads.com
Cover Art License: BigStock Photos / www.bigstockphoto.com
Cover Art Design: LadyDestiny / Sr. Creative Director/ DWP, LLC

Destiny Whispers Publishing, LLC / Tucson, Arizona
AN EXTRAORDINARY JOURNEY ROMANCE NOVEL

www.DestinyNovels.com
www.DestinyAuthor.us
www.DestinyRose-Reads.com
www.LisaSamia.com

A review from author & playwright, Eric Swanson, co-author of the New York Times bestseller, *The Joy of Living.* Also book and lyrics for the play, *EDWIN: The Story of Edwin Booth*

"*My Name is John Singer* is a fascinating novel, rich in historical detail and nuances of character, time, and place. By turns tender, thrilling, and suspenseful, it is a beguiling work of historical fiction and a thoughtful exploration of love and redemption."

With deepest gratitude from
Author, Lisa G. Samia to Eric Swanson:

Thank you for your kind and generous support of "My Name
is John Singer," a fictional account of John Wilkes Booth.
The creative process is one born from desire, passion,
dedication and a relentless pursuit to produce *"that which
was not there before."* The process is both exhausting and
euphoric. And in this world where *like people find each
other*, how extraordinary it is that through your book and the
lyrics of **EDWIN, The Story of Edwin Booth**, an alliance and
friendship based upon the creative process and
all things Booth should indeed be forged.

Warmest Regards, Always

Lisa G. Samia, Author

For My Father
~~ Michael Donald Gentile

Acknowledgements:

To my husband Jim, for his love and support.

To Leslie D. Stuart for all her hard work and editing.
Destiny Whispers Publishing, LLC for their belief in this story.

To Terry Alford, Historian and Author of the award winning
book, *Fortune's Fool, the Life of John Wilkes Booth,*
for his kindness, support and encouragement.

And for the "Agnus Dei."

CHAPTER ONE

To survive war is to survive Hell.

~~ Emma Dixon

It was early May of 1865.

The young woman stood still, her blonde head slightly tipped to hear the field wagon approach on the uneven rutted roads that led to the hospital in Alexandria, Virginia. After working as a nurse here for three years, her ears were trained to listen for the signal that more men were coming who needed care and comfort.

During the war she had volunteered to serve, intending to do her part to help the Southern cause for only a few months, but the need for good medical staff was too great and the war lingered on for years.

Emma never left.

Releasing a heavy sigh as she watched the wagon coming into sight, exhaustion filled her heart.

It would be another long day.

Like every day since the war began, she endured endless hours at the hospital where the work to comfort and tend the wounded never felt complete. Endless days of watching men fall victim to the onslaught of brother against brother, friend against friend, and neighbor against neighbor in the American Civil War.

It broke her heart to hear stories of bravery and sacrifice whispered among the men staying here. Some tales were too heartbreaking to even repeat, stories Emma Dixon wished weren't true and she wanted to forget.

By all accounts of war news recently coming to them, the flow of wounded men would soon stop.

A Southern surrender had occurred.

Just one month prior at Appomattox Courthouse, Virginia, numerous witnesses brought stories of how the Confederate leader General Robert E. Lee gave over to the Union army, surrendering his forces into the hands of General Ulysses S. Grant.

The Civil War had left a bloody path across the United States.

The slaves were free now.

The South had rejoined the Union.

The war was over, yet this General Hospital in Alexandria remained open to receive the last vestiges of the injured Confederate army. Men lay injured across the countryside. The wagons brought them in as the wounded were found in the nearby forests and fields, some barely clinging to life.

As the wagon pulled to the wooden emergency doors of the hospital and she saw other hospital staff hurry to carry the wounded men inside, Emma walked faster. Brushing back stray blonde strands near her cheeks and forehead that had come loose from the intricate knot pinned at the nape of her neck, she tidied her appearance.

She would be needed soon.

Here, a triage nurse might be a man's last chance.

Tonight she had the evening shift, from dusk until midnight, the hours when an injured man had nothing to do but suffer, sleep or die.

Exhaustion and responsibility weighed heavy upon her slim shoulders.

The past few weeks of the war had been especially trying.

The Confederate surrender was welcome news, meaning an end to the conflict and suffering, but fast on its heels came the shocking news of President Abraham Lincoln's murder on April 14th at Ford's Theater in Washington, D.C.

The assassination was conceived and carried out by a Confederate sympathizer. But Emma also knew the famous young actor, John Wilkes Booth had paid mightily for his crime, having been murdered himself twelve days later, on April 26, by Boston Corbett of the Sixteenth New York Cavalry.

Stories claimed the assassin was shot through the neck, much like the martyred President. Booth ran from the law after his deadly deed in the theater, but the Calvary finally trapped him at Garrett's tobacco barn near Port Royal, Virginia. His fellow conspirators were also caught and now sat in a Washington prison awaiting their fate.

A military trial could certainly lead them to the gallows.

So much death.

It wears down the hearts of the living.

Those grievous thoughts saddened her heart as Emma reached the front doors of the hospital and wandered into the central corridor.

The suffering here felt overwhelming today.

For a moment she stood against the well-worn wall and leaned her cheek against it, feeling coolness the early spring evening brought, knowing it was a prelude to the wet summer heat that would soon come.

A brigade of injured men streamed by her, some carried on stretchers, some hobbling on makeshift crutches. Most men were alone, but some were lucky enough to arrive with comrades who felt unwilling to leave their injured friend.

Triage in this field hospital did not always carry a successful outcome.

Emma dreaded the numerous amputated arms and legs that would soon litter the hospital surgery ward, then would be carried away in wagons and buried.

Another loss of war that changed lives.

As she entered the triage ward, Emma saw a previously empty bed was now occupied by the last man brought in by a hospital attendant.

He sat upright in a cot, his face stained with sweat and dirt, the Confederate gray uniform threadbare. The man's expression was tight with lips firmly pressed in silent repose. His casted leg was dirty from the earth and stained red with blood from a possible bullet wound.

It was a sight all too familiar to her war-weary eyes.

Giving the man a curt nod, her mind remained focused upon others with deeper immediate need.

Tonight the numbers of injured and sick men were many, with few nurses to offer aid.

Emma yearned for the day when the broken men stopped arriving, for the night when the war, for her, would truly end.

She wove through the ward, stopping at various bedsides to change injury dressings, bring water, cool feverish faces and bodies, like she had done a thousand times before.

The hands of men needing help and comfort were held out to her, all seeking a touch of kindness she so readily gave.

Hours had passed.

Evening had turned into a warm spring night.

Suddenly she felt a slight shiver as if being touched.

Emma turned slightly, feeling commanded to look. The sensation was eerie, a command without words, motion, or sound. Yet she felt it as real as the air inside her lungs and her heart that quickly beat beneath her breast.

Scanning across the hospital ward, her gaze suddenly stopped short.

Then she saw him again.

It was the man with the threadbare uniform, the one with the broken leg and possible bullet wound. He still wore a reticent composed face. He sat upright in his bed several rows away, his dark eyes fixed on her face.

The commanding power in them drew her.

He bore no smile.

Yet it was compelling.

Emma met his bold stare, unable to turn away. She studied his face, now cleaned of the dirt and grime from earlier in the day.

Someone had shaved him. He was an average sized man with a lean, almost elegant form.

Those eyes captured her.

They were an unrelenting dark color like the depth of night, eyes that gave everything and promised nothing. That piercing gaze seemed to reach into the depths of her heart as if he knew the loneliness that had besieged her these three long years.

The boldness in their locked gaze should have felt uncomfortable.

She should have turned away.

Yet something warm stirred inside her heart, like recognition of something important and vital, bringing with it a strange and powerful attraction.

Emma had never known anything like this.

She lowered her emboldened gaze for a moment, but he still looked. The desire she felt from the man's eyes pulled her back to meet his stare without apology or regard for manners or decorum.

The corners of her lips curved, ever so slightly.

She was entranced, powerless to stop.

In answer, his brow arched, in a question and nearly a challenge.

Without any words or a single touch, Emma knew the man found her beautiful. It was flattering, but this handsome man was certainly not the first to look at her with lust in his eyes.

The good Doctor Bradley, the young and talented physician did it all the time.

But the young physician never made her heart race nor had the natural born charisma that made all other attractive men seem rough and unpolished, in comparison.

This man was different. Special.

She saw his left leg was recast and his wound re-bandaged. Emma hoped if it was a bullet that caused the blood stain she saw earlier, that it passed through soft flesh, not tearing through and splintering bones causing internal injuries that assured a slow and painful death.

If it didn't heal, the swift knife of the surgeon was the only other remedy.

The thought of this extraordinary man amputated with only one leg to work with, to love with, was incredulous to her.

One last time, she met his gaze again. The man was impossible to ignore. The urge to go to him was nearly irresistible.

Yet, she did resist.

Determined to remain in control, Emma lifted her chin a little and across the sea of wounded men, she stood firm.

He never said a word, yet she sensed the power of his will, drawing her into his world.

For long moments, only he and she seemed to exist.

Soon the quiet cries of injured men needing comfort and care moved Emma to continue her work. But with each bedside she visited that night, his intense dark gaze followed her, silent and compelling.

CHAPTER TWO

I was captivated by her beauty.

~~ John Singer

Sleep was fitful for her that night. It was rare for Emma to toss and turn. Normally she felt so exhausted that sleep came swift, dark, and complete. The handsome man whose commanding gaze had followed her every movement tonight, now stole her sleep. She yearned to look into his eyes again; those eyes that must never die; must never see the veil of darkness befall him.

Who was that man?

She had seen thousands of soldiers in these last three years, many brave and courageous heroes of the war, yet none had touched her like this. It made no sense that one man could disturb her sleep. Being honest with herself, Emma knew he wasn't like other men. For the other soldiers she simply felt compassion, but just by watching her work tonight, this handsome stranger made her aware of herself as a woman. Emma sighed and felt painfully lonely, sadly alone. What would it be like to know his loving touch?

The wish brought warm stirrings of a deep and powerful attraction. Perhaps it was her desirous thoughts that made sleep elusive on this particular night. They were quite unusual.

She rose from her bed and stood at the mirror in her modest room. The candle she lit cast elongated shadows on the four walls. This bedroom created her only private refuge from the suffering surrounding the hospital. Emma wondered what the handsome man saw when he gazed at her with such unavoidable intensity.

The woman in the mirror was cast in shadows and golden light. It seemed to accent the strain of this war on her slim womanly frame, a body several pounds thinner than in her innocent youth. Tonight her long blonde hair was loose.

It fell in light waves over her shoulders and down her back. She was considered a lovely young woman, with a curved figure that remained hidden and bound by day with fashionable ladies undergarments that were not meant to expose the beauty underneath. However tonight, her nightgown was just a worn cotton sheath lying over the natural shape her body with curves visible through the thin sleeping garment. Her full breasts pushed up beneath her chemise as if aching to be kissed and caressed. She longed to enjoy affection and pleasure, no longer a woman lonely and alone. Not just touched by any man. Him, she wanted his touch. She leaned closer to the mirror. The eyes staring back were pale blue.

At her eighteenth birthday, just before the war began, her many beaus claimed her eyes were like pools of ice blue water. Perhaps they saw ice because none had never ignited the passionate spark that clearly lit them now.

Emma lowered her gaze as she remembered those boys who had wanted to love her, most gone now, falling and dying for the Cause. *He lit that spark. Just by watching me, he lit a fire inside my soul.* The memory of his silent watchful gaze was so clear, so powerful. Without a word, the man who haunted her sleep seemed to call to Emma, wishing her to come to his side. *Am I in his thoughts tonight as he haunts mine?*

The compulsion to see him was suddenly overwhelming. Emma didn't bother fighting it. She dressed quickly in her normal binding undergarments and slipped into a plain blue dress, then hurried out of the staff quarters where she lived, down the dark road to the hospital. She knew the way by heart, needing no light. She stopped at the doorway where he was, the shadowed room filled with the sounds of suffering, the quiet cries and moans of those lost in grief, pain and sadness. She crept by silently, fearful her decision to see him was wrong.

Several feet away, she stopped. One hand lay over her thundering heart. Spinning around, Emma quickened her pace in retreat.

A rich deep voice inquired, "Why have you come?"

It was him. She knew it without question. No other man had ever made her pulse race like this. She followed that voice, finally lighting the lantern she carried, but had not lit for fear of waking everyone. The flame illuminated the space with a soft golden glow.

Then she saw him. He still sat upright with his back against the small steel headboard frame, the cast and elevation of his injured leg too painful to lay prone. The wound had no blood seeping through the bandages, to her relief. Stopping by his bedside, the candle's flame seemed incapable of outshining the life glowing in the depths of those magnificent compelling eyes.

"I had to come," she simply stated. It was true.

Emma had been drawn here to his bedside in the pre-dawn hours when her hospital duties were clearly finished for the night, only to find him awake and waiting—no other explanation would do.

"My name is John Singer," he extended his hand to her, "And if you have come to give me aid or comfort, I am not in need. But I thank you, Ma'am. Others need your care, far more than I." His voice was low yet melodious as if trained in distinction and pitch. The music of it thrilled her.

She studied John. His jet-black hair fell in waves that seemed to invite a woman's fingers to run through them. Inky black eyelashes were long, framing those enigmatic dark eyes and looked silky to the touch. Clean-shaven, without the mustache he donned when he first arrived, the shape of his face was noble and distinct. He was by all accounts, an extremely handsome man. Accepting the offered hand, his warm skin met hers. She saw no wedding band.

"It's a pleasure to meet you, Miss?" His inquiry hung, waiting. Then he smiled. All her nervous tension fled. Doubt and wonder went with it.

His touch completed her unspoken needs, that smile giving truth to the passion burning inside, making it real. His hand upon hers brought strength to their attraction, a warmth building between them, as prelude to desire.

"My name is Emma Dixon," she softly introduced, sliding her hand away from his. "As you are not in need of care, I shall take my leave." The sensual warmth he inspired inside was unfamiliar, a wild aching need that yearned for more from him, to know John and revel in his touch.

Perhaps she alone, felt it. Her heart lurched and tumbled inside. The boldness of coming to his bedside suddenly felt silly, too impulsive. Before she turned, his voice drew her back.

"Miss Dixon, I forget my manners. How kind it is that you have come to me tonight. I shall recant my earlier indiscretion. I beg you to forgive me for disregarding your concern for my wellbeing." He lowered his gaze, placing his hand over his heart and bowed his handsome head. It was a practiced gesture that bespoke of manners and decorum, manners befitting a gentleman.

"Mr. Singer, you are forgiven."

Immediately, his gaze raced to meet hers again. "Miss Dixon, yes you may do something for me, if you are so inclined."

"Anything you wish." Emma leaned closer, reaching again for his hand. But as their fingers brushed, his hand extended closer and swept back the length of loose blonde hair that had fallen across her breast.

John smiled, just a tiny seductive curve that was certain to make any woman's pulse grow hot. His allure was irresistible. "Your hair is like ribbons of silk," he softly complimented, "how beautiful you are with it falling about you." His fingers toyed with the soft strands. "Perhaps you could sit for another moment and let me gaze upon your beautiful face. And tomorrow you must fashion your hair this way. It pleases me to see it unbound like this."

She remained silent as the touch of his hand so near her breast caused her breath to falter and halt. But a lady never bent to a gentleman's whim.

"Mr. SIngr, it is my duty to provide care and comfort to all our dear soldiers. My appearance is not intended to please one man. Never have I heard such a request." He tilted his head, leaning up from his position against the pillows until they were nearly face-to-face. Only then did she notice his skin had paled. He was clearly in pain.

"Dear Miss Dixon," he breathed, a coy tone deepening his voice, "how lovely you are when your cheeks flush. Does the warm night bring such exquisite color to your face," John flirted, "or is it me?"

Emma gasped, "You presume too much, sir."

But John smiled a little wider, "No denial from your sweet lips, My Lovely? It seems proof enough that your tender heart races for another reason entirely."

"You speak with great boldness, Mr. Singer."

"Gentlemen in your world do not speak to you of desire?"

"No. Never."

That pleased him. "Yet passion lights your pale blue eyes. Your rosebud lips do not deny that you appeared before me tonight wishing for a private moment. Perhaps my words seem bold. You have never met anyone like me; that is why."

With that he shifted in the bed and leaned back on the pillow, lying down at last, his eyes fluttering under the strain of pain and exhaustion.

The pain he silently endured must be enormous. The wound on his leg had seeped a little blood. A red stain now marked the white bandages binding the angry wound. Emma watched John fight it, but unconsciousness claimed him, just the same. A private moment, indeed. One she would not soon forget. Emma waited at his side until she heard the even breaths of a gentle sleep come from John. She then extinguished the candle in the lantern. As she left, she looked back. In the dark she could still see his attractive outlines lying on the bed.

John Singer was an intelligent, observant man. Of course, he had noticed how her heart thundered at his touch. *My Lovely.* His words, spoken with the intimacy of a lover, now haunted her mind. His confidence and genteel demeanor made him all the more attractive. Desire to know him felt like an opiate, a high that thrilled, unrelenting and glorious.

Emma returned to her room and once again undressed for bed, trying to decipher the encounter with handsome John Singer.

His nuances spoke of refinement, his manners practiced and polished. It made her curious. His voice resonated like a man who knew all too well how to use those rich manly tones to reach inside a woman's carefully protected heart and take whatever he wanted. A dangerous venture, yet it was strangely appealing. Lying in her own bed all alone, Emma knew dawn would rise soon. Still, sleep was elusive. Her thoughts were consumed by the late night encounter with John Singer. Of all the hundreds of soldiers she had nursed and cared for during the war, coming from the battlefield needing tenderness, none had truly inspired deep emotions until a mysterious man appeared, speaking openly of beauty and desire, a man whose intense ebony eyes shone with a compassionate light from deep within. Eyes that offered kindness so pure and simple, the naturalness of it beckoned to her very soul.

He must be in great pain from his leg, yet even as that pain drew him into unconscious darkness, no outcry was uttered. Emma felt amazed by his inner strength and self-control. *You have never met anyone like me.*

It was true. Her friend Louisa had met a man who stole her heart. As a nurse, they met hundreds of men wounded from the war, none becoming anything more than a passing memory of pain and the hope for healing. They served with care, but with a sense of emotional detachment. But Louisa claimed when you met the right one, your heart would know. For some, it only happens once, that special connection that made everything else seem trivial.

Jack had won Louisa's heart. But she lost him.

Will I lose John Singer? I can't. I won't.

Closing her eyes, Emma recalled perfectly the way he looked tonight. He seemed so emotionally distant, observing without allowing his private emotions to show, yet he had power. John could draw her close with his dark eyed stare and send her pulse thundering at his bold words.

"You speak with great boldness, Mr. Singer."

"Gentlemen in your world do not speak to you of desire?"

"No. Never."

Hearing his intoxicating voice in her memories, Emma ran her hand over the breast he had brushed against, a fleeting careless touch as he caressed her hair. The fire it created lingered on her still. Remembering did indeed make her wish for private moments, ones far more intimate than tonight.

Emma smiled. Tomorrow she would fashion her hair to please him if only to see a smile pass over his handsome face. Pleasing him would bring her pleasure. She hugged the pillow close, wishing it could be him instead. Exhaustion made those thoughts dreamy, seeming almost real.

"John," she already dreamed, "Sleep well."

Emma's dreamy wish did not reach John as he awoke with a start, his heart pumping violently within his chest. The dream that woke him was a nightmare, one that still haunted him with each attempt at sleep. It was always the same, a torrent of blood, screams and the smell of gunpowder from his small derringer. Then the dream changed, bringing visions of a blazing fire that almost engulfed him. Finally escaping the inferno, the nightmare left him to wander through the Virginia countryside, lost, starving and hobbling on a broken leg, then falling unconscious on a road. Then waking, finding himself in a hospital wagon for the wounded, being tended as one of the last remaining injured soldiers of the Confederate army.

Except it wasn't a nightmare. It was real.

John sat up and leaned back against the metal headboard of his bed, his re-set leg throbbing with unrelenting pain. The leg originally broke from an awkward fall. It wasn't set properly when it happened a few weeks ago and had begun to heal wrong. The young harried surgeon who tended to him had re-set the bone and mended the bullet wound in his thigh. He said to wait and see, reminding the patient how lucky he was that no bullet had splintered the bone.

Needing to escape the pain and think of something else, John closed his eyes, recalling a happier moment from his youth. It seemed so fleeting now, frozen in time and in his memories. She was a lovely young woman. He loved Asia as much as a brother could possible love and care for a sister, and she felt the same for him. Their dear mother called them, "Thick like thieves," for if one were lost the other would surely follow and never rest until found.

He remembered one day as near adults, but still shining with youth. They were at their Maryland farm, in a small hamlet of a town, Bel Air. Tudor Hall was a one and half story Gothic Revival cottage and the farm was not always successful in providing for the owners. This particular day their supplies were rationed. Their mother went to Baltimore twenty miles away, bringing back food and supplies to their family home.

Letting his mind drift away from the current pain in his body, John's memories were vivid. He still could hear his sister's voice floating down from the second floor of Tudor Hall.

"John, I hear horses approaching. We have visitors coming!"

He had checked. It was true. In the distance, he saw a carriage. Asia ran downstairs to him, her black hair neatly pinned into a stylish twist, her lovely face flushed with excitement and fear. Tendrils of her dark hair fell around her cheeks, making her appear even more youthful and beautiful.

"It is our neighbors, four young ladies coming to spend the afternoon."

It was proper courtesy of that time that neighbors would visit, spending all afternoon and evening enjoying the hospitality and partaking of the hostesses table. But they had nothing.

Asia feared the social repercussions of presenting a less than favorable table to her neighbors as it was the custom for neighbors to visit for hours at a time sharing in the bounty of the farm. Not presenting a favorable table would not bode well for the Booth's standing in the community.

His beautiful sister was panicked. "We have almost nothing to serve them." Her hands threw dramatically into the air. "The butter crock is nearly empty. We have only one loaf of bread and a small serving of meat. Mother won't be back in time for the expected meal." Tears filled her eyes. "We shall be humiliated and ridiculed."

"Asia, my sweet," John had kindly reached to dry her tears, his love for her overflowing. He could help her. So deep was his love, he would do anything for his family. They owned his heart, especially his lovely sister. "Let me worry about the ladies coming to call. No one will know of our situation. You set the table in our mother's best china and silver. Get fresh flowers from the garden. Place the butter in the smallest crock so it looks like more."

"What will we serve?"

"I will go into the kitchen and prepare griddle cakes, for they are filling and take the least butter, and place molasses in mother's finest pitcher. We shall slice the meat thinly and place the flowers on the plates as fancy decoration. You pretend there is a servant preparing the meal. When you come to refill their plates, chide the servant for being slow, in front of the ladies."

"But John, we have no servants."

"It shall be I at the stove!" Her pretty mouth gaped at his outrageous idea. "It shall be fine. Now touch up your toilette and prepare for our guests. They expect a fine lady waiting to entertain. And entertain them, we shall." He boldly tilted his head back, laughing. It would be a fun game. For him, acting came naturally.

The afternoon lingered in fine fashion, the ladies none the wiser of who prepared their feast. When the meal was finished, John then appeared, looking refreshed and sociable. His clothes were neatly pressed like a gentleman of wealth and rank as if he had been away enjoying a leisurely afternoon engagement and stopped to entertain the guests. The ladies had been pleased, their eyes riveted on the handsome and charming host.

None ever suspected their ruse. And when the handsome gentleman kindly suggested the ladies return the favor of playing host and invite Asia to visit their home, they gladly began planning an event, eager to please their handsome neighbor. Of course, he would attend too.

The memories faded as John whispered her name. The last time he saw his beloved sister, she was married to a wealthy man, having two young children and another baby coming. Children he adored, deeply. He especially felt a bond with the oldest boy, Jacob, who followed after his own thoughtful inquisitive nature.

Soon, she would be due. But John could never again see her. The war had taken so much. His family believed he was gone. To risk seeing Asia would certainly bring a painful death, for him and for those he loved. One horrendous mistake cost him everything good. The misery and loss of his family overwhelmed John. The physical pain of it went deeper than the wounds on his body. This suffering pierced his heart. His family meant everything.

Exhausted, feeling a fever burning inside, he slowly slipped into the black refuge of sleep, hoping that perhaps this time the darkness would last. His last rational thought was of the beautiful nurse who came to see him tonight.

So lovely. Those wide blue eyes had sparked with life and curiosity, especially when he spoke to her. John was captivated by her beauty. He sensed her loneliness, feeling it as deep as his own. That kinship drew his gaze to her beautiful face, from the first time he saw her.

Life was cruel.

If only they could meet in a different time and place, far away from the war's painful torment and could live in a civilized world, she would be with him now.

He would whisper desire, seducing with his eyes and words.

He knew how to please, to make women sigh.

If he had his way, in that other perfect world, soon they would feel spent and content from a night of passion. Her silken long hair would be his to touch, just as his hands would be allowed to pleasure those full ripe breasts.

He wanted her so much; tonight he had boldly grazed her forbidden curves with his hand.

She noticed, yet had allowed it.

He wanted more, so much more.

"Sleep well dear Emma, sleep well," he whispered, with only the agonized cries of his fellow soldiers around him to hear.

CHAPTER THREE

If war doesn't take these men
It's the disease that takes them.

~~ *Doctor Henry Bradley*

With the early break of dawn Emma awoke to start her day, feeling a buoyant lilt to her heart as she thought of John. She hoped he slept well, for between the pain of his broken leg and the nightly cries of the injured men in the surrounding ward, she feared he had a restless sleep.

She dressed with special care this morning, wanting to leave her blonde waves loose and unbound as John has asked her to do, but in the end her sense of responsibility prevailed.

The call of duty to others as a nurse prevented that.

Once again her hair was twisted and pinned.

"At least for now," she half smiled to herself, "At least for now."

Emma stood gazing at the mirror once again, seeing her subdued appearance and rubbed both palms across the coarse woven skirt. Her soft skin missed the days when only silk or satin touched it. Before the war, she wore beautiful finery fit for a lady.

She especially missed her finest gown: the pale blue silk she wore on her eighteenth birthday, with satin trim and mother-of-pearl buttons. The silk underskirts swished like secret whispered music when she walked.

Such were the days before the war.

Letting out a sigh, she wished John Singer could see her in that lovely ladies gown instead of the drab homespun cotton of her daily duty dress.

Why does it matter?

It mattered because she was compelled by him, intrigued and captured. During their brief encounter the night before, her heart and soul had been claimed by a stranger. He was exceeding bold in his advances last night, yet she was drawn to him like no other before.

But there was more, a desire she saw in his eyes.

They were equally enamored with each other.

The way he spoke melted away the social niceties and drew them right into the truth. Emma felt that he knew her, from the first moment.

Somehow, John Singer recognized her loneliness and secret longings for a man to love. It was there in his intense gaze, in their words unspoken, yet emotions her heart clearly heard. In watching her as she worked, John had sought her out, daring her to see him.

See him, she had.

It had brought her to his side.

His touch last evening was purposeful, meant to comfort her loneliness and incite her passion.

Such thoughts brought a flush to her face.

Emma tipped her chin and in the mirrored reflection, the woman's blue eyes flashed with light. *John Singer did that. He woke me up inside.* The man may be a gentleman raised to display perfect manners in high society, but underneath that perfected exterior was a man who was waiting to claim her.

Yet there was something else in him, she decided as she left the mirror and prepared to leave. Something that was aloof and untouchable, a secret side that he seemed unwilling to reveal. She saw that inner resilience in his firm refusal to cry out in pain, as if there was a deeper pain within him, far more excruciating than the physical pain of his leg.

John Singer was an enigma compared to all other men, a deep and dark mystery.

A mystery she hoped he would soon share.

Prepared for another long day, Emma retraced her steps on the well-worn path toward the hospital ward to where she had just encountered John a few hours earlier. She started off walking, but each step made the yearning in her heart increase.

Picking up her skirts, she ran most of the way.

Her heart felt light today, buoyant with hope.

She didn't care who saw and ignored the questioning looks on the faces of the other hospital workers. She came to the spot where she had stood in the darkness of night and saw his bed was empty.

Her spirit turned cold.

All the hope within her fled.

Frantic with fear, her mind refused to believe. The immediate need to see him only increased. Emma knew what an empty bed meant.

All too many times, an empty bed was a signal of death.

"Doctor Bradley," Emma cried out to him, but the careworn physician was bent over, tending the wound on a young soldier.

This job was sadly familiar.

Despite his medical care, the severe injury would soon bring death to the patient. There was no hope. Finishing, he stood and pushed his spectacles up on his lean angular nose. Peering at her through the lenses, he focused on the lovely blonde nurse whose golden presence here was the sole reason he rose each day. Emma made his life bearable.

If only she knew his heart.

If only he had the courage to win her love, to make her his own.

"Where is John Singer, the man with the broken leg?" She grabbed his upper arm, her expression frantic. "He was in that bed over there." Pointing in the direction of the empty bed, she demanded to know where he was. The Doctor saw fear in her innocent blue eyes.

He'd never seen Emma behave this way.

"Calm yourself, dear."

But she would not calm. In fact, his patronizing demeanor only served to increase her agitation. Soft fingers clutching his arm gripped tighter.

"I just saw him last night. Where is he?"

"Emma, there are many men."

But the war torn physician knew exactly which man she meant.

The dark handsome soldier was the epitome of a grand gentleman who came from fine upbringing. Courageous and stoic, the man never cried out with pain, even when the Doctor had re-set the bone in his broken leg and stitched the wound without any morphine.

Painful procedures, yet he withstood both with silence.

Henry quickly noticed there was more than a passing concern for this soldier on her lovely face. It made his heart lurch.

He told her the truth.

"Mr. Singer drew a high fever last night. I'm afraid it looks like malaria. He was moved to the isolation ward just before dawn."

"No," she gasped. "Not malaria. Not John."

They both knew all too well the slow and painful onslaught of this condition. So many soldiers died from it. Malaria ravaged the body, sending men into delirium from fever. They suffered from coughing, abdominal pain, weight loss with the symptoms lasting for weeks.

Some survived.

Most did not.

"If the war itself doesn't kill these men," he decreed, feeling disturbed by her heart wrenching behavior. "The disease takes them."

"But you can save him. I know you can."

Henry could have listened to her beg him forever. Oh, to be recognized by Emma, exalted as a healer and miracle worker in her lovely blue eyes. "My skills to help him are earthly medicines; this Mr. Singer needs far more than what I can give him."

"No Doctor, you can," her hand tightened on his arm, "please heal him."

For this beautiful and selfless woman, he would do anything.

But to promise a miracle would only bring disappointment and more heartache. "So many have died Emma, dying while waiting for me to tend them, dying from disease."

"Yes, I know. We have lived with death every day."

His gaze swept over her, drinking in her beauty, aching to tell her his private thoughts. "You have given much to this hospital. The men here were grateful to have such a lovely face to gaze upon and a soft hand to hold before leaving this earth."

Modest as always, she simply stated, "It is my duty to ease their pain."

Ease my pain.

See me, Emma. Love me.

But those wild thoughts remained unspoken.

Thoughts like that were dangerous. Yet the distraught look in her eyes was equally dangerous.

How could she care so deeply for a stranger? Henry had stood beside her every day for all the years of the war, waiting for the moment she looked at him with love in her eyes.

Jealousy burned.

"Emma," the young physician warned, "Stay out of that ward. You could easily catch such a contagious disease."

She broke away, shaking her head. "No, I will see him and take care of him."

"You will die, too.

"I don't care."

The Doctor stood silent as she raced to find John. He narrowed his gaze as she ran away from him. A wild urge to run after her burned through him, igniting a secret fire he had kept in his heart for too long. Yet Henry simply clenched his fists.

Wildness was for the weak and uncivilized.

No, Emma must see his strength as a man and protector.

But the wildness bubbled inside, percolating with excitement.

He could give her everything, now that the war was finally ending. A lovely life, riches and worldly comfort, and social prestige in all the highest circles of Virginia would be hers as an honored physician's wife, as Mrs. Henry Bradley.

Soon, he rationalized, she would return his love.

Emma found John lying in a small, secluded hospital ward with no one tending him in his isolation and no one sitting at his side. By all accounts he had been forgotten.

The nurses had too many others to help.

He was pale and feverish, his dark wavy hair drenched from sweat, lying about his face and pillow. His eyes were closed, his breathing raspy and labored from the malaria infecting his lungs. She knelt by his bedside, frantic from seeing the shroud of darkness that had come for him.

"John, it is me, Emma. Please John, please don't die."

His eyes fluttered, but did not open.

No, she could not lose him.

She would not become like her dear friend Louisa Alcott, a woman whose sweet smile had once been filled with kindness and hope, but after losing her special soldier she became heartbroken, devastated by her loss.

Emma leaned closer, boldly telling him of the need for love he had inspired. "You gave me hope, John. My heart chose you. One look from you changed me. Now I cannot go on without you."

He took a deep ragged breath, then another, as if fighting his way to the surface from beneath cold dark vestiges of death.

"Please open your eyes."

But he still took in ragged breaths like a drowning man. His struggle made her heart tear in two.

"Look, John. See, I wore my hair the way it pleases you." With that admission, she ripped out the pins that held the golden length in the elaborate twist, letting the silken mane fall about her face and back.

"John, do you hear me?"

He no longer seemed to be fighting. It seemed the malaria had won. His skin remained pale his breath rattled and made raspy sounds in his chest.

"No, you can't go. We just met."

Emma didn't want to watch him die. She wanted him to live.

Finally a man had appeared who stirred fire in her soul. They were meant to be together. Yet here he lay dying. Why was life so unfair? She buried her face on his chest and sobbed.

"I wanted so much for us. I wanted you as my own, so much."

Hearing her cries and feeling her weight upon his chest, at last his hand caressed her cheek. "Yes, my Lovely. I want you too."

"John?"

Her face lifted off his chest.

He turned his head and opened his eyes, the light of life within them fading and disappearing as he labored under the fever that raged through his body. Then the spark within lit again with admiration as his gaze focused fully, if only for a moment.

"Sweet Emma," he gently murmured, admiring her with his knowledgeable dark eyes. The eyes were windows to the heart and his were profoundly captivating. "How beautiful you are with your hair fashioned that way." Fingers slowly moved to stroke the golden waves that fell loose across her breasts. "It pleases me so."

But he was weak. The hand fell away.

His mesmerizing eyes closed again.

As they closed, her heart plunged into darkness too.

"John, listen to me," she spoke to his heart, knowing he could still hear, keeping her voice firm and even, "You must fight to live. Don't leave John, please don't leave."

A flicker of hope rushed through her as he drew a determined breath and those intense ebony colored eyes saw her face again.

The light in them seemed pleased to see her.

Yet his face was shadowed with regret.

"Darling," he rasped as he drew a deeper breath, "For what I have done, if death comes for me now, it is right and just that I must go."

"Right and just," she cried in exasperation, "What could be right and just about giving up, that death should take you without a fight? No, John I won't let you give up. I shall fight for you now. I will fight so you might live."

"I deserve to suffer," he whispered.

She refused to believe it.

"Whatever you did in this terrible war, it is done now."

His head stubbornly shook, denying her claim.

"So much suffering," Emma plead with John, "so much taken from all of us by this war. I can't let God take you too."

His eyes closed as John gave over to the darkness and the fever. Her hands lay upon his chest. Beneath them, his chest rose and fell in slow labored breaths.

He was weak.

But she was strong.

Emma brought cool water to wash his feverish face and then cooled his chest and arms. She noticed the gold religious medal around his neck as she washed him, cooling fevered skin that was creamy white and pale as polished marble. A gentleman's skin, she was sure. Skin that never saw the glare of the sun.

He was muscular and lean, yet John was not a common man who worked outside, laboring all day in the sun.

He had no tan lines, anywhere.

Who was he to have lived such a privileged life?

Emma was curious about the gold medal around his neck, glittering in stark contrast to his white marble chest. She leaned over to see the script etched on its side "*Agnus Dei*," she knew from her school studies it was Latin for Lamb of God.

May God protect him.

She changed the pillow cover that was drenched in his sweat. The good Doctor Bradley eventually appeared, working and tending to John. But his brow stayed furrowed as he left medicine for her to give their patient when and if he ever awoke.

"I can't work miracles, Emma."

"Yes, I know. But thank you."

Giving him her sweetest smile, she failed to see how that one pure gesture made the young Doctor so happy that he beamed with joy as he walked away.

Emma only had eyes for John Singer.

She stayed next to him, one hand over his heart, feeling it beat beneath her touch, unable and unwilling to leave his side.

After long hours without any change in his condition she began to pray, pouring out her heart's deepest wishes alone in the isolation ward as she gazed upon his handsome face.

"John, this is not the end. No, you shall not die without holding me or kissing me. I have found you now, at the end of this terrible war. This is our time. It is meant to be. I am sure of it. I will not let you slip away. I will not live in loneliness. I shall fight to have you always."

With that promise, she leaned over and lightly kissed his fever raged cheek, savoring the touch of his skin to her soft lips.

"I will not leave you. And you, John Singer, cannot leave me."

CHAPTER FOUR

I shall never be happy until I see your face again.
~~ Asia Booth Clarke

It was late and had been still that cold night in March, the night Asia remembered now with such pain in her heart, the last night when she saw her brother John.

His final appearance on stage was a benefit in Washington D.C. on March 18, 1865 as he performed "Pescara" to the usual thunderous applause and accolades of the appreciative crowd.

He was adored, by fans and family alike, but for different reasons. The public saw his drama, his flair for imagination and action in his performances upon the stage. His family knew the man beneath the drama was a man who thought and felt deeply, too deeply sometimes.

He was the handsomest man in America, a gifted actor and at only twenty-six his youth promising a long and successful career.

He had come to Philadelphia, as he so often did, stopping and staying at his sister's home that she shared with her husband and two small children. He had been mysterious in those last week's, bedding down on the couch in the living room, sleeping in his riding clothes, and having late night meetings with other men—some voices recognizable, some not.

Yet they never came further than the inner sill of her home, their hushed voices like whispered conspirators with a deadly secret.

They brought trouble.

She knew it now.

Trouble that had stolen away her beloved brother, forever.

Now it was May and life as she knew it was forever changed, too.

Asia wiped the tears from her face as she remembered his strange final visit to her home. He had sat late with her that final night, his demeanor excited, yet his appearance was tired and worn.

His dark eyes were always so magnificent with depth and emotion, shining with that vibrant inner life that made John special, but that night they were shadowed with trouble as if he were being driven by forces beyond her knowledge or understanding.

"Asia," he excitedly said, "I have a package I would ask you to lock up in your safe for me. I may come back for it, but if anything should ever happen to me open the package alone. There are directions enclosed. Send the money and letters to the names I have addressed them to."

She had watched him slip a large packet from his waistcoat. Trusting her with his mysterious wishes, her brother placed it in her hands. But an uneasy feeling coursed through her, causing a cold shiver to run up her spine.

"Yes, I will do as you ask." He seemed relieved and smiled in a show of strength, but loving him as she did, Asia saw the exhaustion in his eyes. "You are tired, brother. Stay with us here. Please do not go South again. I fear for you."

"You worry too much."

But the carefree grin he gave was false, a testament to the accomplished actor he had become.

"There is nothing to fear."

She shook her head and reminded him, "Remember when we were at Tudor Hall and the old gypsy woman came by?" He nodded, remembering. "As favor for receiving a warm meal, she read your palm. Remember her foreboding words?"

"No, I do not recall exactly what she said."

"She said that you would have success beyond all dreams, have money and influence and that you would die in a fiery blaze, and that your life while grandly lived, would be horribly short. Money and grand living you have. But the fire, could it be true too? Your behavior now frightens me so!"

"Sweet sister," he scoffed, "Did you truly believe that old gypsy? Her banter was created to give us children entertainment, to make us ooh and ahh at her nonsense talk."

"Was it truly nonsense?"

John smiled. His handsome face became calm and serene.

"Do not allow a foolish old gypsy to trouble your heart. Fame and fortune were clearly written in my stars as anyone could see. Her talk of fire and doom were meant to scare you."

"It terrified me. I've thought of it often."

"Too often, it seems." He lightly chastised. "You are right about one thing. I am tired."

Leading her to the sofa, he sat her at one end while he stretched out on the length of it. Just like when they were children comforting one another, John lay his head upon her lap near her belly that was full with the promise of a new life.

"Soon, I will become an uncle again."

He smiled, full of affection. Oh how he loved his nephews.

At that moment, the baby decided to kick.

Feeling the hearty thumps, John was amused. Laying his palm over the spot where tiny feet proved the child inside was healthy and strong, he blessed Asia with a disarming smile.

"Dear girl, when will this wild child be born?"

"Two more months, I believe."

John closed his eyes and seemed happy, his hand still feeling the baby's feet thump against her tightly stretched skin. His expression was pure devotion. Asia ran run her hand through his thick black wavy hair, carelessly soothing him.

"If this child is a boy, I will name him after you, John."

He liked that. "And if it is a girl?"

"I do not know. Yours is the only name I carry in my heart."

It was true. She had hung a small picture of him above her sleeping children's bed. He was a loving Uncle and he would often stop and tell the babies to pray for him. He loved her children, as he had loved her, all his life.

"I would be honored."

His body relaxed, feeling safe with her.

Asia watched him sleep. His handsomeness never failed to astound her. There was a natural beauty to everything he did, every move he made; a grace and power so few men ever achieved.

Eventually he woke and smiled that she was still watching over him. "You are a lovely guardian angel, my adoring sister."

"I do adore you, John."

They rose up together from the sofa. He gently kissed her cheek. "God bless you, Asia, and the child that should bear my name." He lightly touched her distended belly. "Take care of yourself." With those words he turned from her, the finality of his voice terrorized her spirit and froze her heart.

"Dearest brother, I shall never be happy until I see your face again."

He looked back, his expression shadowed once again by whatever waited for him in the world beyond her home. "I love you, Asia. Never forget that."

Closing the door, he parted from her.

But Asia watched him through the window as he mounted his horse. A tightness gripped her chest. Her eyes blinded with tears, she watched him ride away, staying with him until the darkness of night overcame him.

That was almost two months ago.

When the news came, she died a little inside.

The slaying of President Lincoln at her brother's hand was too incredulous to believe. His ardent love of the South and the violence of the times still gave no explanation for the reasons behind his evil deed.

Why, did you leave me, brother?

Tonight Asia sat alone in her Philadelphia home. Her husband John Sleeper Clarke and her brothers Junius and Edwin were imprisoned. If not for the impending birth of her child, she would be imprisoned as well.

The old gypsy's warnings were true.

His fiery end was horrifying to envision. Asia thought of John running for his life, then shot and burning to death in that tobacco barn.

Tears fell.

Needing to see him, she fingered the collar of her dress and pulled the cord up from between her breasts that held the picture she kept next to her heart, hidden and safe from the vast searches by the government of her home.

She stared at the picture.

His handsome face was staring back at her.

The face that was now lost forever. "Oh John," she cried. The dredge of tears streamed freely down her cheeks, crying for the loss of what was, and would never be again.

The delirium induced by the fever from malaria still raged within John, yet Emma continued to spoon water and gruel into the suffering soldier. She never stopped nursing him.

He sensed her presence there at his side, even as he fought for his life.

He knew he was not worthy.

Only when his breathing eased and the lessened broke did his eyes flutter open to the realities of life. But every time he was able to glimpse her lovely face, the illness pushed him under again, calling him ever closer to the dark shadows of death.

Finally, after three days John awoke fully.

There she was, just like in his feverish dreams. Golden, compassionate, and pure; truly a man's dream come true.

He gazed intently into her ice-blue eyes and whispered, "Let me go, dear girl. Just let me go."

The beautiful woman leaned closer to hear him better while compassionately bathing his hot face with a cool cloth. "I shall never let you go, John Singer. I will save you, for I believe you must live."

"I need not be saved."

Her head shook in denial.

John took a deeper breath, finding more focus with his thoughts. This lovely woman deserved a good man, something he was not.

He was the worst sort of man.

"It's time I meet my maker and let him judge me for the crime I have committed."

She seemed determined to make him see that life was worth living. "I will not stop trying to tend you back to health. You are strong. I know your will is strong. Do not say such words. Don't quit. Please say that you want to live."

"No Emma," his voice became precise and sharp, letting its well-trained tones carry the force of his words. "You must let me go."

The beautiful blonde shook her head in defiance. "How is it you managed to find your way out to the road to our hospital, if not guided by the Maker's hand? He does not want you yet. He wishes you to live. To be with me. I am sure of it. Now, John Singer, you must fight for your life."

Smiling as though sheer willpower could save him, she held his hand in hers. She was a headstrong determined woman. Even in his weakness, she stirred fire in his blood. Touching her brought heat stronger than a fever, but instead of destroying him as the malaria still threatened to do, that fiery attraction brought strength and life to his ravaged soul.

Emma was extraordinary.

"You are a rare woman, my darling."

He raised her hand to his lips and kissed it gently.

Those icy blue eyes sparked with honest excitement that mirrored the passion coursing through his heart.

But he had no right to claim her.

She was pure gold, too good for a man such as him, a man whose horrendous crime against God and Nation was unforgivable.

John released her hand.

"Dear girl, your belief in me is without understanding of what I have done in this war. And please do not ask, for I cannot ever share with you the events that marked the end of my life, as I knew it."

Her smooth brow creased at his cryptic explanation, his refusal to explain mistakes neither God nor man could ever undo.

"Perhaps this is your second chance."

The idea almost amused him, dampened by the wistful yearning that her innocent words might be true.

"There is no second chance for me. For if I shall live, I have a terrible stain upon my soul. Perhaps that is God's plan, to have me suffer here on earth. Once done with my earthly suffering, I shall be banished to gates of Hell to burn for all time for my sins."

She would not be deterred.

"All men commit sins in war they regret. War is nothing but death and pain. Why should your actions be damned above all others? I do not care about your crimes. I care only for you; that you heal and grow strong."

John gave her a kind smile and sighed.

"That you should care about me, dear Emma, or want me to live might be the only glimmer of light in my forsaken life."

Nothing he said convinced her that he was a lost cause.

"Whatever it is that troubles you, John, I promise it matters not to me. I shall never ask about the deep pain that haunts your heart, the regret I hear in your words and see in your face. All I ask of you is to fight to get well, fight for your life, and help me to help you heal."

He was astounded by her unwavering dedication. As the strength began to ebb from his body once again and exhaustion set in, John whispered, "And why, may I ask, it is so important to you that I live?"

"It is my deepest wish," she simply replied.

John wanted more, to hear her truth.

"You have shown me such kindness. Your medical care has brought me back to life and your beauty has touched me. It has left me wanting more. With you."

He watched her lips part as she gasped, yet she didn't flinch and leave him, Emma leaned closer.

Her unbound hair brushed across his arm.

Unable to resist, he stroked it with his fingers.

"I ask you again, as I have truthfully told you of the evil within me. Why is it so important to you that I must live?"

Emma moved so close he could inhale the soft womanly scent of her skin, giving a clear bold response, "So that you may kiss me John, kiss me today and for the rest of my life."

His heart, ever so full of grief and sadness, gave over in that moment to the one light of hope, to the one person who opened her heart to him, who not of his crimes but asked only that he live, and live for her.

John leaned up from the bed, drawing her toward him.

He felt her full breasts pressed into his bare chest. He wondered what it would be like to have them bared and caressed by his lips.

He kissed Emma.

She gasped and he almost smiled.

John kissed her breathless lips gently, yet leaving an emotional imprint of the promise of his passion and desire, of things yet to be fulfilled. Her sweet full mouth was heavenly.

Weakened, he leaned back into the bed.

She was breathing fast and flushed, and by any man's measure, remarkably beautiful. A sight to inspire a dying man to live, but he was fading fast.

"Dearest Emma," he whispered, memorizing her face to carry that memory into Hell. "There is your kiss, for today and for the rest of my life."

The exhaustion overcame him.

Eyes closed as the fever once again raged within.

Late that same night the delirium was especially fearsome. Emma sat at his bedside and sponged his head and bared chest while carefully watching the rhythm of his breathing. Alone in the isolation ward, the room was silent. Knowing none would hear, not even the man whose malaria threatened to steal him away from her, she spoke to him.

She would not live a lonely life.

She needed someone to love. And that someone was John Singer.

"My dearest John, I know nothing of your past, about your people, your life before the war, or the burdensome secret you keep. I care nothing for it, only that you must get well and live. Somehow, you have stolen my heart. None ever touched me as you do. You must see that I need you. I want you to take me into your heart and to your bed and never leave me."

The silence wore on. With each passing hour Emma became more worried. The fever would not break.

John Singer's life hung dangerously close to death.

When burning up, tossing in a delirium late in the night, he called out from the secret whispers of his heart.

"I did it for my country, I thought he was a dictator," he groaned in regret and pain, "the gun, my leg, the fire, the pain. Oh God help me what have I done?"

Emma listened and told no one.

His secrets were hers forever.

CHAPTER FIVE

There is really not much more I can do.

--- *Doctor Henry Bradley*

He was thrashing with fever and John's head turned in violent waves from side to side. Emma feared he would hurt himself. Finally leaving his side, she ran to find Doctor Bradley.

It was late, nearly midnight.

For three days she had sat in isolation with John.

She looked in the hospital ward where injured men slept and realized the hour. The Doctor would be preparing for bed if not already asleep. Since tending John, she had lost all sense of time and day.

Time mattered not.

With the reminder of the taste of his lips on hers and the feeling of his bare chest pressed against hers, the hour, the day, even the year mattered not.

Only that he must live.

One kiss, a kiss and promise of tomorrow.

She vowed it would not be their last.

Emma found herself outside the office Doctor Bradley had called home for the last four years. He was already working here when she arrived, surrounded by blood and death from the war. They were friends from before the war, neighbors in Richmond and Henry was grateful for her nursing skills.

She knocked gingerly.

The physician was a dedicated man, determined to save lives. He sometimes worked for days without rest and she knew the screams of the wounded was a nightmare without end that lay deep in the heart of the overworked Doctor. His skills were no match for the constant onslaught of enemy fire.

At least the war was over now.

Emma knocked again and waited.

"Who is it?" she heard him call through the closed door.

"Doctor Bradley, it is I, Emma."

She heard rustling noises and a chair scrape back as the Doctor rose from his desk. The young physician opened the door and came out past the threshold. As the hour was late, Emma noticed his disheveled appearance and realized he had fallen asleep at the desk, a rest that was well-deserved.

When the war began Doctor Bradley had recently graduated medical school from the University of Virginia. He stayed to help care for the wounded. The tall wiry man was only a few years older than Emma, yet stress from the war had aged him another ten.

"Please, come help John Singer."

Henry saw the distress in her face.

"I told you not many men survive malaria," he declared with great care, "plus he was weakened due to exposure. God knows how long he was exposed to the elements with a broken leg, dehydrated and starving. Mr. Singer has lasted far longer because of your tending. There really is nothing more I can do."

"Please," she begged, "Please come with me. He is talking out of his mind and thrashing about from the fever. He could hurt himself." Emma faced him fully, merely inches away as she plead for the other man's life.

Henry took full measure of her beauty.

This was not the first time her face had captured his gaze.

In a different place and time, away from this wretched war, perhaps she would see his finer qualities and feel the same devotion for him as she felt about her dying soldier.

A misguided affection, he reasoned, surely just a passing fancy from a lonely woman who had seen too much death and pain.

He knew. Henry felt that dark weight too and wished for release from heartache and lonliness.

He yearned for a reason to smile.

"Your heart is too tender, Emma." He gently chided. "This lost man does not deserve the miracle you wish for."

"But he does," tears now glistened in her ice-blue eyes.

The good Doctor sighed.

She was so beautiful, so full of life; even here amidst this life-stealing war. She was a young woman born to laugh and dance, to live every moment of her life like a highborn lady. Yet she chose to be here, volunteering her kindness at his hospital.

The war was over.

Soon their duties at the hospital would end.

He could return home to a prosperous private practice in Richmond, purchase a large luxurious home where he planned to live out his days loving one woman.

This woman.

This perfect golden woman was destined to be his.

Henry fancied taking Emma on the dance floor in a swirl of a beautiful silken gown, her golden hair curled to lay about her lovely face, woven with pearls and ribbons of lace.

She belonged with him. He was a gentleman, a man of honor.

Soon, she would be his.

He would court her, win her love. Not here in this hospital full of death and dying. He looked into those pleading eyes, clear blue as sunlit seawater, and realized he could not refuse her pleading.

"He may yet pass," the Doctor warned.

"But you will try?"

Nodding, Henry gave a resigned sigh and shrugged into the physician's jacket he had removed only an hour before. Placing various supplies into his pockets, he was ready to try to perform her miracle.

"Come now. Hurry. He needs your care." she declared.

He was shocked when Emma snatched his hand to tow him along with her, nearly running toward the dark, forgotten corner of the hospital where a man who did not deserve her pure devotion lay dying.

They made their way quickly.

Upon entering the isolation ward, he saw John was still thrashing about. He would prove his worth, be the hero Emma deserved. The Doctor began his care. Reaching into his pocket, he gave his patient sips of quinine, a remedy that perhaps could help break the fever. It was the only remedy available to him and there was very little left.

He called to several other night attendants to help move John to a clean dry bed. Between the wet humid springtime air and the blinding fever, the sheets were once again soaked.

Emma looked grateful, which pleased Henry.

"Bring cool water," he instructed.

She nodded and hurried away.

The young physician took time to examine the soldier the golden beauty found so compelling. The leg he had reset when John first arrived had accepted the new cast and he saw no signs of gangrene in the wounded leg.

He was fortunate.

While the leg would heal, the poorly casted leg John Singer had originally suffered from would leave its mark on the bone and the man would have a decisive limp for the rest of his life.

But at least he would have the leg.

Not like the thousands of legs, arms, hands and feet that the good Doctor had been forced to amputate to save lives. Now they were broken men, alive, but never again whole.

One could not think of it, not for long.

The horror of the war would threaten any man's sanity.

The quinine appeared to be taking effect. His fevered thrashing began to cease. His body lay limp, worn out from fighting. Emma returned with the water and found John resting, breathing evenly once again.

"You did it. I knew you could."

The way she beamed at him made the Henry wish to take her into his arms, right in that moment. But he said and did nothing as the attendants rushing to move John to the clean dry bed. Emma ran to the soldier's side when he was settled in the clean sheets, cooling his face and chest with a towel dipped into the cool water.

She sponged him with the utmost care.

The young physician watched her tender caresses. At the soul of him, deep inside his heart, jealousy burned deep. But he dare not speak of it. Yet a part of him did rage, silently inside.

No, he could wait.

Wild emotions would not rule him.

Soon, Emma would see his finer traits, she would know he was the better man. She would desire a true gentleman as her husband, not toss away affections for a man not worthy of her heart.

So, let her try to save this one.

Perhaps the effort kept her from drowning in the loss of so many others, too many others who they could not save.

In the end, the better man would win.

Henry knew it would be him.

Coming to her side, he placed on hand softly on her shoulder. Even that benevolent touch secretly warmed him. "Emma, should the fever rage again, spoon some quinine into him. It helped this time. It is no cure, but perhaps it may help. The fever must break for him to have a chance."

"It must break," she stood, facing him.

He watched her expression and silently wished for the day when he sparked such devotion in her heart.

Soon, very soon.

"Doctor Bradley," she cried out, throwing herself into his arms, "Thank you for helping John."

As Henry held Emma in his arms he didn't feel gratitude like she must be feeling, or even the comfort of one war weary friend soothing another. No, he ached to kiss her, to tell sweet Emma of his plans for their future, to share his true feelings for her.

Instead, he stepped back, holding her by the slim shoulders.

Soon, his heart whispered. *Soon.*

"Good night," he said gently. "God be with you both."

Emma sat in the wooden chair next to John's bed and wept openly for the first time. He was in so much danger. A fever such as this could destroy the strongest of men.

Tears fell for what may never be if he did not get well.

The taste of his kiss was still on her lips, the promises of that moment had burned into her heart, and the memory of having felt the closeness of his bare chest next to hers was maddening to her very being.

He was to her, all-consuming.

Nothing else mattered anymore. Only John Singer.

These years at the hospital she had tended many wounded men, often sitting next to them to bring comfort and had wrote many a letter from a dying soldier's bedside to be sent home to a mother or a wife. Each one written with a broken heart for the recipient of the dying's last words.

Yet now at the end of the war her world had turned to chaos, all because John Singer looked at her, had embolden her to seek him out and fall under his charismatic spell.

Emma shook her head in disbelief of her actions.

But spellbound she was; couldn't shake it and did not wish to be free. Somehow, he had claimed her.

With one look, she became his.

When John had watched her those dark eyes glowed with an inner fire of life, a fire that now burned through her, that could only be quelled by him.

Yet his ease with sparking that desire, also gave her pause.

How many others may have fallen under his spell?

His diction and clarity of speech revealed a trained and educated background. The ease with which he touched her, pulling her toward him also bespoke of a confident and practiced lover. These things made her worry. Yet deep inside she knew it only mattered that he must get well.

But could he?

Maybe Doctor Bradley was right.

John's exposure on the road, no real food or water for days on end, suffering from a broken leg may have set him firmly on the path to death.

"No," she whispered, stroking his hand while he slept quietly now, "You shall not leave me. I only just found you."

But he might die.

Tears wet her pale cheeks at the thought. Wiping her face, she recalled his fevered outburst from earlier, mutterings that revealed the mental agony raging within him. Crimes, he had claimed, sins that would send him to hell. A man's conscience cried out to right the wrongs, even when his mind was not aware.

Emma wondered why he said he thought a man was a dictator? And fire and pain, he had yelled, so much pain. She may not openly tell her of the secret he carried within his heart, yet the delirium exposed the raw layers of dark secrets he fought so hard to hide.

John had said all his family was gone and there was no one.

Being alone was a terrible fate.

Surely someone was missing him.

As with all wounded when they arrived from battle, his uniform had been stripped away when the attendants changed him into the plain white hospital gown he now wore. Sometimes soldiers carried a carte de visite of themselves inside their uniform, with pictures of their family or perhaps a letter from a loved one from home.

But undoubtedly as was common practice, his uniform was already burned to prevent the spread of malaria and disease.

Any identifying items were lost.

Emma gazed at him, tears escaping her exhausted eyes. She had not slept, but faithfully stayed all this time, tending to him as best she could. The other nurses kindly brought her meals occasionally.

But no one stayed for long.

Malaria was for most, a death sentence. Hope was futile.

She admired John while he lay still in the bed, the quinine working through his body, his only hope for a cure. His marble white skin was such a contrast to his thick dark wavy hair.

Another hour passed with only the sounds of his breathing to mark the time. The delirium had passed now. The handsome man lay sleeping, silent and innocent as a child asleep in their bed. She waited by his bedside and covered him with the thin white sheet.

She felt his forehead and found it cool to her touch.

Was it possible the fever had broken after all?

Had God spared him? She bowed her head in gratitude, hugging herself, then absently ran her hands over her slim frame, feeling the sharpness of her bones though her duty uniform.

She was so very thin.

A woman should have curves, lush and inviting curves.

But like the war itself, Emma had been worn down, stretched to the point of nearly breaking.

Although not wise in the sensual ways of men, John's confidence with her combined with his perfect face and dark eyes were impossible for a woman to resist. She recalled how his hand lightly touched her breast when he reached to touch her hair.

It was no accident she knew.

And his kiss, lips soft and gentle just pressing her for more and drawing out her passion as if he owned her very being. His arms around her had been strong. Her breasts had pushed and been held against him.

She could not draw breath. Could think only of John Singer.

In that kiss, he touched the very essence from her heart.

There was no turning back. She would never let go.

Now she understood the pain her dear friend Louisa must have endured, praying for her soldier to live, dying a little inside when he passed.

"We will not pass, John." She swore aloud. "We have only just begun."

As if he heard, a tiny smile etched the corners of his lips and he drew a breath that seemed easier that those before.

He slept peacefully now.

Emma caressed his face.

Too exhausted to stay awake any longer, she turned to take her leave of him. But still drawn to him by a magnetic force, she turned her head as she stood in the doorway, hesitating long enough to look once again at his resting form. Seeing him sleeping comfortable now sent warmth through her body as if drawing life from the very sight of him.

CHAPTER SIX

My God, where is my uniform
Where is my diary?

--- John Singer

The next morning found John still sleeping as Emma made her way to his side once again. She felt his forehead and was pleased to find it was cool to her touch. The fever by all accounts had broken.

The miracle Emma prayed for was granted.

John Singer would live.

She sat by his side, impatiently waiting for him to wake. She couldn't sit still. Anticipation made her fidget. She had to touch him and couldn't resist rubbing his hand. Soon his eyes fluttered and the dark silky lashes opened to reveal his dark and shining eyes.

"Emma, my Lovely. What has happened these last few days?"

"Doctor Bradley believes you have been afflicted with malaria. You suffered through quite a fevered delirium, but he gave you some medicine. The fever was finally broken last night."

Emma smiled at him, her heart racing to see him awake and aware.

John met her gaze for a long moment as if his mind were still putting together the facts, "You stayed by my side?"

"Yes, certainly."

Affection lit the depths of his intense eyes, drawing her closer. She leaned forward, their faces mere inches apart.

"You have given me so much." His fingers caressed hers, "Your will to help me to live, your care and your belief in me," he sighed and looked overwhelmed, "it is humbling for me to accept such kindness. I am in debt to you. Tell me, how shall I repay you?"

Emma thought only of his sweet stolen kiss, although it had been given in defiance of living and was his way of saying goodbye, she wanted another one more than anything else.

But ladies did not speak of such bold things.

"You must get strong now and eat," reverting to her nurse duties, she sat back and avoided his emotionally laden question. Truth was, he had stolen her heart completely. Worry for his health and life only compounded it.

But those honest words felt heavy, too soon to be spoken and burdensome. The only repayment she needed was looking at her with deep brown eyes, his dark curls mussed from sleep, and her miracle had a slight curve at the corners of his supremely kissable lips.

Nodding slowly, he seemed to understand, but insisted, "Answer me, My Lovely Emma. How could a man be so lucky that the sweetest angel in all Alexandria chose to guard and protect a sinful devil such as I?"

He was daring her to speak the truth.

"Every life is precious, John. Especially yours."

It was the most honest answer she had.

Helping him sit up to lean against the metal headboard, she fussed and tucked the pillows behind his back. "You must take care now, that the physical part of yourself shall heal," leaning down, she was close enough again she felt the brush of his hot breath upon her cheek.

Boldly, she looked him in the eyes.

"And as for whatever sins you believe you committed, that is in the past. You survived death, to begin life anew. Can you forgive yourself enough to let go and let your heart heal as well?"

He swallowed hard, "What right have I to a second chance?"

His words were laden with regret.

Emma sat in her chair again, the position moving their faces too far apart for this intimate conversation. Nervous by needing him, she tucked the chair closer, leaning in slightly so they could quietly speak.

"In your fevered state you called out, saying things about a man. You believed he was a dictator, and you did it for your country. You spoke of the fire, the gun and the pain. What did you mean by this?"

It took him a long tense moment to reply.

"I committed unspeakable acts, Emma."

"Are your actions in the war so unforgivable?"

"Speak no more of it," he begged.

"Well then. Appreciate the new life you have been given, John Singer." She tartly demanded. "Prove to me that saving your sinful life was not wasted effort. Prove to me that a man such as you deserves to hear my private thoughts, to know my mind, and to feel my kindness. It's only then that we can begin to discuss repayment."

Dark brows arched in shock, "Prove to you?"

"Certainly. I deserve no less than your highest effort."

The corners of his lips curved. "Sweet Emma has an edge, when pushed too far." His smile widened, "Adoring you will be a privilege, my Beauty."

For a happy moment, they simply shared a triumphant smile.

She had given him something to live for and John had proven he was not a man willing to shove aside a challenge, especially one that promised so many private pleasures in the end.

The lady had won.

Emma pushed back her chair, giving her skirts room as she stood. "You must be hungry. You have not eaten in three days. Let me bring your breakfast."

John reached for her hand and as he brought it to touch his lips, then he turned it over, placing a kiss in the center of her palm. It was a persuasive charming gesture that stirred the very essence of her being as a lady.

His touch was gentle, yet commanding.

This was a man who could hold her deep into the night, bringing far more than physical comfort or an end to her loneliness. This was a man she could love. Emma felt a wave of warm affection stir her heart.

"Is this your promise, John?" She quietly asked.

"Yes," He solemnly vowed, then tenderly cradled her open palm against his face, enjoying the feel of her skin on his cheek. "Thank you."

"For?"

"Reminding me how deeply I crave feeling a fire burning deep inside the soul," he eloquently explained, "And for shedding light upon my darkness. Tis a great day when a condemned man wakes to find himself reborn anew."

The way he spoke was beautiful.

It made her feel extraordinary.

"Now you must rest and heal." Emma said matter of fact to him. "I will stop by to see Doctor Bradley and then bring your breakfast to you. I will be back very shortly."

As Emma smiled at him the shine in his eyes glistened with renewed life, chasing away the gray pallor from his skin and making his face incredibly handsome.

John's promise would hold. She felt it deep inside.

"Thank you, too," she sweetly allowed. "I look forward to our time together."

It was the biggest promise she had ever given a man, but the only one that mattered. Her cheeks flushed with excitement as she turned away from him, skirts lifted as she hurried to find the Doctor to share her good news of their recovering patient.

John watched her go and felt the brightest blaze of that fire inside his soul go with her. She was a woman to surpass his dreams, a woman worth living for. He knew it when they first met. She was completely irresistible, both to his heart and to his body.

That body ached still. He was lucky to be alive, far luckier than anyone could ever know.

It must remain his secret.

His thoughts returned to the day he had first entered the hospital.

John's blood froze as he realized his uniform had been stripped away and an ordinary white hospital gown covered him. The pain from his leg and the delirium of the last few days had addled his senses. Clear-headed now, he realized what was missing.

Where is my uniform? Where is my diary? I must have that diary back.

John barely remembered stumbling out of the woods onto the road, his compass gone, food and water gone, the pain from his leg unrelenting. Yet he held firm to the inside pocket of his uniform, where he kept his secrets, secrets that must never be revealed, not to anyone, ever.

Especially not to Emma.

She must never know.

His heart thudded with fear.

John had to find a way to inquire about his uniform and the diary he had tucked into the inside pocket. If it was burned or otherwise destroyed, then so be it. However if it was not destroyed, then he must find it.

His mind raced to all the places it could have been lost; on the road, in the ambulance that brought him here, in the triage ward where his leg was tended to, or somewhere here in isolation where he was recovering from the onslaught of malaria.

Too many places for a man with a broken leg to search.

This inquiry must be done carefully. The diary was the only possible link to his sordid past, a past that must remain dead and buried.

John closed his eyes, wishing none of the past few months had ever happened. Regret was a mountainous weight inside, crushing his heart. The choices he made were foolish, so rashly championing a cause that he could not win. A cause that destroyed everything he loved about his life.

He had been so wrong.

Emotions ran tight and high, making his eyes sting.

He recounted every mistake in his mind and thought of Emma.

She was his second chance.

"My name is John Singer, my name is John Singer, my name is John Singer."

John uttered the name again and again as the tears slowly fell and his heart ached with waves of grief and sadness. He was alone, in more ways than ever. Here, he gave himself one last private moment to mourn all that was lost, and everything that could never be again.

Emma's pace quickened as she hurried into the triage ward to find Doctor Bradley. She was anxious to tell him the good news and thank him for John's recovery. She found him in an all too familiar scene. The young soldier the good Doctor had been tending just yesterday had recently passed.

She watched in reverent silence from the doorway as Henry covered the young man with a sheet. Giving a shake to his head, she heard him call to his medical aids to remove the body.

Emma hesitated.

John was spared, yet that young man was not.

It confirmed her belief that God did not want handsome John Singer amidst his heavenly hosts; not yet. He was given life and that second chance was hers, too. She felt the hope warm her soul.

She respectfully approached the Doctor.

"Good morning Doctor Bradley. I am sorry for yet another loss," she nodded politely at the attendants moving the body of the young soldier away, "but I wanted to tell you, John Singer's fever has broken. He is awake and speaking."

"Your soldier refuses to die," he grimly noted.

"Yes, it appears he was spared. I was on my way to bring his breakfast and I wanted to tell you he is recovering. John will live."

The young Doctor was keenly aware of the joyful light in her pale blue eyes as she spoke of John. The sad impact of the other young soldier's passing was lessened for a moment.

The joy in her face was beautiful to witness.

How many times Henry wished for her face to brighten at the sight of him, a light he hoped to see in her eyes; the light of love.

"Emma, it is with favor that God has given John the elusive gift of recovery. He is fortunate indeed."

Doctor Bradley spoke with the authority of a physician, maintaining his stoic demeanor, yet he was just a man. A man who felt the pangs of jealously ruminate though his heart.

Maintaining control, he let out a tense breath, "I have been told no more wounded will be transported here. The triage area will be dismantled and only the hospital will remain to tend those who will need longer care. It is time for you to go home now," he sighed again, "and start our lives. The war is over Emma."

He said this wishing her infatuation with John had faded, wanting to tell her of his feelings, hoping that the war being over would mean they could start their lives together. He wanted to court her, properly. In time, she would love him far more than this passing fancy for an injured soldier.

Emma heard this news with a look of happiness but the smile quickly faded. "Home is not as I left it, I fear."

Henry knew her joy was numbed by the realization of what was left of her home. "No, it is not."

The city of Richmond was burned and leveled in the last days of the war. He knew her family's home neighbored the large house given to the Confederate President Jefferson Davis to serve as the Confederate White House and his army to use as their headquarters.

How her home fared, he did not know.

But the city she loved was in ruins.

It was rumored that President Lincoln, in the last days before his assassination went to Richmond and sat at the desk where Jefferson Davis had plotted the Confederacy and commanded Robert E. Lee and the Army of North Virginia. Perhaps the neighboring homes had been spared, used by the army as housing.

Emma's mother and young sister were all that remained of her family. Her dear father and older brother were lost to the cause. When letters detailing these losses arrived to their hospital, it had ripped through her heart. Afterward Emma had dedicated herself to saving every soldier possible.

Perhaps this explains the infatuation with John Singer.

Henry realized he was her last soldier to save.

Watching her work so hard was difficult, but he had remained her friend, offering strength that might make her life less agonizing. "You have given so much to the care of so many soldiers. I thank you, for all you have done here these last three years," he said simply. "Go home, Emma. Your responsibilities here are over."

"But Doctor, what about you?"

"I can't leave here yet. My commitment to the completion of care for these soldiers is my duty. There are several young physicians interviewing to be in charge of a medical facility," he tried to express the importance of his station. "When one is chosen, I will return home to Richmond to begin a private practice. My family has prepared for my homecoming. My medical career is already arranged."

"That is wonderful. You deserve it."

Henry almost asked her to come work with him, but he couldn't court her as his attending nurse. The business of his patients came first. Emma must be free, a lady free to choose, who would love him as an equal and become his wife. He always believed he would have time when the war ended, yet now he felt time was running out, as the presence of John Singer hung over him like the dark cloud of death.

"Your life is outside these walls, Emma." He carefully advised, "This soldier John Singer is someone who has captured your heart today, but it seems to me that this happened so quickly and under dire circumstances. Your devotion to his health is admirable, but as your friend I wish to caution you. What do you know of him?"

He again felt the stirring of jealousy for the man that captured her heart in so short a time.

Emma lowered her face, letting the cautionary words of the Doctor resonate within her. "Doctor I know nothing of him really, not where he is from or what he did before the war. He didn't have the will to live when he arrived, even after you set his leg. The pain in his body appears to be not nearly as agonizing as the pain inside his heart."

"How do you know this?"

"John speaks of terrible deeds he committed during the war. He refuses to speak of it, but the past tortures his mind."

"He is a soldier," Henry rationalized, determined to prove himself a worthy friend. "Like us, he has undoubtable been forced to witness death. It marks some men. Perhaps his memories are best left in the past. It is his future, who he is today and his intentions now that the war is over, that should concern you more."

Emma nodded to accept his advice, but did not seem content to allow the mysterious man his secrets. "Is his uniform is still here, or has it already been burned and buried?"

"Why do you want it?"

"If I can see his uniform, perhaps there is a clue, something to learn where he is from and to help him contact his loved ones. He says his family is gone. Surely there must be someone who is looking for him, someone who is waiting to hear word of his wellbeing."

The Doctor paused, "You mean some woman, yes?"

She nodded.

"If there was someone who claimed his heart he would not have captured yours. Think about that. But as to the uniforms, as you well know, most are burned or buried as they are carriers of lice and disease. Check with the attendant Old Sam that deals with such matters and see if it exists."

"Thank you."

Letting her pursue John Singer was torture, but Henry vowed he was still the better man. Forcing her to see it would only cause anger between them.

"If you are adamant to learn more, then just ask him. This is a request born of an honest desire to help him contact loved ones," he tipped his head, wondering, "or is there something you aren't telling me?"

Lowering her gaze, she bit her lip.

"Emma," he gently encouraged, "what is it?"

He saw the look of confusion cross her lovely countenance and waited for her to speak. "I cannot fathom what it is exactly. He is a charming, obviously an educated man who seems most comfortable and practiced in the ways of women. He claims no woman is waiting for him, yet I need to know for myself."

"If he is healing, he will leave soon."

"Yes, it will be time to go home, for all of us, yet I cannot bear to imagine letting him leave without me." She finally looked him in the eyes, speaking bold and true. "My heart says we were brought together for a purpose. I must pursue it."

The young Doctor felt angry heat prickle up the back of his neck at Emma's words. The pangs of jealousy that had been festering within him, now raged. Yet he still chose his words carefully as he plotted.

The trust she gave to him meant everything.

Better to keep her friendship and earn her love, especially when her precious soldier proved to be unworthy of her affections.

"Yes, I understand. Your John Singer has been through unspeakable horror as we all have. Such things weight on anyone. Perhaps he will tell you and he may not. It is up to you to accept who and what he is; if you truly love him."

She took a deep breath of realization, her eyes gleamed with emotion. "Yes, yes I believe that I do love him, no matter who he is or what he has done."

"Then you have your answers."

He smiled at her outwardly, yet inside the agony Henry felt over her words of professed love for another man piercing his heart. He wanted to rage, to yell at her, but he simply clenched his fists.

"Go now to find the uniform, if you feel it will help you."

As Emma ran from his side, Henry realized this John Singer was now a rival, and cursed the cure that he himself provided to bring this man back to life.

Emma rushed to the back of the hospital where the freed black attendants were preparing to burn the latest pile of uniforms. The burning fire pit was a constant reminder of the disease that lingered here and of dead men who no longer had need of their uniforms.

"Stop, please." Emma asked the men, intending to comb through the pile in hopes of finding John's uniform. "I need to keep the one that says 'John Singer', please. Can you help me retrieve it?" She smiled at one man in particular, the attendant known as Old Sam, a towering heavyset black man who she had seen every day since coming to the hospital. He was devoted to his work and to serving Doctor Bradley.

Old Sam frowned, "I don't know why you'd want this Miss, nothing but lice and disease on these old things."

"Yes, I know. But please check."

Old Sam turned, wading through the pile of bloodied and torn uniforms, poking and lifting the diseased and bloodied garments with a large tree branch. "Miss, it looks like we be leavin' here soon. It time we all be getting home, 'cept I don't have no home. Doc Bradley says he is stayin' on for a while, so I be staying on with him. He's all the home I got."

Her heart went out to him.

"But you know Miss, I is free now. Massa Lincoln, he done that for us and a madman done struck him down."

He shook his head in grief.

"Yes I know, such terrible things have happened to this country. Southern or Northern does not matter as we are all back in the Union now. It was a shame our President was struck down. We needed him to help the country heal."

"Yes um," was all he said.

In the very last pile of uniforms that Old Sam picked the name Singer appeared on the cuff sleeve of the left arm.

"Sam," she cried, "that is it."

He carried it to her, letting it dangle from the end of the stick as if Old Sam were afraid the jacket was contaminated.

"Don't be touching it, Miss Emma," the big man cautioned in his simple way of speaking. "I'll look in it for you."

He patted down the jacket with big dark hands, flashing her a shiny white grin when he discovered something hard and rectangular hidden amid the soiled cloth. "Look there. There is something in the jacket pocket. It seems like some kind of book."

He tugged loose the handstitched threads keeping it in place, pulled it out of the threadbare uniform jacket and handed it to her.

"Why Old Sam," she exclaimed. "It's a diary."

As he handed it to her several pages that looked like news clipping slipped out to the ground. As she bent down to retrieve them, she realized they were not only news clippings, but carte de visite photos of not one, but five very pretty young ladies.

"Well there Miss, I guess he knows some ladies." Sam peered at the photos that were fashionable for people to trade in relationships. He wrinkled his brow, "And then some, too."

"Old Sam," Emma evenly instructed, "Say nothing of this to anyone. If anyone should ask, say we found nothing. Do you understand?"

"Yes ma'am, I do."

"Thank you."

"But look here, it's none my business, Miss Emma, but Mr. Singer sure looks to be sweet with the ladies. Old Sam knowed you for these last three years. We seen lotsa bad things, but I tell you this here man must be some kinda man, if he has all those photos of them ladies. Watch out, is all I say."

With that warning, Old Sam picked up the uniform and threw it onto the fire. Emma stood and watched it burn to ashes.

She grasped the diary with both hands and ran back to her room to look at it later. What secrets would this reveal? Should she tell John about the diary, was he even looking for it?

She decided to wait. Emma pushed away thoughts of the carte de visite of all those young ladies. While it wrenched through her heart, she had always known women probably adored John. His social ease and outright handsomeness were impossible to resist.

But right now, she was late getting his breakfast. Tucking the diary in her dresser drawer, hiding it among her white petticoats, she hurried to the kitchen to prepare his food.

The very idea of another woman loving him pierced her heart.

She pictured his handsome face, the way his eyes focused so intently upon her, burning her with sensuous desires. It was new and profound. It stole her breath. His kiss was addictive, especially to a lonely nurse who had spent too many years surrounded by pain and death.

Her spirit yearned for love.

Rushing with his breakfast, the desire to see him again grew stronger. She thought again of the diary with the five carte de visite from very attractive females. Whoever they were to him, she was here now. She had saved his life.

She would read it tonight.

Soon, she would have answers. Emma decided being near him was like a heady fragrant spring rain, his presence like a euphoric opiate she had become addicted to.

Soon it would be time for her go home.

What of John; where will he go?

I cannot think straight. What is this spell he has cast upon me? I have lost my heart to a man I know nothing about. It matters not. I must be near him. And if he feels the same, I will never ever let go.

CHAPTER SEVEN

Why Mr. Singer, has anyone mentioned
you bear an uncanny resemblance
to John Wilkes Booth?

--- *Walt Whitman*

While John sat quietly in his bed, thoughts of his missing diary resonated within him. The very idea of it being discovered was enough to freeze his blood cold. His second chance would be over before it had properly begun.

Emma must never know.

Misery once again crept back into his heart.

As he turned his head to hide the pain, he noticed a gentleman coming towards him. He was an older man, short of stature and heavy set around the middle, with scattered white hair and an equally white beard.

Without hesitation, he sat in the chair next to John's bed.

"May I introduce myself? My name is Walt Whitman. I have spent much time in Washington DC area hospitals, helping soldiers from both the North and South in whatever way I can. Doctor Bradley informed me a soldier named John Singer recently survived malaria. It is a miracle."

"Yes, I believe it is."

The man smiled, "I ask if perhaps there was letter I could write for someone at home, tell them your good news. I am at your humble service." With that said the old gentleman bowed his head in deference to the injured man in the bed.

"Mr. Whitman," he sat up a little straighter, "I am familiar with your writings and poetry. You are truly gifted. If there was someone I had waiting for me, most certainly I would be honored to have you write to them. But as it stands sir, I have no family, no one for you to contact. My family is gone."

"I am sorrowed by your circumstance."

"This war has taken much from all of us."

Mr. Whitman's face turned solemn, if not by the war but by something deeper. Familiar with the look of the misery of pain, John recognized sorrow in the gifted writer who sighed and nodded his head. "Indeed, it has taken much." His chin tipped as elderly eyes studied John. "You believe my writing and poems are a gift?"

"Yes, creative greatness in any art form is a gift. But might I ask you sir, what has saddened your soul? I can see the pain in your eyes."

The poet looked relieved to have found someone to confide in.

"Yes Mr. Singer, I have such pain, as all we do from this war, but never so much as when my dear friend, our President Abraham Lincoln was struck down by a madman."

It made John's heart almost stop beating.

"He was gunned down by a Southern sympathizer," the elderly man continued, "a great actor of the famous acting Booth family of Maryland. Utterly unexpected. I saw John Wilkes perform in Boston. His art was pure and deep, the performance perfection. I heard ladies claim he was the handsomest man in America. I cannot believe an artist of such high acclaim would abandon his art and cause such devastation to mankind by this one evil act."

John listened, unwilling to say anything at all.

But Walt did not notice his silence.

He was simply grateful for a listening ear to hear his thoughts. "It has caused me great disbelief in humanity, for the wasted life of a great President and the wasted life of so talented a young man."

"Yes, a waste, to be sure," he managed to agree.

The old man eyed the young handsome stranger.

"If I may be so bold as to ask Mr. Singer, as I said, I saw John Wilkes on stage in Boston; by chance have you heard how closely you resemble the man?"

"Never."

The writer persevered with his claim. "If we were not so sure he was shot and killed in Garrett's Farm," his white head shook in disbelief as he studied John, "well, you are clean-shaven and he was known for always having a bold mustache. But you resemble him so closely. Perhaps it is in the eyes, so dark and intense. Where is it you come from again?"

John quickly turned the conversation to the old gents art, thinking it may dissuade any further inquiries.

"Tell me Mr. Whitman, what is your latest piece of prose?"

A broad smile lit his weathered face.

The distraction worked. "It is a dedication to my friend and our late President, Abraham Lincoln."

"Would you be so kind as to share it with me? I would so love to hear you recite to me, it would please me so."

The old gent hesitated a moment and thought long and deep at the request. Reciting it would certainly open the wound that would take his lifetime to heal.

"Mr. Singer, yes most certainly I will," He then took a deep breath and began, "The name of the poem is *O Captain, My Captain!*"

John listened to the words of the poem, the orator's voice resonating and falling with each stanza as he described the passing of a leader, the flowers and wreaths of death laid upon the form of the fallen Captain. It was the litany of a broken heart to his friend, a tribute to the passing of his hero.

A hero I struck down.

When he finished the prose, John could see the tears welling up in the red-rimmed eyes of the elderly gentleman. "My apologies, Mr. Singer. As you can see my pain over the sudden loss of one I loved and respected is still so very fresh. Our President was indeed, a good man."

John simply nodded.

"Mr. Whitman, thank you for the recital. Your words are riveting and beautiful, a poem born by love and loss," he sincerely complimented. "Thank you for stopping by and sharing your gift of words. Your writing is a gift born of devotion and passion."

The poet wiped his eyes, staring once again at the man in the bed. Clearly the nagging insistence of his uncanny resemblance to the one who had murdered the President bothered the old gentleman.

"Mr. Singer," the writer inquired again, "where were you born?"

At that moment Emma came rushing in with the breakfast tray, making joyful noise that John welcomed. She smiled her greatest smile, obviously reveling in the sight of him sitting up, speaking to someone. Her gaze was riveted on his face as she entered.

"Good morning Mr. Whitman," Emma happily greeted, "I see you have met our Mr. Singer."

"Why yes, Miss Emma, I have. We were just becoming acquainted."

"That is wonderful."

"I have heard this hospital will be closing its doors very soon, and I gather you will be going home to Richmond."

John sat silent in the bed, listening intently, as he knew as little of her as she did of him.

"Yes, Doctor Bradley explained it will be time to go home soon. In their last letter from home that arrived a few days ago, I learned my little sister and mother have moved back into the family home in Richmond."

"Your home is safe from the burning?"

"Yes, it is higher on a hill at the edge of the city. We were fortunate as it is next door to the house used by President Jeff Davis, which served as part of his headquarters during the war. I had heard General Lee and General Stonewall Jackson were frequent visitors to our home. We were more fortunate than most as our home was not burned on the last days of Richmond before it fell."

"Most fortunate," Walt agreed. "You know, in the three years I have known you dear, you never spoke of your family."

"Perhaps because my brother and father were lost to the war."

"Yes, the pain of loss is difficult to speak of."

Emma carefully placed the tray of food on the bed, but not before plumping John's pillows and straightening the well-worn sheet that lay over him.

As she fussed over him, she gently pushed back a raven lock of his hair from his forehead, combing it back with her fingers. It was a gesture that needed no words as it spoke volumes of love.

The old man obviously recognized the moment had come for him to leave. Clearing his throat, he rose from the chair beside the bed. "It is time I take leave of you both and continue my rounds for those in need. Mr. Singer, please continue on your recovery and Miss Emma, I bid you farewell."

Emma watched the old gentleman leave, then turned all her attention to John.

"So now you have met our Mr. Whitman. He's been a regular presence here for years, offering his assistance to administer to those in need. What did you think of him?"

John hesitated, choosing his words carefully.

"He is a great writer and orator, who is grieving for the loss of his friend, the murdered President. Certainly I can understand loss."

He lowered his gaze, feeling a sharp sting left from the old writer's use of the word madman.

"Yes he is a talented man. His kindness towards all, both to Northern and Southern hospitals were known in the capitol at Washington and here in Alexandria. He was dear friends to the President as he had told me repeatedly; he is lost right now in his grief, but still tries to help those in greater need."

She sat in the chair, her smile gone, lost in her own thoughts about the war and all it had taken from her.

He could see the private sorrow etch her face and dared not ask.

Suddenly, she abruptly stood.

"I must tend to the others now John, rest and eat. I will return."
Before John could stop her, Emma dashed away.

Emma had only left his side for a few hours, but forcing herself to stay away from John that long felt torturous. She had not intended to leave his side, but the conversation had become far too painful. She hated thinking about the loved ones she had lost in the war.

She wanted to focus on John.

"I apologize for leaving you so abruptly," she softly told John as she sat at his bedside again.

"What troubled you so deeply?"

"Death. Losing my brother and father are not something I like to speak of. I cannot allow myself to wallow in sadness, mourning the past. I must move forward with hope. Believing life will be happy again is all that keeps me going. I hope you understand."

"More than you can imagine," John honestly confessed. "My losses are deep, my mistakes many. But a lovely wise woman believes I've been blessed with a second chance," he smiled, a playful seduction warming his voice. "You've made me hope, Emma."

His hand reached to touch hers.

She felt the warmth of promise as his fingers laced with hers.

Slowly, asking for permission with that sweet touch, his dark-eyed stare remained focused upon her face as John affectionately pulled her close to him.

She did not resist.

Heedless of the injuries he suffered, he pulled her closer still and lifted himself ever so gently as to reach her lips.

"Are you my second chance, Emma, my love?" He whispered against her cheek, his arms holding her upper body pressed against his.

"Yes, just as you are mine, handsome John Singer."

John kissed her then, drawing the sweetness of her lips to his, teasing her mouth with unspoken promises of so much more.

Emma had never been kissed like this.

His touch, while gentle and sweet, took command of her senses. Denying the fire between them was impossible. It consumed every ounce of resistance, pulled her into his world, body and soul, making her burn for more.

This was more than a mere kiss.

This kiss was the beginning of love.

Her breath quickly became labored as her passion was drawn out by his obvious desire. John Singer was skilled. Every touch, every tender caress of his body against hers made her feel beautiful and adored.

He slowly released her.

Emma realized the hand that had once held hers was now resting just beneath her breast, palm spread to feel her slender ribs, possessive fingers waiting for the time when he could physically claim her body more.

"John," she struggled for words, needing to speak her heart, finding his kiss had given her courage. "I cannot bear being alone any longer."

Her breath was raspy with emotions.

"I have not known a man, have never experienced the intimacies between a man and a woman, but I am drawn to you like no other. I ask you not to toy with passions or take my feelings lightly, but to take me into your heart, love me and never let me go."

A tiny smile curved his soft lips, "It pleases me that no man before me has shown you the great and wonderful mysteries of love. I will be honored to share them with you, when the time is right."

Of course, he knew more about loving than she did.

Emma should have felt embarrassed.

Instead she felt excited to learn. From him, only him.

Her thoughts went quickly to the diary, the pictures of the women, the news clippings, evidence of who John may be, evidence that was hers. But looking at his handsome face she decided whatever the diary revealed, it would not change her mind.

"Emma," he murmured, "My sweet darling. Our time together will be soon, I promise. I am growing stronger by the hour. Your care has given healed me."

She looked into his eyes and searched them, trying to see past the secret depths of their inky blackness.

"They will be closing portions of this hospital soon. Doctor Bradley has released me from triage duties. Don't you see, dearest John, I will be leaving soon for Richmond. I will be going home."

He clearly understood.

"And so you are wondering what will become of me, where shall I go, and to whom do I go home to?" She nodded and held his hand tighter. He sighed, "I have no home, no family wondering of me, and no woman whose bed is waiting for me."

She boldly asked, "Where will you go when I leave?"

He gazed into her beautiful face, giving her a loving smile. "Wherever you go darlin'. I will too; that is, if you will have me. I have nothing to give you presently, no station nor status, only my heart."

She held his hand and lowered her gaze.

Emma wanted to tell him of finding his diary, the carte de visite of the five women, and the news clippings. It was at her very lips to tell him of her discovery, yet she held back. He was so cryptic and cautious, revealing so very little of himself.

She wanted trust between them.

John read the distress in her face, "Emma, what is it?" She did not reply. "You do not want me, is that it?"

"Of course not, this is all happening so very fast. You cast this spell on me just by the look in your eyes." She honestly revealed.

"Most people only get one real chance at love. This one is mine. Nothing of your past, or what you did before the war will change my mind. Such is the admiration you have prevailed upon me. Yesterday will never matter to me, only the man that you are today and tomorrow."

"Others may not be so forgiving," he softly acknowledged. "What if tomorrow I bring trouble into your life?"

"I will stand with you, for today you have made my heart smile."

With her heartfelt words, John blessed Emma with a smile of his own, answering all of her questions.

He needed her, too.

"When I am able, my Sweet Emma, we will go to Richmond," he promised, "and will go together."

Her heart filled with joy.

"I will write to my mother to say when I return home, you will be with me."

"And how is it you will introduce me in this letter?" John asked.

"As a Confederate soldier that fought for the cause, and who now fights to live and love again, that you are the soldier and man who loves me. How is that?"

"Perfect. You are perfect, my love. No man could wish for more."

His desire of her showed in his adoring gaze, she could see it clearly. Emma felt his growing love and knew with it came passion. He toyed with their attraction, teasing her in his deepest most intimate voice, "Come to me darling, and I will show you love."

He was impossible to resist, but she shook her head to break his spell, if only for the moment.

She picked up his empty breakfast tray and stood.

"You must rest now. I still have duties to perform."

"I will rest, if it pleases you."

"Your swift recovery would please me greatly."

He smiled, revealing his perfectly white, even teeth. He looked noble, yet almost wicked in his perfection as a man.

Surely, she wondered as she admired his face, he might be the work of the devil with his strange and cryptic ways. But the spell he cast over her was swift, complete and all-consuming.

She drank in his handsomeness feeling awestruck that he wanted her as deeply as she needed him. Her gaze never left his face.

John Singer was her future, every tomorrow would be spent by his side.

"Good day, Sweet Emma."

He took her hand and kissed it, like a true gentleman.

As she pulled away her thoughts returned to the diary she had found and what secrets it may reveal.

"Rest well," she turned and took leave of him.

John rested his head back down and closed his eyes, in awe that life had given him a second chance, praying Emma never discovered his true identity. As he thought about beginning life anew with the beautiful blonde nurse, his thoughts drifted back to another time, at time that was hard, yet was full of love and youth.

His memories always drifted toward his favorite sister and their times together at Tudor Hall, in Bel Air Maryland.

John whispered to himself, "Dear sister Asia," he missed her deeply, mourning the loss of her love and friendship, "remember the last winter on the farm, aye, but it was harsh. We were almost starving. Mother, you, sister Rosalie and brother Joe were there."

He remembered how they set out traps, far beyond the gates of Tudor Hall and they both walked in snow drifts five feet high. Asia became stuck in the drifts and John rescued her from the mounding snow. Remembering, he felt the chill from that deadly winter. They found the traps filled with poor creatures who were as starving as his family.

Having a tender heart, Asia begged him to let them go. John didn't have the heart to kill them for food.

He whispered again, lost and alone in his thoughts, "Remember mother said it was because we named every creature on the farm as to friend it, and could not by nature kill the befriended beasts? Remember that Asia," he quietly cried out to her, "remember that time?"

He remembered it clearly.

"Aye," he sighed, "those times were hard, but we survived them."

MY NAME IS JOHN SINGER

He would give anything to have a moment back with Asia, to see her face again and let her see he had been given a second chance.

John's sister would never know.

He began to lament to loss of his family.

It was a private pain, one he could not share with Emma for he aimed to bring joy and love into her world, not heartache.

"Dearest sister, such pain I have caused our family."

John knew he could never explain his actions or see his loved ones again. He was alive, yet his family and the world believed he was shot and died in a horrible fire.

That is how it must remain.

The man who shot President Lincoln must stay dead.

He sacrificed his youth, his family, his famous acting career all for the cause he believed to be right and true, only to realize that one decisive act was not a heroic one, but a heinous one.

He had believed the President was a tyrant and thought the South should never have surrendered. He envisioned his actions would help the South, but this single act was not heroic, but rather the act of a coward.

"I thought death had come for me, yet I was spared." He whispered. "Is this God's joke or God's Blessing?"

He turned his head and closed his eyes, he allowed himself to see his sister in his mind. She was pretty, intelligent and thoughtful. In his mind she rode alongside him on his horse Cola, the day was warm and bright.

They laughed and talked, never thinking those youthful memories it would come to this end.

He pondered that scene for another moment as the harsh reality of what is life would be from now on came into focus. It was time to heal and start making plans to move on.

That old gent Walt had frozen his blood cold.

He wondered how the writer could think he recognized him when the world believes John Wilkes Booth was murdered.

John recalled his performance in Boston, seeing the famous author Walt Whitman was in the audience one of those evenings. He was also a guest of the wealthy Sumner family of Boston.

Perhaps he should have paid a bit more attention, but his thoughts at the time had been otherwise engaged with the young woman Isabella Sumner, who found her way to his dressing room and never quite left, followed John to New York to his next engagement.

If Walt Whitman recognized him, John knew he must heal quickly and leave this place soon, for if the old gent saw the truth he could convince others the same. He then thought of the young beauty Emma, who offered her love without knowing anything of his past.

She offered a place to go.

As soon as he felt well enough to travel, they would go to Richmond to her family's home. She has offered an escape and a true second chance, only asking that John love her.

He could and he would, with all his heart and soul.

Her profound beauty and honest heart claimed him completely.

Yet I can never tell her who I am or what I have done, there will always be that part of me that she will never know. That she must never know.

It is time to make plans, John decided, the first of which was to share himself with Emma, to take her to his bed and show his devotion.

He closed his eyes and pictured himself making love to her, devouring her body until she cried out for more.

Oh how he wanted her as his own.

He wanted to love her again and again. It was that thought that closed his weary eyes, hoping the nightmares that plagued him would dissipate.

Mr. Whitman had since moved to another area of the hospital, to spend time with any soldier who welcomed his visit. While he was finishing talking with a young soldier from the Ninth Infantry of North Carolina, while making his rounds, Doctor Bradley passed by him.

"Well, good morning Doctor Bradley," the old gent greeted.

Doctor Bradley turned from his patient and smiled at the writer. His visits to the hospital were so welcome by not only to the patients, but by all the hospital staff. He was always willing to stop and recite his writing or sit for a while and write letters home for those who could not.

"Good morning to you, Mr. Whitman. How does this day find you?"

"It finds me well, good Doctor, I thank you," he smiled and bowed with refined elegance. The banter between the old and the young was quick and heartfelt.

The elder man informed the physician. "I saw Emma in the isolation ward this morning." This caught Henry's attention. "It seems our dear nurse is smitten with a rather handsome soldier, a Mr. John Singer. And it appears he is quite taken with her as well."

The young Doctor held his feelings in check, but said through gritted teeth, "Yes, I noticed their attraction. It happened rather fast. Emma has devoted several days to attending to him. Mr. Singer was one of the last soldiers brought into this hospital after the war was declared over."

"How was he injured?"

"His leg was broken. It had been casted, but was poorly done and had started to heal improperly. Then shortly after I reset the leg, he contracted malaria and was delirious with fever. Emma sat with him and practically willed him back to life. The fever has since broken. Mr. Singer will walk with a limp the rest of his life, but he will completely recover."

"Her devotion is admirable. He is a lucky man."

Henry did not agree.

"The strange thing is, Emma stopped by earlier this morning, asking if Mr. Singer's uniform was still here. She told me that John was cryptic of his life prior to the war and says all his family is dead."

"A terrible loss, I'm sure." The writer sympathized. "I wish Emma well. She has been an angel of mercy here, bringing comfort to so many wounded men. I hope she chooses wisely. It would be a shame for that handsome man to break her tender heart."

This time Henry agreed completely.

"I believe she questions his past, which is wise. Emma thought if the uniform was about, perhaps there were papers as to learn where he is from."

"She is right to question his past."

He wrinkled his brow and asked the old gent, "It seems your concern for our Emma has been peaked, but for what reason? Has he said or done something that makes him seem dangerous to Emma?"

"No, he was a complete gentleman."

"Yet, you are concerned."

The statesman simply asked, "Does he perhaps remind you of someone?"

"Ah, Mr. Whitman," the Doctor sighed, "I have seen so many men. They all remind me of death and pain. John Singer is no different."

The old gent firmly explained, "From the first time I laid eyes on him, heard his voice, watched his practiced manners and charm, I felt certain I had seen him before. The resemblance is uncanny. This Mr. Singer is a dead ringer for John Wilkes Booth, the man that murdered our dear President and my friend. I saw him perform in Boston, his performance was truly a tribute to the fine art of acting."

"Looking like a famous man is no crime," Henry argued.

"It was more than his appearance. The women, Doctor. The women were driven mad by him. I saw it for myself. Like a careless spell he put on them, heedless of hearts or feelings."

"It was said John Wilkes Booth took up with a sixteen year old, Isabella Sumner from a good family from Boston's Beacon Hill. She was so entranced, she followed him to New York without a chaperone. Her family quietly married her off after the interlude as to preserve her name."

The Doctor hesitated to give weight to these claims.

"Mr. Whitman, the murderer of our dear President and your friend was murdered weeks ago on Garrett's Farm. This man John Singer is someone who unfortunately looks like Mr. Booth, that is all. Do not bring trouble to Emma and an innocent man. It is your grief that is talking right now. You are tired, come rest."

The Doctor took the old gent by the hand, tending to him, and he noticed the exhaustion in his face.

"So you don't think Mr. Singer is Mr. Booth?"

"No, I do not, unless the man in the barn was an imposter, and you must know that is not the case. Now please come with me. You must rest."

The poet acquiesced and allowed the Doctor to walk him out of the hospital and found an attendant to escort him home.

Returning to his duties, the conversation stayed with Henry.

He kept thinking of that very narrow possibility, that John Wilkes Booth was indeed John Singer and that perhaps yes, an imposter was killed at Garrett's Farm. The physician had heard that no Booth family member was invited onto the Montauk, the US Navy ship anchored off the Potomac where military officials housed the body of Booth.

He thought of his friend's ranting and dismissed it, yet the seed of doubt had been planted within him.

It festered in his mind.

As he stalked down the hospital hallway, his white physician's jacket flapping against his lean frame, Henry muttered to himself under his angry breath, "I shall find out more about you, Mr. Singer. Emma was promised to me. You won't take her away from me. She belongs to me."

Striding into his own room, the pent up fury raged.

He slammed the door, taking long strides across the floor.

Finally alone, his fists were balled up in the air, shaking above his head. Feeling the stinging pain of jealousy, he repeated over and over, "She belongs to me, she belongs to me!"

Meanwhile in Philadelphia, the young expectant mother sat quietly in her living room, the sweet smells of an early spring breezing by her face as Asia gazed out the window, remembering the brother she loved, the brother that everyone believed had assassinated President Lincoln.

Her brother caused the wrath of the United States Government and all its power to fall hard upon the Booth family.

The hand of justice was swift and without mercy.

For the Government officials believed most certainly the family must have known John was capable of such a deed, and that yes, his loved one's must have known his devious plans.

Such beliefs could not be further from the truth, the young mother sighed.

The great actor and brother Edwin Booth was an ardent supporter of President Lincoln, the opposite of John, yet he was taken to the Old Federal Penitentiary in Washington DC for questioning, along with brother Junius Booth and her husband John Clarke.

Their dear mother was beside herself with grief and suffered in agony for the loss of her dear sweet boy John. The elder Mrs. Booth loved all her children, but it was widely known John was her favorite, her favored boy. It was always John who her heart ached to see.

Asia pulled the lace curtain aside as she peered out the window. The spring morn had no beauty for her aching heart. She ran her hand over her distended belly, full now with child, remembering her promise if this child were a boy she would name him John.

This would not happen now.

The mere thought caused her even more pain.

She remembered her brother John's words at her wedding, as he was not pleased with her choice of this husband and warned her that Clarke was a procurer of names for his own benefit, and the Booth name was a handsome one to procure.

His words were true, for her marriage was truly an unhappy one. Her husband now distanced himself from the family.

She could only whisper to the walls that surrounded her, "Dear John how right you were, and no matter what you have done, I will always love you."

With that said she fingered the pendant of him that lay between her breasts and pulled it up to gaze again at that handsome face. Asia kissed him and placed it over her heart.

How it is that our Edwin or Junius or even mother were not invited to view John's body on the Montauk?

She shook her head.

It made no sense to her, yet nothing that happened these last few weeks did make sense.

She moved away from the window as not to give onlookers a chance to see her. The lace slipped out of her fingers and fell back in front of the window. As she turned, walking into the next room a young soldier that was commissioned as her guard followed her.

Her anger at this invasion was too much.

She snapped at the young blond soldier, "Sir you needn't follow me about, as I am nine months pregnant, there is little chance I should bolt anywhere and run away."

"Yes ma'am I understand, but there here are orders from Secretary of War, Edwin Stanton, so I have no choice. I must follow orders."

"Young man," she coldly stared, "And what is you think I might be hiding that would incriminate myself or my family in this heinous act committed by our brother John?"

The young soldier had no answer.

The young expectant mother was a victim of the crime her brother committed, persecuted and ostracized like all her family and his known associates and friends.

Two young boys suddenly ran to find their mother, surrounding her with their energy and love. Asia's sons quickly dispelled her grievous and heart wrenching thoughts.

"Ma'ma ma'ma," the five year old yanked at her skirts. "When is Papa coming home? And why is there a soldier here in the house with us? Why is everyone mad at Uncle John?"

Asia bent down to her oldest child, Jacob, as to see him face to face. She gathered him in her arms all the while favoring this beautiful boy, for the resemblance to his Uncle was uncanny. He had the same stern expression and black silky lashes, noble shape of his face and those same black eyes that were filled with depths of kindness.

It was like seeing John alive again.

"Jacob," she said to her child, "Papa will be home soon. The soldier is here to keep us safe," Asia lifted her head to the young soldier who nodded in understanding.

"Mama, do you still love Uncle John?" Jacob asked.

"Of course." She swung her arm to encompass both boys. The pendant swung free from his mother's neck.

While she knelt, he looked at it. "This was the picture that was in me and Joshua's room."

"Yes, it was."

"Uncle John used to ask us to pray for him when he'd come to visit."

"And so what do you think we should do now," his mother asked of him.

"Mama, I love Uncle John. Me and Joshua should pray for him."

"That would be wonderful."

The young mother hugged the child and kissed his silken head, then did the same to Joshua. The morning scents of breakfast called their attention to the kitchen.

The boys ran through the house again.

The young soldier followed the children out of the living room.

Walking a distance behind, Asia fingered her apron pocket, touching the letter she knew by heart.

It was a letter from John's fiancé.

Asia learned of this secret engagement from her brother Edwin. In the letter the young woman poured her heart out in agony for John's alleged crime and subsequent murder.

A lovely young woman Lucy Hale, was the senator's daughter from New Hampshire. One line in the letter haunted Asia.

"I should have gladly gone to the gallows with him."

As this was written to brother Edwin to explain the extent of her love for John, it brought Edwin a great sadness. In his reply he tried to empathize and explain that which was unexplainable.

Shortly after the letter was received by Edwin, they learned that Lucy Hale's father boarded her on a ship to Europe hoping the wide breadth of the Atlantic was enough to keep the name John Wilkes Booth out of his daughter's life and keep her from the hands of the government as well.

Everyone had distanced themselves from his crime.

The child in Asia's belly kicked and the delicious scents of the morning feast called to her body that needed nourishment for this child yet unborn. She walked into the dining room, grasping the picture of John tightly in her hand.

His crime was unforgivable.

But her love for the man he was inside would never die.

CHAPTER EIGHT

It is not my wish to ever leave you.

~~ Jack Clayton

Since John was recovering Emma had returned to general hospital duties. Work was easier with no trauma patients rushing in, clinging to their last moments of life. Now medical care centered around healing the men who remained. Today she bent to bathe the brow of a fevered young soldier from the Seventh Infantry Division of Murfreesboro Tennessee.

"Ma'am, thanks for your care of me," he said with appreciation. "Doctor Bradley said I'll be mighty fine in just a few more days." A wide toothy grin followed this hopeful statement.

"That is good news."

"Well, I've been luckier than most. See here, the bullet passed right through the fleshy part of my arm, nothing really. Soon I'll be good as new. I just wrote my wife and little girl that I will be home just as soon as Doctor Bradley gives me the ok."

Emma took the pulse of the soldier.

"Hmm, you seem quite strong, Sergeant Riley Jacobsen. I hope that Doctor Bradley sees favor in your recovery and sends you home to your family, as soon as you are able."

With her encouragement, the young soldier from Tennessee laid back in his bed, "Yes, ma'am!"

A flurry and swishing of skirts caught her attention.

Since the conversation and medical observance of this young soldier was completed, Emma moved to the next room where the swirl of skirts had stopped and a petite brunette woman waited, offering a bright smile.

"Louisa!" Emma was delighted to see it was her friend and mentor, Louisa May Alcott of Boston, Massachusetts, whose desire to help all those soldiers needing care during the war had brought her to serve as a nurse in the Washington DC area, just as it had brought Emma from Richmond to Alexandria.

"I had no idea you were here," she ran to embrace the slight and steadfast woman.

"Emma," her friend kindly smiled, brushing one hand up to smooth the neat up-twist in her long brown hair. "How wonderful to see you, as well."

She had met Louisa here at this field hospital in Alexandria over three years ago and was instrumental in mentoring Emma on tending the soldiers by sharing whatever medical training she could provide.

Beyond that, Louisa was strong and independent, a woman to be admired. She helped Emma realize her own worth as an intelligent woman, the importance of her contributions to society.

The Civil War increased need for nurses. This was a new career field for women where none had existed before. Louisa was compassionate and kind, making her an excellent field hospital nurse. Willingly, she left behind her comfortable life in the pastoral setting of Massachusetts. While Louisa only actively served for six weeks before falling victim to a terrible bout of typhoid fever that left her weak and ill, she remained a champion for women everywhere who sought to show their strengths.

Emma respected Louisa May Alcott greatly.

"What brings you here today?"

"I am returning soon to Massachusetts. I stopped to say goodbye to Doctor Bradley as I heard the hospital here was closing. I assumed you would have left already. Ah, it seems we were both incorrect in our assumptions, yes?"

Emma took her friend gently by her arm, and cautiously asked, "Are you ok to leave now, really ready to leave Jack behind?"

One hand went over Louisa's heart and she drew a sharp breath, "Oh yes, you remember the story, don't you dear?"

"Yes," Emma gently pulled her into another compassionate hug. "I do."

At the beginning of the war, Louisa was asked by Clara Barton, the founder of the new institution of nursing, to assist with training nurses at the Alexandria field hospital. When Emma met her a strange and grievous event had beset Louisa, one in which all who knew her still could not conceive such a kindhearted woman could suffer such a terrible tragedy.

Louisa was tending the steady stream of soldiers coming in from the battle of Blackburn's Ford, the prelude battle to the first battle of Manassas, Virginia in mid July 1861 that left both North and South mortally wounded, with a multitude of the dead.

While she attended to this stream of carnage coming through the hospital doors, she noticed a light haired man on a stretcher. He was a large muscular man, healthy and well sized. Except for a bandage wound around his shoulder, he appeared to be otherwise in a non-fatal condition.

A miracle considering the number of dead.

His eyes were blue, colored like the breaking of dawn, a fair shade that shone from such a distance from across the rows of beds, his eyes seemed to brim with beauty and innocence, the eyes of a child.

The soldiers all around him screamed out in pain, begging for water or quinine or ether to stop the suffering. Yet he remained prone and silent, his arms by his side, never raising them as to ask for help. His sun streaked light hair swept back from his face only lending to frame his handsome countenance.

While Louisa helped soldiers around his bedside she felt a slight tug on her skirts. She knew without turning was the handsome soldier.

That tug on her skirt also seemed to tug at her heart.

Louisa asked if he needed anything.

"No thank you ma'am, I be getting along fine," the accent was distinctly Southern, a smile touching the corners of his full lips. He seemed pleased with himself to have her attention, even for just that short moment.

"Perhaps later, I will sit with you."

"I'd like that very much, indeed."

Finishing her rounds Louisa found Doctor Bradley and asked about the man. In his haste to tend patients he would invariably lose that night, he gruffly explained, "Yes, Louisa. That is Jack Clayton. He is the smithy that tended my horse here in Alexandria. He is from Charlottesville." The Doctor looked up at Louisa, his hands wrists and forearms covered in blood after losing more men than he could save. "Such a shame this one must die. All the deaths bother me. But his will be such a painful slow death, and I have nothing to help ease his pain."

"But it is only a shoulder wound, surely he can recover from that?"

"Louisa," he said gently, wiping his blood-stained hands. "The bullet struck the shoulder and hit his lung. It is lodged there. I cannot operate. Each breath he takes must be agony from the pressure inside his lung. I am sorry; there is nothing I can do."

Louisa retreated in horror. Such a fine man, this cannot be.

She returned to where he was laying, still prone in the bed.

"Evening ma'am," he greeted. His voice was sensuous yet soft and gentle.

"My name is Louisa May Alcott, and yes, good evening Mr. Clayton."

Louisa immediately helped Jack to sit up, leaning his back against the pillow. She knew he must be kept in upright position, to prevent him from drowning in the fluid in his lungs that would soon suffocate him. He motioned her to sit and she pulled a chair closer to him.

"Is there someone perhaps I could write to," she spied a thin worn gold band on his left finger, "a wife or sweetheart or mother perhaps, to let them know you are in the hospital?"

The blonde man lightly tossed his head back and smiled at Louise showing an even white perfect smile. Surely the Doctor must be wrong. That robust strong man could not be dying.

"I am not married, Miss Louisa. The ring is my dear mother's. Her gift to keep me safe." He fingered the well-worn band, twisting it in a nervous gesture. "So you can see, it has worked and I am safe."

With those brave words, tears sprang to his eyes at the realization that death was near and inevitable would come. His bravery combined with his utter lack of concern for himself was compelling to Louisa. The idea that this vital and handsome man should no longer cease was unthinkable to her.

Her heart skipped a beat as she reached for his hand. "Mr. Clayton, might I stay with you and visit for a while?"

"Why yes Miss Louisa, please stay a spell, and you must call me Jack." He tilted his face to the side and smiled.

Her heart was lost.

From that time and through the next three days, Louisa sat with Jack, talking and reminiscing about childhood's dreams and life experiences. It was less of a deathwatch and more like a social visit. With each day she sat with him, their hands twined even more. She sponged his face and chest with the coolest of water, but the pressure to breathe and the fluid in his lungs built, caused him great pain.

He was the bravest man Louisa had ever known.

In the early dawn of the fourth day, after a hard night of breathing and pain, his eyes firmly planted on Louisa's face. Jack gasped to her, "It's time for me to go; it was not my wish to ever leave you."

The light in his eyes extinguished. Louisa kept holding his hand as they always did. Her grief was so overwhelming, she would not leave his side. She refused to have his strong body taken away, hidden and buried under the earth.

She sat by his side for hours, the tears flowing like a stream of heartache that had no ending or beginning. When Doctor Bradley was called to her side, she finally looked up. He was her friend and understood loss.

"Not this man, Doctor, just not this man. Look how handsome and humble he was. You cannot take him away."

"Louisa," the Doctor gently soothed, "he is gone. You must rise now and leave his side."

She looked at him and said simply, "I cannot."

"But it is time. It is not right for the dead and the living to be entwined."

He began to pry Jack's hand from hers, all the while Louisa crying a fresh veil of tears. With each finger of Jack's that was pried away, it would once again entwine with hers. Even in death his hand sought hers. It was a situation the Doctor had never witnessed before. Believing it was the right thing to do, Henry took off the gold band from Jack's finger and placed it into her hand.

"I believe it would be his wish," her friend kindly stated.

"Thank you."

Emma had been witness to this heartbreak.

Afterward, she took Louisa back to her room for rest and comfort. The women hugged while Louisa cried. She had not slept since the day she met Jack. Finally finding comfort with Emma watching over her, she fell asleep with tears still falling, even as she dreamed.

Emma had never seen grief so deep or so true.

She now understood what it meant to be "bowed down in grief."

Louisa fell ill shortly after that with typhoid fever. After weeks of illness, she recovered enough to return to Massachusetts, but remained in fragile health for a while. Throughout the rest of the war, she employed her perceptive writing skills to inform the public of the conditions within the hospitals, to use her keen mind to write stories and poems that stayed in the hearts of her readers, just as Jack stayed in hers.

Her writing was as eloquent as her tender heart.

Her visit at the hospital today was a bittersweet goodbye to her dear friends and for her heart to have one final goodbye to Jack. "Ah Emma, the war has changed all of us. We began it as naïve youths tending the wounded, but all that death and grief stripped our hearts and souls bare. But look at you. How beautiful you are."

"Thank you."

"You must be readying for your trip back home, to Richmond."

"Yes, soon I will leave."

Louisa was always compassionate and kind. "I was sorry to hear of the loss of your dear father and brother. This war has taken so much from all of us," she shook her head and Emma noticed the worn gold wedding band on a simple gold chain around Louisa's neck.

It was the wedding band.

After Jack died, Louisa had said with one look of his eyes and the simple gesture of him tugging on her skirt, and she was never the same.

In those moments, they were husband and wife.

Having befallen under John Singer's charming spell she now well understood what Louisa had meant. "Oh yes Louisa I yearn now for home, for my mother and little sister. But I won't be leaving alone," she smiled gently at her friend, always mindful of Jack's impact on Louisa and the loss she so wholeheartedly felt.

"You have met someone?"

"More than someone; the someone."

Louisa tossed her head back laughed aloud with joy, grabbing both of Emma's arms in an embrace. "I am so happy for you. You must tell me all about him. Where is he from?"

Answers Emma did not know.

"I would love for you to meet him."

"Perhaps later," Louisa promised. "Today I must stop in to see Doctor Bradley and let you finish your work. We will talk again, too."

The women hugged one last time.

Always compassionate, Louisa seemed genuinely pleased for Emma's good fortune in finding a good man who owned her heart. She drew back to look her friend in the eyes. "Emma, how incredibly brave and good you are. I'm proud of you. Throughout the war you have stayed here, working hard, giving of yourself so others might suffer less. And now life has given you the gift of love."

"You will find it too, again."

"I hope so. Surely my heart is meant to love, and be loved, someday."

With a fresh veil of tears brimming her eyes, Louisa rushed passed to find Doctor Bradley.

<hr />

The sounds of footsteps woke John from his brief morning slumber. Wisps of dreams filled with fire, pain, and regret drifted through his thoughts like smoldering embers from a dying fire. Even the smell seemed to linger in the air, yet as his mind left the dream, a deep breath of fresh hope filled his lungs.

It was the breath of a second chance.

He shook his head remembering where he was and reassured himself that the approaching footsteps did not mean approaching soldiers and certain death. He sat up as Doctor Bradley approached his bed with a large black male attendant by his side.

"Well, Mr. Singer," began the Doctor. "First, I must say how pleased we all are your battle with malaria was ceased. The color has returned to your face." He touched the forehead of the man in the bed. "The fever has passed as well."

"Yes, I feel much better."

He frowned, "We almost lost you. Now let's look at that leg, shall we?"

John sat quietly as the Doctor checked his leg, finding no signs of gangrene or infection in the bullet wound, which had closed and was beginning to scar. The bone was healing nicely. "Soon you will be well. It is time you began walking again, to strengthen the muscles and help the bone grow strong. Although I must warn, I believe you will walk with a slight limp for a long time, possibly the rest of your life."

"It is a small price to pay for a second chance."

"You are lucky, that is true."

He motioned to his attendant, Old Sam, who held a crutch. The large black man was free, yet he was always at the Doctor's side, devoted to his duties.

"Do you feel strong enough to use these?"

"I am certainly eager to rise and escape the confines of this damnable hospital bed," John swore, amusing both men. "I will gladly walk to Richmond and back if your medical advice requires it."

"Perhaps just to the end of the hall, to start."

"Agreed."

The Doctor assisted John, helping him slide to the side of the bed. Old Sam stood at his side to support and help him balance. He rose to his feet for the first time in over a week. Once steady, the men stepped away and John stood with the aid of the crutch.

"This is good, very good indeed."

John hobbled as he started to walk slowly. It hurt and his weakened muscles complained, but he felt happy to be out of that bed.

While standing near John, watching him maneuver on his new crutches, the Doctor got a good long look at his patient. Walt Whitman was right. Henry had seen the wanted posters of Booth. The resemblance was uncanny. Henry sized him to be about five foot nine, not all that tall, yet his manner was stately.

Yet all knew that John Wilkes Booth was murdered.

The questions raced across his mind.

As the Doctor prepared to leave, he turned to John and said flatly, "Tell me Mr. Singer, has anyone ever told you bear an uncanny resemblance to the man that murdered our President Lincoln."

John took a deep breath and stopped walking. "Well yes Doctor, the old poet, Whitman mentioned that. Yet my name is John Singer. We all know Booth was murdered at Garrett's Farm. It is my sorry fate to resemble him in appearance."

John's eyes seemed cold and steely, making Henry uncomfortable with the dark stare. "Perhaps Whitman was mistaken."

"Clearly, he was. Do you have further ugly gossip to discuss, Doctor?"

Henry felt foolish, "My apologies, Mr. Singer."

Doctor Bradley stood silent as he watched John limp out of the ward, and when he was gone he asked his ever present attendant. "Old Sam, did Miss Emma ever find Mr. Singer's uniform?"

Old Sam's gaze focused on the ground. "No Doc, we didn't see nuffin."

"Well, I guess it was a long shot at best."

"Yes'sir," Old Sam muttered under his breath, "allot more than you think."

CHAPTER NINE

Take me John, take all of me.

~~ Enma Dixon

The warm spring days that followed strengthened John and eventually drew him outside. Hobbling on his crutch, he walked out past the triage ward toward the hospital entrance. His hospital gown was gone, in favor of used trousers and a shirt, items he was sure the former wearer would no longer need.

John could feel his muscles respond as he moved ever so slowly past the front entrance. He breathed in the fresh fragrant spring air and enjoyed the sunlight on his face. The street was rutted by the spring rains and from the ambulances hauling patients back and forth to the hospital for many years.

But the street was quiet now. The war was truly over.

John hobbled away from the hospital and noticed a brook further past the rutted roads. It was surrounded by the blooming dogwoods whose pink blooms covered the sky and small petals blanketed the green grass.

It was beautiful, utterly serene. The place enticed him to come see.

Using his crutch for the healing leg, he carefully picked his way along the path to the nest of blooming trees, noticing while the trees were visible from the hospital, the area along the brook was not.

It was a perfect secluded spot.

Arriving beneath the shade of the trees, pink petals littered the grass. It reminded him of weddings and roses and all the soft lovely things in life. John leaned up against the biggest tree and stared across the brook. It's watery noise was welcome music. It was good to be free of those prying eyes within the hospital, yet he realized hiding in plain sight might not be the best approach either.

I should be dead in any case.

The dark thoughts came rushing back.

Should be dead in Garrett's Farm, I didn't know James William Boyd was in the area, making the switch at the last minute as I took my escape and he took the bullet. Then I stole a dead Confederates uniform and ending up here. It's all too much. I must find help from Knights of the Golden Circle. They don't even know where I am. They promised passage to the Far East once I agreed to do their bidding.

But his dark thoughts again stopped as he heard his name called from the top of the hospital steps. Still leaning against the tree trunk, he turned slightly.

It was Emma, looking for him. Seeing her always brought back a smile. He waved and called out. She found him immediately and returned his smile. Seeing her always brought back a smile. He waved and called out. She returned his smile. Her face was flushed as she came upon him, lifting her skirts as she ran. Her joy was youthful and incredibly attractive.

"John," she scolded with a laugh, "when Doctor Bradley put you on the crutch it did not mean for you to walk so far so quickly. Why it's been just shy of a week or so."

"The day is too beautiful to stay inside." Shouldering his crutch, they slowly strolled across the grass together, disappearing further beneath the canopy of the flowering pink trees.

It was, to his recollection, the most peaceful day he had ever known. The air smelled rich with blossoms and the golden woman at his side looked at him with adoring eyes of love. Second chances were for lucky men and today he felt lucky, indeed. Finally they stopped, settling together on a grassy knoll beside the creek, far away from any reminders of the hospital or war. He slowly lowered himself to the grass, leaning his back against the welcoming tree.

"It's lovely here."

"Yes, it is."

She spread her skirts and sat next to him. Their hips touched. His arm encircled her slim form, snuggling her up against the curve of his body.

"This is lovely, too."

"Lovely," he grinned, "and wickedly alluring."

He loved when she laughed. But she was accustomed to his boldness now. She no longer flushed when he flirted, but seemed to enjoy it. This was the closest they had ever been to each other, their bodies warming together where they touched. Their passion teased and was tested now to the very brink. John reached for her hand, bringing it so her palm was caressing his cheek.

Her nearness was maddening.

"Emma," he whispered, "I tell you from my heart, the love I feel for you is real. I have nothing in this world to provide to you except my heart and my love. This second chance is all because of you. I vow to you now, my heart and my body is yours, should you have me."

He bowed his head, waiting for her answer.

Her smile was radiant. "John, from the moment I saw you and looked upon your eyes, I knew you would be mine."

So much truth.

With her it came easily, but he hesitated for a moment.

"There are things about me I cannot tell you, things that I can never express, a part of my past that I cannot ever share with you. If you accept that, then my darlin' I shall take you now and forever. And take you as my wife to Richmond."

"You wish to marry me?"

"With all my heart."

He said this to her not knowing what was truly going to happen to him, if he was abandoned by the Knights of the Golden Circle, as they had sent Boyd in his stead, his escape from Garrett's complete yet with no real plan how to contact them. The Knights of the Golden Circle was a secret Confederate Society, men of prestige and power from the South were members, responsible for blockade running and the spy network that infiltrated the Union.

They had originally decided to kidnap the President to hold him hostage as to continue the exchange of prisoners from South to North, but the South surrendering gave no reason for the Circle to kidnap the President. Decapitation of the Government by murdering Lincoln would do their bidding and help the South rise again. Booth's ease into all societies, his charm his money made him the perfect person to commit this heinous deed. They promised he would be a hero to the Cause and guaranteed safe passage out of the United States.

If he did find passage, what of Emma?

Would she leave her family and live with him as a fugitive? He hoped so. Due to his heinous act, a life in hiding was his only choice. Regret was bitter. His hatred of the North, the ensuing surrender of the South, his ardent support of all things Southern had caught him up in it, never truly considering the horrendous price. His wealth, his social connections, his ease into the highest society along with his long list of female companions made the case for the Knights of the Golden Circle to have Booth commit this crime. They won him over.

For this indeed he did, leaving his family, his career and youth. Given over to this crime, now his life was destroyed, the country destroyed and in mourning.

His knowledge of all this and the agony of loss could never be shared with anyone, especially Emma.

He had just a glimmer of hope for happiness.

She was right here, if she would have him.

Emma's thoughts went back to the diary and the carte de visite. She had the diary, yet never looked upon it nor told him about it. Perhaps she was afraid to know the truth. Yet she knew she had to face her fears.

She watched John resting under the bloom of dogwood trees, his crutch by his side, his raven hair glossy in the spring sun, as it fell in waves around his handsome face. He awaited her answer.

The look in his ebony colored eyes was intense, shining with kindness and love. His natural grace and elegance were more evident, now that he was free to move about.

Marriage. She had expected to discuss it eventually, but John's proposal beneath the dogwood trees was truly romantic and came sooner than she had even dared to hope. She wanted it.

Emma's heart pounded.

Marriage to John Singer, it was his promise for a lifetime of love.

He needed her; that much was true. And she needed him.

"John," she whispered to him, "I accept."

John took off the small pearl and platinum and diamond ring he wore on his smallest finger and placed it on her ring finger. It fit perfectly.

"There. We are bound now."

"As husband and wife?"

"Yes, today in our hearts we are bound. In every way that matters, you are mine Emma, and I am now yours." His tender words made her smile. "And when we return to your family in Richmond, we will have a true wedding with all your loved ones. But here beneath the trees," his gaze peacefully wandered upward to the canopy of pink blossoms, "I cannot think of a more beautiful place to bind our lives, our hearts into one."

He watched Emma's eyes gleam with emotion.

She was everything he wanted.

This second chance meant nothing without her.

"I love you, John Singer. I am honored to become your wife."

"You have made me very happy."

John then gently pulled her toward him, shifting her body until she straddled his legs and her skirts spread around them. Emma molded herself against him. It felt so good, so right. Taking care to foster her desire, he kissed her flushed sweet warm lips.

Her soft sounds of approval were music to his ears. He gently licked and tasted, sweeping his tongue inside her open mouth to kiss her deeper and fuller. Her breathing was aroused now, her hips slowly moving against his in an instinctive dance of seduction. Even innocent in the ways of loving, she knew what she wanted.

It was a joy to him, a pleasure beyond words.

He trailed kisses to her neck and nuzzled her there.

Emma's body was responding, warming against his as each touch was new and thrilling. John recognized the excitement in her face as his caresses pulled her closer towards their intimate desires that had yet to be fulfilled. Today it was enough just to hold her like this, to feel the promises of passion that would someday be his and his alone.

This woman would become his wife.

She was his to have and hold, to honor and cherish in this wonderful second chance at life. A second chance he knew he did not deserve. He would do everything in his power to insure Emma loved him.

"Wait," she smiled, laughing a little as she caught her breath.

"What is it?"

"My hair is bound."

He grinned, understanding. "Yes, it is."

"You like it falling loose."

"I certainly do."

He leaned back and watched Emma unravel her hair. It fell past her shoulders. The soft gold waves, like wheat in a field, gently moving about her body in the light spring breeze.

"You are glorious, Emma."

"Please, touch me," she breathed the bold words, her cheeks flushed with desire, "please show me your love."

At her request, John then fingered the back of her dress; expertly releasing female underpinnings that kept her body bound. As the dress slid from her shoulders, he gazed at her full ripe breasts, straining now for his touch as he toyed with the satiny laces of the corset chemise.

Once unlaced from the corset, he placed both hands upon her breasts, perfect and untouched. She drew in a breath that was pure pleasure. Her soft curves arched into him, begging for more. He caressed and cupped them until her body was driving into him as he kissed each one.

"I want you, John," she begged. "I love you."

He could see the fires of passion had risen high enough. Although making love was his desire too, his beloved wasn't ready. Kissing Emma to calm and sooth, he whispered to her gently, "tis beautiful you are, yet the first time will hurt you."

"It will?"

He could tell by the panic in her pale blue eyes that such truths were not discussed among ladies. It made him love her even more that the trust between them allowed for such private things.

"Then why does my body crave something that will hurt?"

John smiled at her reasoning.

"Because joining as man and woman makes us stronger, more as one. Intimacy deepens our love. I promise you, it will be the only such time it hurts. But when the time is right, before the pain I will release you from your passion so you will feel ready. Then it will be easier."

Emma searched his gaze, breathing fast. Her hips that had instinctively rocked against him driving them both with need, now held perfectly still.

"Darling, you are God's perfection and in His mercy, he has given you to me. I never want to cause you pain." John assured, "I shall cherish you and love you until the day I die."

The love and trust he saw in her face swept over him like the gentle fragrant breeze. Without hesitation, she slipped the chemise from her body, and was now naked to his gaze and highly aware of his passion. Fear of the first time seemed to disappear. Her voice was soft and heady, full of sensual emotion.

"Dearest John, you know I have had no other man. I am wholly yours to love. I am afraid, not for the pain, but because I don't know what to do."

His heart bursting with love, John held Emma's beautiful face in his hands. He laughed aloud with the joy, making her smile too.

"Darling, you simply love, that is all."

"But I might not please you."

"Impossible. Every breath pleases me. You gave me the will the live, brought me back from the depths of death. I welcomed death, begged for death, and it was you and your kindness that saved me."

"I had to save you. I love you."

He smiled, seeing it was true.

No woman had ever looked at him with such certainty, such purity of heart. "Know this act of love is from the deepest part of my heart, that I share with you all that I am, and take you soon as my wife before God and family, forever then bound together throughout this life, if you will have me."

He bowed his head in deference to the pure and perfect Emma. She ran her hands through the silken waves of his raven hair, making him meet her gaze.

"John, from the moment I saw you my heart was yours. Your eyes following me about the hospital. I turned, and I looked. I knew there could never be another. I was born for you. So take me, my darling. I am not afraid. Take me and love me. All I ask of you is: don't ever stop loving me."

"Here, beneath the dogwood trees?"

"Yes, here in the beautiful forest where we are alone at last."

His hands caressed her lush curves, "My sweet Emma."

"Take me John, take all of me."

He removed his clothes, letting her watch. He lay the shirt upon the fresh spring grass, protecting her soft skin from the ground. Her hands touched him; hesitant at first, but soon her fingers greedily consumed the marble whiteness of his skin and his masculine body.

The passion was too much. He needed her. John kissed her sweet lips and gently laid upon her. He knew there would be a moment of pain. He did not want her to feel that physical pain, albeit brief, a pain that he would inflict in the name of their love.

But her hands pulled him closer, guiding where she wanted him to be.

"Are you sure, Emma?"

Her breath came is warm gasps. "Please John, I must have you."

And so he did. Moving within her, the moment of pain was sweet and fleeting, only serving to awaken feelings and desires that John knew how to quench and satisfy. Her arms were holding him close.

He loved Emma, made love to her.

Desire for one another fueled their passion. His movements were slow and tender, as gentle a possible, making every moment of their union become the sweetest surrender of body, heart, and soul.

At last she cried out, arching beneath him, shuddering with joy.

That moment too, was one he would always remember.

John kissed her tenderly, "You are mine now, Emma."

"Yes, yes I am."

"To have and to hold..." he whispered.

"Never to part," she finished with a smile.

John leaned back, drinking in the perfection of her body. Her golden hair splayed about her face and shoulders, their silky ends half covering her ripe lush breasts. Her flat white stomach sloped into supple slim hips and down into long legs. She was perfection, and she was his.

"We will marry, very soon," he assured.

"Of course."

"My love you have always, along with my heart and all that I am. This much, I vow." As he helped her reassemble the chemise and dress she became silent, the joy fading from her eyes.

"What is it, darling?"

Emma spoke in a careful yet fearful voice, "You are practiced in the ways of love. Have there been many before me?"

"Darling," he assured, taking her again into his arms. "Yes, there have been others. Yet fear not for the past no longer exists. None won my heart. No woman ever touched my soul. Nothing matters except having you as my wife and beginning our new life together."

His words soothed her fears. But they were both aware they had been away from the hospital for a while. The sun glint further down off the surface of the rippling pond and shadows were gathering beneath the dogwood trees.

"Come to my room tonight," she offered. He nodded. She held out her hand him, enjoying the strength and promise of him being both a lover and a husband.

The walk back to the hospital now as lovers showed in their faces as they passed by the daily workers of the staff.

The happiness was impossible to contain.

John rested his hand on Emma's arm as she helped steady himself with his crutch as they crossed the rutted road. In their moment of togetherness, he noticed Doctor Bradley peering through his office window, watching the two lovers walking back into the hospital as one.

The Doctor's face contorted in rage.

CHAPTER TEN

May I ask Mr. Singer,
which division did you fight with?

-- Sergeant Beauregard Jackson

The Doctor could not believe his eyes. It was too late. She had been with him. He could see it in her beautiful face as they passed by, too engrossed in one another to notice him watching. That vexing, evil man now had Emma under his spell; a spell forewarned by his dear friend Walt Whitman.

Could this indeed be Booth?

The Union firmly stated he was killed by Boston Corbett of the Sixteenth NY Calvary, shot through the neck and died the next morning. What made him question it? Resemblances happen all the time.

This war, he shook his head, has changed everyone forever.

He had loved Emma since being invited to her eighteen birthday party at her parent's home, and then at the hospital had feigned friendship in hopes of the prospect of love, but she showed no signs of interest in him other than as her superior. Yet he dreamt of undressing her and taking her to his bed.

And now she belonged to this man, Singer.

He was loving that beautiful and lush body.

Hate burned through his body, hate for the man John Singer.

Emma walked back to the hospital ward with John and helped him back into bed. He was no longer in isolation, but bunked with others who needed long-term recovery. "I should think you should be tired after our activities this afternoon," she whispered.

John replied with a sly smile, "No my darlin, I will wait for the 9:00 hour. Then I will once again show you my deepest and most passionate love."

The smile reached from his lips to those deep black Baltic eyes, eyes that felt spellbinding and haunting, even as she turned to leave. He had awakened the passion within her, a passion for life ignited by the fire of love, a passion that could only be quelled by him.

Today had been beautiful, indeed. Emma would never again look at dogwood pink blossoms without having a smile.

Shortly after Emma left the soldier lying nearest John began to speak as he had been privy to the sights and sounds of Emma's devotion and had remained silent until now.

"Mr. Singer, I believe is your name sir," came the thick heavy accent of the deep Southern voice. "Might I introduce myself, seeing as we are bunk mates for this unfortunate bit of time. My name is Sergeant Beauregard Jackson of the First Infantry division of South Carolina."

"Pleasure to meet you, Sergeant," he responded to shake hands, noting the man was missing one arm, the sleeve of his skirt tucked and pinned at the shoulder. "It would seem you have an unfortunate time, indeed."

Jackson nodded. "I was at the Battle of the Wilderness and managed to crawl out from carnage with just my right arm gone. I was luckier than most." He smiled at that victory over death.

"That Battle was horrid. I been fightin' for four long years. Never did I see such death and suffering. The night before the Battle the cold breeze swept across the land, seemed to rattle through the frozen skulls of them boys that done died there."

"It sounds horrifying." John suppressed a shudder.

The burly Sergeant agreed, "The spring rains opened up them shallow graves of our dearly departed brethren. We was witness to our poor comrade's unburied bones."

"Well now nothing could be done but to rebury them, but well, it was the screamin, such screamin I done heard, screaming until my ears could stand no more and my blood froze clear to my bones."

"See them flint rifles set the whole underbrush afire from the pieces of lit linen that fell into the dry and thick layers of underbrush."

"Didn't matter none, I tell ya, North or South, hearing them screams for our fallen comrades that were being burned alive because we couldn't get to them injured and half dead in the brush."

The burly Sergeant shook his head as if to shake out the horror he had witnessed. "Doctor says this here hospital will be cleared out soon. Those able to walk will be sent home. The other poor unfortunates will remain. Hopefully our Doctor Bradley can help them."

"He is a fine physician," he allowed, although John silently disliked the man. Something about the good Doctor nagged at him. Perhaps he too was hiding something.

"And you sir not only survived a broken leg, but the onslaught of malaria. Some divine providence must be looking after you," the Sergeant grinned.

This interested John.

"So you believe divine providence saved me from a certain death?"

"Why yes, that and our devoted nurse Emma."

John had to smile, "She is divine providence, indeed."

"We arrived the same night, you know. That sweet lady tended to me without much of a fuss, but she saw you and," he let out a whistle. "Whoo-wee. She likes you pretty fine, I say. May I ask," Jackson continued, "which infantry division were you with? I seen the green embroidered name Singer on your braided cuff, when they brought ya' in."

The Sergeant paused and waited. John didn't like the new line of questions. "So you saw my uniform when I arrived, yet I did not have it afterward. I wonder what had happened to it?"

"Usually if they are burned, any personal belongings returned to their owner. Was there something in particular you were looking for?"

He had enough of this inquisition. "And I wonder why that question should be of any interest at this point, sir? The South lost and we are all now one Union, so as a Southerner on the defeatist end of this battle; why should a uniform matter now?"

"Just conversation amongst fellow soldiers is all."

"The South lost, Jackson. Hundreds of thousands died. The country is in ruin, cities destroyed and families torn apart. It was a tragedy, at best. Let the matter go."

Now Jackson seemed deeply sorry, "I was just asking, especially since our Emma has found favor with you. And so many visitors seem fascinated to look upon and speak to you. Your background seems like a mystery, also like maybe you are trying to hide for someone or sumptin."

John sighed, feeling weary of the Booth speculations, "Yes my stay here has caused quite a stir, my resemblance to this Mr. Booth notwithstanding. The wretched man died in that fire."

It was true. The man he was had died that day.

"Gossip is for old ladies. My name is John Singer. Emma and I are engaged. We are leaving soon for Richmond to be married there." John turned his back to the inquisitive and annoying Sergeant and said no more, he was just waiting for the nine o'clock hour to rendezvous with his beautiful fiancé.

That evening while Emma was back in her room, she sat at her desk writing her mother, explaining she was coming home, but with fiancé as well. She worded this very carefully, for John spoke of no background or education or profession to write home about yet his diction, manners and command of language bespoke of something grand and wonderful.

She wondered how her mother would take this. Her family had held such high hopes for a good match. Her eighteenth birthday saw many suitors. But all were gone now. The war took them. Those days of parties and cotillions seem so long ago. Emma closed her eyes for a moment, remembering her life in Richmond just before the war, and the bounty of their family life. Her favorite memory was the beautiful blue silk dress that offset her pale blue eyes. She wore it with her mother's wedding pearls woven into her hair for just that one special evening.

Her father a successful Richmond banker, never believing nor having slaves in his house. He had servants, paid and housed comfortably. He was an anomaly in the nearby slaveholding plantation owners. He and his son Caleb joined the Army of Northern Virginia under the brilliant General Robert E. Lee not to fight for slavery, but to show he would fight for Virginia.

That was the final party before the war. The blue silk was gone. Her beautiful home was located next door to the Confederate President, Jefferson Davis' house and had been used by the Confederacy and their army during the war, given over by her father. It was even said a horse had wandered freely into the expansive front foyer before being moved out by its owner. Her mother wrote the horse left a dent in the marble flooring at the base of the exquisite staircase.

Emma was glad their home survived the burning of Richmond. Right after the end of the war, the citizens of Richmond burned their own City, rather than handing it over to the North. She was fortunate indeed, at least she had a home to return to.

President Abraham Lincoln himself stopped at the Confederate Jeff Davis house next door and sat at the very desk used to command the Confederacy. Emma wondered if the President had walked by her home. She visualized the tall statesman holding the hand of his youngest son Tad. Only a few days after his visit to her hometown, he was cut down and assassinated. Emma knew Richmond would be nothing like her memories, but at least she had John.

She was so shocked by her own boldness earlier, not waiting for the marriage bed. But she did not regret it. He was a practiced lover, giving generously to ensure her pleasure. John appeared at her door at the appointed time. At his soft knock, she opened the bedroom door. His handsomeness as always seemed so stunning and his lovemaking had made her weak, wanting to beg for more of his tender touches.

"John," she welcomed, "come in please." She closed the door behind him and they were alone. "I just finished writing mother of our engagement, informing we will soon come home."

"Ah Emma," he hobbled closer, "Each time I see you I see the beauty that haunts my heart and drives my desire, until I can stand it no more." He sat up patiently waiting to hear how she was introducing a man of whom she knew almost nothing into her world.

Emma absently ran her hand across the flatness of her belly.

John smiled at her as he noticed her gesture, "We are engaged and will be married. No need to worry, darling. It often takes many times for a child to be conceived, if by chance that is what you are thinking?"

The worry fled from her heart.

"Shall we try again soon?" John teased, but she could feel the heat of his desire thicken the air.

"Yes, of course. But first listen to my letter to mother." Emma began to read.

Dearest Mother, it is with my heartfelt love for you, I sit tonight and write. The war is over. I am coming home. It seems like an eternity since those wonderful lazy summer nights of my youth, enjoying the mint julep drinks father was so famous for, or the balls we attending in our finest dress. Our tables always had flowers from your beautiful garden, set in the finest silver and china. There was plenty for all who came and enjoyed our home.

I know such times are behind us. They live as memories. With Father and brother Caleb gone, we will go on as best as we can. Every day I think of dearest Father, the loss deep and the wound unhealed. I miss our dear boy Caleb too, gone now with only memories of his bright infectious smile.

Emma continued to read on, but John's thoughts reverted back to the loss of his own loss of his father, while only fourteen. His father, the great actor Junius Brutus Booth was away performing, dying from the drink or the madness the drinking brought forth. It matter not, the loss of his father too resonating inside John, remembering a happier time. He was the most favored child.

He recalled sitting on his father's knee on a sunny summer afternoon by a stream near their Tudor Hall farm, all the while his father stroking the beautiful boy's black coal hair. He said to his son, "Dear sweet Johnny, tis your father's favorite you are," and hugged him.

It was a good memory. One he liked.

John did not realize he was lost in his thoughts until Emma called out to him, "John, have you not heard anything I have said?"

"Ah yes, I have heard it all, such a beautiful home and life you had. But losing your father and brother in the war has made me sad. For my father died when I was only fourteen, a loss like that never heals nor goes away. Such is this pain we share."

"That is the first time you have mentioned family to me. Please tell me more." She held out her hand as if to carry his pain through her. Instead, he drew her close and slowly unpinned the length of blond braids, each strand falling like silken cords of the finest silk. It was sheer seduction. Emma had never experienced, the intimacy of being undressed by her lover.

"Let us speak not of sadness," he murmured, "but celebrate the joy of being alive." The sweetness of it made her sigh and forget about the letter.

John wound his fingers in her hair, kissed the ends and laid her down gently on her bed. He unfastened her delicate undergarments and removed them.

She started to object, but he kissed her lips until they melted to his will. He explored her mouth with his tongue and as he did so, leaned into her to let Emma feel the weight of his body.

Gently his hands kneading her full breasts and nuzzling there in prolonged pleasure until he felt her body twist and arch with desire. He kissed her flat soft belly and continued to kiss her body until he tasted her sweetness.

The intimacy was so unfamiliar she squirmed beneath his touch.

Teaching her, loving her, John softly soothed in a dusky voice, "Let go, let me have you," he begged her to trust. Emma did.

As his kisses intensified and the intensity of her pleasure reached a crescendo, she suddenly cried out his name as her body bowed in passion.

Only then, when her body was heated and her heart satisfied, the desire for their union made Emma wild, he gave himself to her warmth and loved her fully until he too reached his crescendo.

In the aftermath of their lovemaking, John teased, "I guess you had better finish reading me that letter, my beauty." He chided her with that broad beautiful smile that reached his dark expressive eyes giving his gaze infinite depth and kindness.

"Let me get dressed first," in modesty, she slipped into her nightgown and John watched as she tidied her hair and clothing. To appease her modesty, he pulled on his trousers. Emma began to re-braid the length of hair and his hand stopped her from twining.

"Leave it free, darling. It is much too beautiful to be bound."

She did as he asked and proceeded to read the letter. John leaned upon the bed, sitting up with pillows behind him and began once again to listen.

Although I know you had hoped that Doctor Bradley and I would find favor with each other, having known each other as childhood playmates, and neighbors, but the fact remains I never have felt anything but kind friendship for our dear Doctor.

"You knew he hoped to marry you?" John sat up in earnest when he heard Emma's description of Doctor and her lack of feelings for him. He was not surprised the dear Doctor was enamored of her, and he was wholly thrilled to learn she had rejected him.

"It is impossible to miss his obvious adoration."

"Your family will be disappointed."

"Not when I tell them about you."

John thought with a smile with all Henry's kindness, fancy educated manners and family background she rejected him. He smiled deeper at the thought that he was loving a woman the dear Doctor never had a chance with.

Emma continued reading.

But dearest mother, I have indeed fallen in love with someone. A soldier of our glorious South, his name is John Singer. He came to us a few weeks ago with a broken leg. One of our ambulances found him as the war ended and brought him here to Alexandria. He was the last soldier from our dear brave Southern boys.

Mother what happened next is something I never knew existed here on this earth. He was brought in on a stretcher, uniform torn and bloody, but with such a countenance and depth of character in his eyes that I had never seen before. I had hundreds to attend to, but was riveted by his magnificent stare. As I made his acquaintance, offering aid, he said nothing; there would be no letter writing, no family missing him. It was evident he was in excruciating pain.

Doctor Bradley re-casted his leg, but he contracted malaria and we almost lost him. By the goodness of God he was spared and I more grateful than anyone, as we have fallen in love and are engaged. John gave me a platinum ring with diamonds and a pearl in it for our engagement ring. We would like to be married as soon as we come home to Richmond. With your blessing, I would like to be married in the front parlor, as we had always dreamed I would be.

I know not to expect the grandeur of our old lifestyle. Life has changed. A simple wedding will do. What matters is that I am coming home with my fiancé John, and that our family will embrace him, as I have.

I will write to you of our departure date.

All my love, Emma

"Does the letter say everything it should," she tentatively asked.

"Enough for a mother to see her daughter has found love." He was pleased she respectfully did not offer details about him to her family. They would judge him for themselves and John felt confident he could win their hearts.

"Once in Richmond we will marry immediately, in my front parlor, just like I dreamed I would before the war started."

"Darlin, that sounds wonderful."

Emma suddenly looked worried and ashamed. "John, being with you before the marriage bed, is not how I was raised. It was forbidden. But you are for me, my total love. I went against all I knew to be with you before marriage. But please, at home with my family our behavior must be above reproach."

"I understand, not to worry," he slid off the bed and she aided him with his crutch. But as she came near, the thin gown revealed the outlines of her body, a temptation too great to resist. He grabbed her then and kissed her fully, caressing her breasts until once again she was weak.

"John, we should stop. The hour is late."

"Yes darling." John continued to kiss her. Soon Emma forgot about stopping and smiled wide when he laid her down on the bed once again.

It was very late indeed, before John finally slipped out her door.

CHAPTER ELEVEN

If it is true you are alive I will find you,
I will never betray you.

~~ Asia Clarke Booth

Doctor Bradley saw the handsome patient just outside Emma's door leaning on his crutch, leaving Emma's room at such a late hour. His body shook as the anger bubbled within him, raging like an untreatable cancer, festering and destroying his mind.

It was too much to bear.

It was madding to him, the thought of that strange and evil man making love to the only woman he ever wanted.

The only woman he ever loved.

And now she was taking him to Richmond, back to the very house where Henry first made arrangements with Emma's father to court her. But the Major in the great Army of Northern Virginia died and the elder boy Caleb Dixon was gone too, falling together on the battlefield early in the war.

But there was still Emma's mother, who might still be in favor of his marrying her.

Perhaps he should pen a letter to Mrs. Dixon, a friendly sort of letter, with hints of suspicion regarding the man Emma is bringing home and mention his uncanny resemblance to the murderer John Wilkes Booth.

Henry smiled at his plan, thrilled at what would happen when Mr. Singer appeared at her door.

He rushed to his desk as he began to pen, *"Dear Mrs. Dixon..."*

As he sat and began to write a soft knock interrupted him.

He rose from the desk and opened the door, a smile crossed his lips upon seeing his guest.

"My dearest Louisa, how wonderful to see you. Please come in."

That same night in Philadelphia the child inside Asia was in no mood to sleep. She rose from her bed as the child moved within her. Perhaps the baby sensed her anxiety and fear from still waiting for the return of her husband and her brothers who were arrested and taken to Washington for the conspiracy for the murder of the President.

The Government already had eight conspirators in prison, rumored for the gallows, possibly four of them would hang for their part in the conspiracy. One was John's boyhood friends from Catonsville Academy and another was one of the mother's of the conspirators. The poor woman had somehow become woven into the fabric of this scheme.

Asia's heart cried out, "John, how could you do this, dearest boy? Was your love of the South so reverent that it should destroy so much good?"

She did not believe her brother acted on his own. She had heard whispers of John's allegiance to the Knights of the Golden Circle of the South. Asia believed they influenced him.

She knew it was because of his fame, his charm, his money, his ease and grace that made him their perfect choice to do this heinous act.

Asia felt deeply lonely without her brother and yet so distressed.

He was the favored child, a true friend and devoted brother. She resolved in her heart that no matter what is said or what happens she would love him until the day she died.

All she had left of him was the locket with John's picture.

Asia grasped the locket, the picture of his handsome face forever burned in her heart and mind. She pursed her lips in sadness. The government wouldn't even allow any Booth family relative to see him as to say farewell aboard the USS Montauk, the ship that housed his body for autopsy.

She bowed her head and walked the floors of the elaborate home, all the while still not wanting to believe John could do such a thing.

The child inside her kicked.

Asia rubbed her distended belly, hoping to soothe the child within her, a child being brought forth in the midst of this terrible time for her family.

A scenario that Asia hated.

How could their sweet, temperate John commit such a terrible deed? The newspaper headlines rang out with stories that their famous acting father Junius was mad. Asia read they were now calling the whole family the "*Mad Booths of Maryland.*"

It broke her heart.

"Such a time to be born into, little one," she whispered to her child.

The baby kicked as if hearing.

"Such a terrible time."

Asia knew nothing was written or spoken of John's generosity and kindness, only now hearing the rumored story of the little program boy who worked outside Ford's theater where John had performed so many times.

The little boy of about seven or eight worked in the cold, his hat threadbare and unable to keep the child warm. John took the child by the hand to the haberdashery in the town and bought him a proper newsboy hat to keep him warm. There were more stories of his generosity and kindness, but Asia feared they would never be told, overshadowed by this most heinous deed.

She thought too of the times John would stay at her home in Philadelphia, sometimes sleeping on the couch in her living room, but not long for sleep when the boys would see their Uncle and such a raucous playtime would start. She smiled, recalling nights when he would rest on the front parlor couch, so tired he kept his high black riding boots on. She tried not to remember the pistol she saw slid into the uppermost part of the boot.

Those whispering voices from his meetings haunted her.

The Knights of the Golden Circle Secret used him to the murder the President. So where are these men now? Scattered like the wind, hiding from the swift and mighty hand of the government.

"John," she softly said his name, "Could you be alive?"

Rumors persisted of the man autopsied on the USS Montauk, rumors of an older man, with freckles and red hair. Asia heard rumors even his own personal physician Doctor Frederick May did not agree the man on the Montauk was John Wilkes Booth, but that it was "in his best interest" to agree it was indeed Booth.

The name of James W. Boyd was whispered on the many nights when John was here. It seemed no coincidence that his initials were JWB, just like her brother John had initialed onto his finger with India ink when he was just a boy.

She pondered again why no Booth was allowed to view the body.

Because she realized, it was not him.

"John," she cried out his name in the inky darkness of her hallways, "are you alive? How do I find you? Who do I trust?" She could not trust her husband John Clarke, as he was furious for what John had done, and was distancing himself from the family.

Her brother was right, she should not have married him.

John had warned her the Booth name in the theatre world was a tempting dowry and not to marry John Sleeper Clarke, as Clarke was known for not only for his comedic prowess on stage, but as a very successful theater manager as well. Certainly, his alliance with the Booth name brought favor to his career.

Asia worried about the danger to her and her children and family as she thought how to lay plans to see about who the government claims they autopsied. She realized too, the treason such plans could bear, with the hatred of world upon the mere mention of the name Booth.

She needed to remember those who met John here at her house in the weeks before the assassination and find them, to learn if they knew where her brother might be hiding.

The more she pondered, Asia became convinced John was still alive. It soothed the ragged edges of her heart to think of him, somewhere out there tonight.

She walked back towards her bedroom, the child within her finally resting as if in agreement with the mother's decision to learn what really happened at Garrett's Farm.

"Dearest John," she said into the silence of the night, "If you are alive, I will find you. I will not abandon you and leave to you the gallows to die a second death. You have my word on this."

The peaceful feeling grew stronger.

And with those words said, she closed her eyes only to see the handsome face of John in her mind's eye as she drifted off to sleep.

It was late to be sipping the very first drops of hot tea that Doctor Bradley had poured for Louisa, but this visit was important and the conversation quickly turned to Emma and her fiancé.

"What do you know of him, Louisa?"

"Oh Henry," She put her cup down, using his familiar name, as she had not only worked for him briefly, but they became friends as well.

"I know nothing. I only saw Emma in passing, but she mentioned there was someone."

"Yes, she seems quite taken with this John Singer."

Louisa nodded, "I could see by the look in her eyes, I know that look. It was the same feelings I had for Jack," she fingered the chained ring around her neck. "I am so happy for her, as I can't imagine enduring life here these last three years. She stayed and worked to help all those soldiers, so many of them lost. It is hard to bear."

"Death weighs on us all," Henry agreed.

"And now she has someone to love." Louisa looked thrilled for Emma. "I plan to see her tomorrow. You treated John Singer. What kind of man is he, where is he from, what did he do before the war?" She smiled and wrapped both hands around the warm teacup, enjoying their chat.

"Yes, I did treat him. He arrived with the last group of our fallen boys. Word was he was found out on the road, passed out, using a tree branch for a crutch for his broken leg."

"The poor man."

"Funny thing though, it had already been casted, and not set right. It bothered me. If the leg was broken and casted why was he on a road trying to walk on it? Surely he was told by his physician to rest. But I reset it, properly. He was lucky. But no sooner than he arrived, he contracted malaria and almost died. Emma pulled him back from death, almost with her sheer will. I had never seen anything like it."

"She is a marvelous nurse."

"But there is more," he sighed. His face became crestfallen as he hung his head with the pain.

Louisa put her hand over his, "Henry, what is wrong?"

The Doctor knew he could tell Louisa of his feelings for Emma and of his suspicions of John. He knew his kind and dear friend she would not betray him. Her compassion was extraordinary.

Meanwhile John hobbled back toward his bed in the hospital. It was late. No one was awake.

The moon was full in the starry sky, lighting the land with silvery light. He felt restless, unable to sleep.

His bed could wait.

Without questioning why, he found himself returning to the grove of dogwood trees where just that morning he had made love to Emma. Those were beautiful moments, memories he wanted to cherish.

He leaned against the tree, lowering himself to the ground.

Being alone held a certain freedom.

Hiding in plain sight was trying indeed.

John realized the time was upon him that he would forever be bound by the alias he had stolen. He knew nothing of the real John Singer who he found dead on the side of the road.

It was too perfect that the Confederate Singer's uniform was just the right size. While threadbare, it was less recognizable than his normal black riding clothes that were exchanged for the uniform.

The diary was inside that uniform.

But it was destroyed when they burned the uniform. It was fortunate, for the reader of this diary would understand that indeed, he was John Wilkes Booth.

The evidence would be irreversible and deadly.

It was gone, burned along with the rest of his past. The secret of his real identity was safe.

Still, worry gnawed at his heart.

But it was more than that, he slowly reasoned.

He had become a wanted man, an assassin who found little help from fellow Confederate spies who were unwilling to take in Herold and himself while on the run. It had all been planned. Then when trouble struck he was deserted.

But at the eleventh hour, Boyd came through.

The switch at the barn at Garrett's Farm by James Boyd was at the last minute. He recalled the shot that felled Boyd and the swarm Union officials came. He simply slid out one of the barn slats and ran into the forest. John heard fellow conspirator Davey Herold in the distance telling the officers the man they shot was not John Wilkes Booth. And from his vantage point deep in the forest, the Union Cavalry didn't seem to listen to the moaning of the captured Herold.

John realized as time passed, it may become impossible to elude questions of his past. The horror of the war would only carry silence so far. He needed a story and he must earn a living without calling too much attention to himself. John had believed that by doing this deed for the Knights of the Golden Circle, he would be a hero.

Instead, he found himself alone.

But that mattered not, for the hour of reckoning for meeting Emma's family was nearing. It was time to leave the hospital, escape the prying eyes and curiosity seekers.

He would start the next chapter of his life.

With his new alias, it would be as if John Wilkes Booth were truly dead.

As the world thinks, then it is so.

"Asia," he whispered her name in the moonlight, as his brilliant black eyes burning with unshed tears. He imagined the pain he had caused her and his dear mother and family. "Asia," he cried out, "if you can hear me, I am alive. I thought what I did was right to avenge the South."

Regret burned his heart, streaming down his cheeks.

Alone, he could cry.

"I am alive!" he screamed to himself. "Asia, I am alive. Please forgive me."

He wanted beyond anything, to see his sister again.

But his life was with Emma now. She was his second chance. If she knew who he really was, he would lose her too.

He gave over to the tears that rained upon his handsome face.

The night had turned cool with a breeze. Eventually he was forced to return to his bed inside the hospital.

But he tossed and turned in an effort to sleep. Once again, his dreams were filled with the flashes of blood, gunpowder and screaming as this heinous act replayed in his tortured mind.

At that moment in Philadelphia, Asia woke suddenly from her sleep. The child inside her was still, yet she wondered at her awakening. A subtle awareness shivered over her skin as the night breeze blew against the lace panels across her window. Sitting up, she thought she heard John's voice crying out to her in pain.

"I'm alive." she heard him cry, "Please forgive me."

The agonizing sound of his voice made her heart lurch.

Could it be true? She had always been a sensitive woman, keenly aware of things most ignored. The intuition Asia had learned to trust felt honest and true inside, speaking to her heart.

"Dearest John," she whispered into the dark, letting the night breeze carry her words, "if it is true you are alive, I will find you. I would never betray you."

A calm warmth washed over her.

Asia suddenly felt unbearable weary.

The weight of her unborn child and the impending birth felt like a daunting task. Her strength would be needed. Thinking of John, missing her brother, she rested her head back down on the pillows, giving into the blackness around her and fell back asleep.

CHAPTER TWELVE

That I should be hunted down,
with every man's hand against me.

~~ John Singer

"Henry, tell me please what is it?" Louisa insisted, "You are upset. We are friends. Please trust me to understand." She leaned closer supporting him.

"It's about Emma." She held his hand gently as he gave over his secret emotions to her. "It's this man she is in love with, and may marry, I can't understand it. He won't tell her anything about his people or where he from or what he did before the war. It is like there was no life for him before the war. That just cannot be. It makes no sense."

"What makes you think they will marry?"

"I saw them together today."

Henry could see Louisa did not understand the subtle hint. "Yes, she is taken with him."

"They were together today in the forest," he tactfully clarified. "I saw them afterward. It is clear they are lovers. Emma chose to give her love to that man. For all intents, I believe she loves him. I have no doubt they will marry."

Louisa looked shocked, "Emma made love with him?"

He sadly nodded, "Of this, I am certain."

Now his friend looked sad, too. "I am sorry."

Her compassion for his devastated feelings sparked a deep and festering anger inside. "How can she consider a life with a man like that? I could give her everything. She would reign over her household like a queen. I can give her so much, yet she does not see me."

"When Emma came here to work I had hoped being around me and seeing what a far superior man or husband I would make, would resolve her heart to be mine. She never paid me any mind. It was like I was invisible."

"Then right at the very end of the war this John Singer comes to the hospital, handsome, silent and compelling, yes compelling even to me. He is a mystery." Louisa held fast to his hands, nodding for him to continue. "There's more." He drew a deep sigh, "Have you seen him?."

"Not yet, I was hoping to tomorrow."

"He is a dead ringer for the murder of our President Lincoln."

"Impossible!"

"It is implausible I know, yet it nags at me. Walt Whitman brought it to my attention. I scoffed, believing it was an old man in mourning for his friend."

"It is true. Mr. Whitman was very fond of our President."

"Then I went to see John and asked if he realized how much he resembled John Wilkes Booth. He said yes, he had heard that, but no one would be interested in him if this Booth hadn't murdered the President. He's canny this one. I honestly think it is him. It has to be him! And he has fooled our Emma, and she is going to marry him."

He bowed his head, overwhelmed.

"Henry, the heart goes where it does it has no will. For it cannot, for love finds each of us in different ways, ways sometimes we don't agree with. All this time, I never knew of your feeling for Emma, nor that her father had given permission to court her."

"I spoke of it to no one, not even Emma."

"Believe me I understand of your unrequited feelings. Likely you would treat her like a queen in her household, but maybe that is not what she wants."

"How could she not want that?"

"Think about it, all this time all these soldiers, boys and men in agony, dying quicker than you can save them, and she withstood it all. Then she finds someone who loves her, just as she is ready to move on with her life. Perhaps it is fate."

He refused to believe it.

"Henry, all I know is in three short days I fell for Jack. If he lived, I would have married him. His death destroyed me. If it weren't for you, I never would have let his hand go after he passed. And you said words I will always remember: It is not right for the dead and the living to be entwined. Only then could I let go of him."

"Yes, I remember that."

The tears gleamed in her eyes, "When they lowered him down into the grave, it felt as if I should go down with him."

"That is how I feel, right now about Emma."

"Love is something we never expect until it happens. She loves this man Henry. It is not for us to judge. I am so sorry for your pain. It is for the one left behind who is the most devastating of all."

"Yes, it is true."

"And as for him resembling John Wilkes Booth, we all know he too was murdered just a couple of weeks ago."

Henry was shaking his head.

"How it is our dear Walt could convince you that is it actually John Wilkes Booth?" Her hands motioned up and down in disbelief of this information.

The Doctor stood up, resolved in this statement of fact to his friend. "Because it is him, Louisa, it is!" He bowed over as if the pain in his heart was beating him down in grief. Louisa was deeply concerned about her friend. His mounting hysteria about Emma and her fiancé was frightening. His belief he was actually John Wilkes Booth was clearly taking a toll on the Doctor's mind and heart.

As Louisa helped to steady her friend, he begged her, "Go to Emma in the morning and meet this man. See for yourself. Then come back and tell me it is not him!"

***

Emma was preparing for bed, running her hand over her breasts still feeling the heat from John's lovemaking. She was powerless when near him, unable to resist his passion.

Yet he was shrouded in mystery.

The diary could answer her questions.

She had it in her possession from the time he came to Alexandria, yet feared to look upon it. It was time to look within it and find out more about her John. She had the power of knowledge at her fingertips. It was time now to use it. It was her future too.

Her resolve to John was that she did not care about his past, yet in all honesty she did and she knew it, for the diary stood as a testament as to his innermost thoughts. Getting it from her dresser drawer, she sat at her wooden desk, lit a candle and opened the red leather book.

But as she opened the cover, the faces of those women of the carte de visite stared back at her, their expressions seemed to wonder too as to whom Emma was and the connection to John. She pushed past those faces and found news clippings. She opened the worn page and began to read.

Confusion rushed past her. The clippings were from a Washington DC newspaper that was condemning the murder of the President, stating a manhunt was under way to find the person named as John Wilkes Booth and bring him to justice.

Emma shook her head in confusion, wondering why John had this clipping and what it meant to him. She then opened the next clipping and saw the wanted poster.

She stared at the photo of John Wilkes Booth.

Her heart beat faster in recognition of the man in the poster.

Surely it is by coincidence that there is such a strong resemblance. We all have a double out in this world. How was it she never recognized it before?

She then looked at the first entry in the diary, dated April 16th, yet noticed several pages ripped out before that date, then pushed towards the end of the diary dated April 25th noticed more pages ripped out and began to read. "that I should be hunted down with every man's hands against me, for avenging the South from this tyrant..."

Emma felt the blood freeze in her body.

"My God, no this cannot be so."

She read everything again. There was no mistake.

"The man I am about to marry, the man I have made love with and given my body and my heart to, is the murderer John Wilkes Booth!"

The agony of the truth was devastating. She fell to her knees sobbing while holding the damning evidence of John Singer's true identity. He had seemed so perfect. This was monstrous. Emma tried to scream but the pain of the truth stuck in throat, the reality of her loving the most wanted man in the United States burning and choking her breath.

Her denial steadfast as she murmured, "His name is John Singer," she said over and over, "his name is John Singer." She refused to believe otherwise.

She then thought of his conspirators, soon to be tried and possibly hung in Washington. Fear gripped her as she realized the damning evidence she now held in her possession was evidence of treason.

Her mind was reeling.

Who was killed at Garrett's Farm? The uniform that John wore had the swirl of the name Singer embroidered in gold thread upon the faded and worn cuff. Emma's body began to shake as the gravity of the ruse was exposed.

She took a deep breath and steadied herself, noticing an envelope in the back of the diary addressed to Asia Booth Clarke, Race Street, Philadelphia, PA. Her heart racing, Emma opened the envelope began to read of its contents.

Dearest sister Asia, This is the end for me, hunted down like an animal, my leg broken, my heart heavy. I thought the end of the tyrant would hail me as a hero, not as the murderous villain the newspapers claim I am. It is you I would turn too to understand why I did this act, aided by the Knights of the Golden Circle. Their belief was that I was the only person that could conceive to carry out the assignation of the tyrant in the White House. Dearest sister, tell mother I did it for my country.

Emma could barely see as she read; blinded by tears over this revelation. Whether the man was known as John Singer or John Wilkes Booth, she was deeply involved now and there was no looking back or going back.

Thinking of her own family, she then cried, "I am bringing home the most wanted man in the United States. A man that committed murder," a man she had recently lain with taking extraordinary pleasure in his unleashed passion. The shock settled within her, "a man I will still marry."

It was a vow and a promise.

But could she keep it? She tried to absorb this unbelievable discovery, almost wishing she had never found that diary.

Emma realized too if discovered with it, she could be tried and hung just like his conspirators; her only crime, loving the man hiding in plain sight. The man she nursed back from his deathbed, who wanted to die, yet Emma willed him to live. A man who promised to love her and her alone yet found evidence to contrary with the carte de visite of five women. She agonized as to who they were to him.

"Are they now crying out for you not merely for what you have done, but for the love you gave so freely without care or worry about the broken hearts left behind? Is this to be my end as well?"

Her thoughts returned to the name on the letter, "Asia," she said the name out loud. John's sister. A family member now revealed. Emma spoke aloud as if Asia was in the room, "Oh that I can find a way to see you Asia, to return the letter that was written by John, to tell your dear brother is indeed alive and safe with me, that he will be married to me. I should want you to see him."

Yet if she did this, John would know she kept the diary, and that she deceived him by reading it. Emma imagined traveling up to Philadelphia and arriving at the Clarke house and announcing to the mistress of the house, that she had married John on May 27, 1865.

Would Asia think she was mad? Perhaps, but it was a risk worth taking.

"John," she whispered, deciding at last. "Your secret is safe with me."

Life had driven them together. She could not let go of him. She too was culpable in this life long deception and was driven by a love that did border on madness.

"So be it."

She put the diary back together, the faces of the women in the carte de visite staring back at her in solidarity for the man known as John Wilkes Booth.

The pain of their broken hearts now joined by Emma's.

CHAPTER THIRTEEN

It is the least I can do
for one who brought me back
from the depths of despair.

~~ Louisa May Alcott

It was at Louisa's insistence not to leave her friend's side in his hour of such painful revelation. "Please you must rest, Henry. It's over now. Time now for all of us to try to move on and find some happiness in this life that has been so filled with grief and sorrow."

"Here," she gave over a hot cup of tea to steady his shaking hands, "Drink this and I will sit with you for a while. It is the least I can do for one who brought me back from the depths of despair."

Henry took the cup, holding it steadfast, his crystal blue eyes swimming in tears as he let them fall, the pain of Emma's leaving and the pain of her love to another too difficult to bear.

After drinking it, he leaned over and held onto to Louisa's hand tight as if drawing strength from her hand and into his heart. He had held his feelings in for so long, the secret kept within now exposed. The revelations of his feelings were for naught, for Emma would soon be married.

"Louisa," he begged, "You will see this man John, who Emma is in love with. You will stop and see for yourself. I know it is the murderer John Wilkes Booth. Our dear old friend Walt started this rant, but he knew. Don't you see, he is hiding in plain sight."

"You have convinced yourself, but you may be wrong. He may be innocent. The man would have to do more than appear to look like Booth, to convince me."

"Then ask what battle he was injured in. I guarantee he has no answer because there was no battle. He broke that leg when he murdered the President, injured Major Rathbone, who was guest along with his fiancé Clara Harris, of the President and Mrs. Lincoln, and leapt over the side of the balcony at Ford's Theater."

Louisa could only gasp at the implications.

"That is who our Emma is going to marry."

He did not realize that his hand had slid away from Louisa's grip and he held his hand in a fist pushing it up past his head.

"Henry, I will do this for you. I cannot deny any request you ask of me, yet this scenario so very improbable. From a logic standpoint, it makes no sense."

He was shaking with inner fury now, both fists clenched.

"Even I am not immune to his charming ways and his powerful presence. He casts a spell. If I cannot look away, then Emma and her heart would be an easy causality. Watch out for yours Louisa, watch out for yours."

Louisa could only sigh and nod her head to agree with her friend. His pain and loss were playing havoc with his mind.

As John returned to his bed, the sound of his crutch echoed throughout the dim ward. He was trying to be quiet as to not elicit any questions as to where he had been. The persistent thump of his crutch however, exposed his absence.

He had just hitched himself up and laid upon the thin worn pillow when his neighbor, Sergeant Beau Jackson said in a loud and distinct Southern voice.

"Well there John, so where did this night take you? I can only imagine what it was like. We see that sweet beautiful Emma working here. Every man here dreamed of having that girl for our own. Some men have all the luck. She sure is a beauty."

John was so used to adulation, the ease of women and their wares, and the equally ease at manipulation of men with his eloquence and charm.

He had no patience for his neighbor's coarse words.

He was leaving in two days, just two days and he would start his new life, safe in the South he loved so much and with Emma.

He was anxious to leave this hospital and Alexandria.

It was so close to Washington. His conspirators were caught and would surely be put to death. He was saddened that Mary Surratt had been arrested. Her knowledge of the plot was truly vague. Her only fault was welcoming him into her home and enjoying the celebrity he brought.

He drew a breath to settle his ire towards his neighbor and spoke evenly. "Sir, may I say your comments about Emma are rude and not welcome to me. She is mine most certainly. Luck had nothing whatsoever to do with winning her."

"I say Mr. Singer, where again did you injure your leg, you never did tell me what battle it was. Or even where you are from."

John raised his head from his pillow and swung his leg onto the floor the space between the beds small and narrow.

He bent down to the Sergeant and said in a threatening tone.

"None of your business Sergeant, doesn't matter now much anyways, our glorious South surrendered to the tyrant that governed the North and paid mightily for it, did he not?"

John had leaned so far into the Sergeant that he thought he could see flames spire up into the midst of those black eyes.

The burly soldier put his hand up to push him away from his face.

John hoped he would not speak to him again.

He sensed trouble from this man with all his questions.

Backing up into his bed he laid his head on the pillow and waited to hear the sleeping sounds of his neighbor.

Only then did John close his eyes to sleep.

"Rest well Henry," Louisa bid him good night. "The war was a siege to endure, your sacrifice beyond reproach. Your heart is broken for an unrequited love. It is too much to bear, but you must rest now. I will see Emma and meet John. Please, just rest now."

The Doctor took her hand and kissed it gently, proving the war had not stolen his gentlemanly manners, then closed the door.

Alone in the darkened room he wept.

Louisa's thoughts were spinning, her compassionate nature sparked to save her friend, remembering too well that it was possible to die of a broken heart.

For she felt close to that when Jack died.

Louisa turned on her heel, determined to talk with Emma. The morning was too long to wait. She left the Doctor's quarters and walked over to where the nurses were housed.

One faint light was on, a small flame from a candle.

She approached the door and knocked gently.

It was very late, but perhaps Emma was still awake. Without asking who it was, Emma flung the door open. She was dressed for bed and clearly had expected to see someone else, perhaps John.

"Louisa," Emma cried in shock, "please come in."

"Thank you. I was going to visit you in the morning, but I was on my back from visiting Doctor Bradley and saw you were up. I hoped we could visit. I am sorry for the late hour."

"Oh Louisa," Emma hugged her friend, pulling her into the sparse room, "It is never too late for you to visit with me, ever."

Together they say on the edge of her bed. Louisa noticed her pillow looked as if a restless head had left its imprint and looked wet with tears. Emma's eyes were pink, her skin pale. She knew all the signs of pain, yet wondered why the tears, when just earlier today she was beaming with the look of love?

Emma took a deep breath and realized now the deception would begin, that John's secret was now hers. She had proof of his true identity, and would for the rest of her life be culpable in helping him hide in plain sight. It was a difficult burden that might take its toll, yet she would do anything for his love.

"So you were visiting with Doctor Bradley," she inquired to Louisa, knowing full well the answer.

"Yes I was. I saw your light on." Ashamed to have been caught, Emma's gaze lower to the ground. "Did something happen today with your John? I see you have been weeping."

"Oh Louisa, no nothing has happened honestly, why John was just here an hour or so ago,"

Emma tried to smile, remembering his power over her, taking her again and again, and his ease with lovemaking.

It bespoke of one who had many women in his past.

"John was here? At such a late hour," she gently chided her friend.

"Yes, I know. I was not brought up for such behavior. Yet I cannot resist the passion. We are taught to court and wait for the marriage bed, but when you meet him Louisa you will see. We will be married very soon upon arriving home, home to Richmond." Emma extended her hand to Louisa, revealing the pearl and diamond platinum ring on her left hand ring finger.

"Emma," Louisa smiled to ease her worries, "We have been through a bloody miserable war, hundreds of thousands lost. Wartime does strange things to rules and decorum. It nullifies them. There is no time for proper courting in war. If you are to be married, then no one is the wiser, my dear friend."

Emma's heart was bursting to scream out of the deception she now was a part of, but her loyalty to John stood firm. "I love him. That is all that matters, in the end."

"It's true," Louisa agreed. "Love takes us when we least expect it. When I first saw Jack and felt the tug on my skirt, I thought he was barely injured. A shoulder wound. But no, he was dying. I fell in love with him immediately. If I thought he could, I would let him make love to me, and not be ashamed of it. I was raised the same; that courting was a necessity and heard whispering of the great mysteries of the marriage bed."

"Great mysteries, indeed," they shared a small laugh.

"Wartime changes all of that. It just does. I will stop and meet your John tomorrow," she promised.

Emma raised her eyes from the floor and looked at her friend, petite with dark hair surrounding an intelligent face. She felt understood.

Louisa's compassion and empathy were beyond bounds.

"Thank you."

"You know, Doctor Bradley wished to court you." Louisa simply confessed.

"He is my friend, that is all, not someone I would wed. He is a gentleman, a fine Doctor and decent man. He will make an excellent husband for someone, but not for me."

"Perhaps you should know Henry believes himself in deeply in love with you. I am inclined to believe him. He is dangerously jealous. He saw John leaving your room at this late hour, it nearly killed him."

Emma gasped at having been caught, but Louisa shrugged her shoulders, "He wants you to be his queen."

Emma pursed her lips and said evenly, "This I cannot help Louisa, I cannot help his delusions. I never misled him, never being anything more than a nurse and his friend. His beliefs are unfounded. Never once have I desired a man until I saw John. My feelings for Henry are purely professional."

Louisa shook her head, "There is something else. I told Henry it was impossible. It's idle gossip, really. Something started by our old friend Walt Whitman." She clearly changed her mind about discussing it. "Forgive me. I should not repeat his rantings."

"Please tell me," she begged of her friend.

"Well," she said carefully, "for some reason he thinks your John Singer is really John Wilkes Booth."

Emma felt her heart turn cold with fear.

"Henry believes my wonderful John is the assassin, John Wilkes Booth?"

As she spouted with shock, the deception festered in her heart, the lies causing heat to rise and prickle the back of her neck.

It was a denial to practice for her lifetime.

"I believe the Doctor is saying this because he is jealous. Perhaps there is an uncanny resemblance. If we knew his background, I am sure everything can be explained."

Emma steadied herself. Her tone was even and firm.

"So then because my handsome John Singer resembles the murderer of the President and does not explain where he calls home, then he is believed to be this Booth? It is preposterous. Who was killed at Garrett's farm? An imposter? A government cover up? A conspiracy?"

Louisa looked ashamed for mentioning it. "I'm sure your John simply resembles him. The murder is fresh on our minds. It haunts our country. Certainly he is who he claims to be."

Emma looked at her friend, the deception a success, but her heart felt like a stone in her chest. "I love John. We are leaving the day after tomorrow to be married in the front parlor of my house like I always dreamed about."

"I wish you both the very best in your new life together."

Emma hugged her friend, yet wondering and fearing what life ahead of her with John would really be like.

The morning sun rose with the promise of another sweltering day. The early onslaught of heat and humidity of summer visited upon the South causing yet more suffering for those caught in the wet thick air.

It did little however to impede Louisa from visiting John Singer.

She awoke from her bed in the nurse's quarters and made haste to her toilette. It was indeed very early when she made her way over to the hospital. While on the path, she met up with Old Sam. She waved to him as to catch up to him as they proceeded to walk and talk.

"Old Sam, good morning," she greeted, but he gave her a blank look. "You remember me, it's Louisa Alcott? I was here about three years ago. I remember your kindness to me, and your devotion to Doctor Bradley. I was only able to stay here several weeks, I became very ill, recovered and was sent back to Massachusetts."

The large black man stared at Louisa for only a moment. "Yes'um I remember you, I remember that man you done took care of, and he done died and I thought for a spell you was gonna die too."

"Yes, you are right. The pain of that time still lingers in my heart. Coming back here only reminds me of dear Jack." She fingered at her collar and pulled the well-worn gold wedding band out as to show Old Sam.

He peered at it from his height advantage since Louisa was a petite woman. "Yes'um, I know it. I remembered that Doctor Bradley done took it off his finger and done give it to you. I seen all of it there, Miss Louisa."

He narrowed his eyes and said gently, "I seen his fingers grab yours when Doctor Bradley pulled 'em loose. It was somethin to see and we just don't talk about it, we just don't. It ain't for me to say what happened, 'cept some souls just don't wanna go."

Louisa's eyes brimmed with tears.

"I know something unspeakable happened, something not of this world. I came back here to say goodbye to Emma and Doctor Bradley. The war is over and the need for this hospital will be gone, thankfully, but Doctor Bradley is staying on for a while to help those patients that need long term care. Are you staying, or are you going home?"

"Seeing as I don't have nothin' or no one to go back to, I'm figurin to set right here with the Doctor. I been with him all these long years and we seen allot together. Why he is my family, Miss Louisa, I can't be leavin' him now."

Louisa reached out to Old Sam and held his care worn hand. "God bless you. Keep a close watch on him. I am worried about him."

"Yes'um, I will.

They continued to the front of the hospital when they both stopped at the entrance. Old Sam asked, "Miss you here to see someone? I gotta git that cookin fire good and hot. No matter the heat today, them poor souls inside needin some fixins."

"Why yes, I came to see Emma's fiancé, John Singer. They are leaving tomorrow to go to Richmond to be wed. I wanted to introduce myself as it would please Emma greatly to visit with the man she will marry."

Old Sam faced Louisa, his expression solemn.

"I know John Singer. I was here the day they brought him in. Was sitting upright on one of them stretchers, dirty and silent. Never said nothin. But them eyes that just followed Miss Emma about staring at her, until she looked over at him. Never seen that before, like a spell he cast."

Old Sam just shook his head.

"I said too much Miss Louisa. I'm just a runnin' at the mouth today. You go see for yourself. You go sees."

Louisa took his hand and thanked the black man. "Old Sam, thank you. Stay close to Doctor Bradley." With those last words she swept past him, finding an orderly to direct her to the bedside of John Singer.

Louisa came upon his bedside ever so gently, some of the surrounding patients just waking to the day. She could hear in the quiet of the room the echoing of sobbing and cries of pain. She remembered those sounds all to frequent when she attended those early on in the war.

She noticed then the raven-haired man turn his face slightly, as if acknowledging her presence. She moved to his side.

"Mr. Singer, my name is Louisa Alcott. I am friends of both Emma and Doctor Bradley. I was a nurse here at this hospital about three years ago. I live in Massachusetts and heard this hospital was closing soon, so I came to say my goodbyes. I was told you and Emma are engaged to be married."

"Yes, we are."

"I have come to offer my congratulations."

John's eyes missed nothing as they swept her body from her foot to her head seeing a slight frame and pleasant face with deep-set intelligent green eyes. His black penetrating gaze then settled on her face as Louisa noticed how very handsome this man was.

She held her breath, feeling those eyes look into her very soul as if he could sense her thoughts and draw her out against her will.

Henry was right.

It was almost impossible to look away.

John sat up from his sleeping position and motioned for her to sit. "Why Miss Alcott it is a pleasure to meet a friend of my sweet dear Emma," his voice melodious and sensuous, the impact of his magnetism was immediate and compelling on the visiting stranger.

John extended his hand to Louisa in a gesture of friendship and as they touched she suddenly froze despite the early morning heat.

His hands were not roughhewn like someone whose living depended on them, but rather smooth and hard like white marble. The feeling of his hand in hers was like white heat that inflamed her very being and touched her in the most womanly of places.

Such power. It was compelling and irresistible.

She found her voice finally, embarrassed by the feelings of his hand in hers and said in a cracked low tone, "Why yes Mr. Singer, it is a pleasure indeed."

She waited until he released his hand then and fought back the urge to grasp it once again.

My God, they were right.

He was utterly magnetic.

Facing him, she easily observed his beauty. His raven hair was set in waves about his face, the perfect features of his profile were impossible to ignore. She looked deeply into his eyes, their blackness seeming like an inky pool of uncertainty, revealing everything and nothing.

His lips looked to be soft and inviting. Louisa quickly looked away from those lips, certain of the deep passion resting behind that beautiful face.

It took her only just a moment to agree with her friend Henry.

This man was the look-alike double of the man who murdered the President. If it was not him, then his double on this earth was destined by some trick of fate to be known as the twin of John Wilkes Booth.

All that she had heard of the handsome actor was of his exquisite beauty, great talent, and of course his heinous act of murder.

She had heard of the rumor of madness in the Booth family as well, his father a great actor, yet the drink drove him to an early grave. Rumors of the elder Booth missing stage appearances, wandering streets, and just walking off the stage were dismissed as eccentric acts perhaps, but eccentric acts disguised as madness.

She gathered herself quickly, "You were a soldier in the cause of the South, Mr. Singer. Tell me where you come from?"

She settled back and waited for a response, knowing it might be cryptic, but could not help but ask it of him.

John pulled himself up and plumped the thin pillows behind him, as he did so partially unbuttoned shirt parted to reveal a solid muscular white chest.

"Why Miss Alcott, or may I call you Louisa?"

He purred her name and she acquiesced to his request.

"All right then, Louisa. Yes, I am from the glorious South, and a believer in the cause of what is right in this world. I never could understand Mr. Lincoln's conviction that black slaves should not only be free but should give citizenship. Next they will be given the right to vote. You see, I believe in the higher order of things. And the black slave should have stayed a slave. That's what I believe."

"And pray tell me Mr. Singer, ah yes of course then, John, if it is your conviction as a Southerner that the black man should not have been freed, it begs the question: did you have slaves where you are from?"

She smiled at this and felt she had him.

"I am a gentleman of the South, born of Southern convictions and Southern beliefs. That is where I am from. Now, you must excuse me. I wish to see Emma."

As John rose from the bed and found his crutch, Louisa persisted.

"How it is you bear such a strong resemblance to the murderer of our President, the man known as John Wilkes Booth? Have no others mentioned this to you?"

She stood and faced him, defiant in her questioning.

"Miss Louisa, I believe a man's past from the war should remain in the past. No deed committed at wartime is ever good. Please forgive me, but I do not wish to live forever in the past. Do you?"

Her head shook.

"No, I also wish for something better now."

Somehow, he had convinced her that his silence must be respected.

Oddly, it felt right.

He truly was a master at weaving a spell.

"As to my resemblance to the murderer John Wilkes Booth," he calmly decreed in a haunting voice, "That people find this resemblance so fascinating is truly pathetic. However what they should be asking then, if this is so curious a subject and by some misbegotten twist of fate, if indeed I am the murderer John Wilkes Booth, then how arrogant of me to be hiding in plain sight."

Louisa felt shaken and confused.

"Don't you agree?"

"Yes. I suppose I do."

He smiled from the side of his mouth then, bowed in deference to the lady before him and limped away. The sound of the crutch on the wooden floor seemed like an echoing hammer into her heart.

Louisa was dumbfounded by him, confused and yet strangely driven.

She had to find Henry.

CHAPTER FOURTEEN

I am dead to you and all who have known me,
yet I am unable to run to you to tell you I am alive.

~~ John Wilkes Booth

The young mother in Philadelphia awoke with a heaviness in her distended belly. She knew the time was near for the child within her to be born. She called for her house servant Mrs. McLeary to send a message to Washington to try to bring her husband back to Philadelphia in advance of the child's birth.

She wondered as she steadied herself for the onslaught of birth if he would even come. As he was imprisoned in Washington, it was highly unlikely yet even before all this tragedy, John had distanced himself from his role in the family and as husband. He cared little about her or his children, distancing himself from the Booth family even more since John's heinous act that had befallen them all.

"And this poor child to be born in the midst of this unhappiness," She rubbed her belly, speaking to the child. "Should you be a boy, I will name you after your Uncle John, secretly, for your dear Uncle loved you so very much. Know that you are loved and the man I name you after was a beautiful and dear man; no matter what is being said of him and what he did."

She felt her abdomen lurch in pain as the contractions started. No time now for her husband to come. The child was upon her.

Louisa stood and tried to comprehend what John has said to her. It was all nonsense, just plain nonsense. She began to take leave of the hospital bedside when a baritone voice next to John's bed broke the wailing sounds of the hospital ward and said to her.

"Ma'am look here, I wouldn't cross that man for nothin. See I been this here's Singer's bunk mate from the time they brought him in. He got up in my face and dang near threatened to punch me cause I said how lucky he was to have Emma."

"Oh, perhaps he found it disrespectful."

"Now look see here, ma'am. I didn't mean no disrespect, but that Miss Emma is sure right pretty. He just lucky is all, I mean he got all his parts, and some of us we got some missin. Hard to be going home to the Missus not quite the same way we left. That's all I meant. He got real angry. I been in battle. I seen and done some terrible things. But the look in his eyes scared me some, burning they was like the fires of hell."

"That sounds overly dramatic, sir."

"I'm sorry ma'am, but you just watch out for him. I sure hope Miss Emma loves him allot. Not gonna be easy with that kinda temper in 'em. And what's he done mean if he is the murderer John Wilkes Booth, I don't understand that? For we all know that fool Booth got himself killed for his wicked murdering ways. And deservedly so. Singer better watch out cause he does kinda look like Booth, a name not taken so kindly these days."

"That will be his burden to bear."

The soldier nodded to Louisa, contented he had said his piece against his hospital roommate.

"Thank you. I wish you a speedy recovery and a trip home."

"Why yes'um," a smile spread across the care-worn face, "I be going home down to the sweet smells and home fires of Charleston, South Carolina to my wife and daughter."

With that he smiled at Louisa, and as she turned to leave she noticed his right side which was facing her had an empty sleeve where his right arm should have been. She hastened her leave and made her way over to see Henry.

At the physician's office door, Louisa knocked gently. She was not sure if he was awake, as it was still early, just past dawn. Henry came to the door and forced a smile. It failed to hide the red-rimmed eyes and tear-stained cheeks that told of a night not well spent.

"Please come in Louisa. I was just going to have breakfast, care to join me?

Louisa smiled at her friend, "Yes I will join you for breakfast." She stepped inside and he closed the door. "I stopped in to see John Singer. I have just come from his bedside."

Henry's red-rimmed eyes widened in anticipation of Louisa's reaction, but interrupted her suddenly. "I was up all night. Come and see. I spent the night writing to Emma's mother, telling her of my suspicions of her daughter's fiancé. She should know he is not worthy of Emma and to warn her of the dangers. I am preparing to send it today. That will fix things, most certainly. Mrs. Dixon knows I am the better man for her, not this murderous miserable fake."

He was raving now, his eyes wild.

"We should contact the Government and tell them that the man killed in Garrett's farm was not Booth, but a fake planted there. They will want to know. They must know of this."

Louisa placed her hands on either side of the exhausted physician's face, thin, gaunt and drawn to the touch. The feel of her hands relaxed him. It stopped his rant for a moment.

"Henry, There is no doubt he is Booth's double, his dark and mysterious ways, only adding to a compelling presence. I too felt the magnetism of this man, his words leaving me with more questions than answers."

"What did he say?"

"He said if he was Booth, how arrogant it would be to be hiding in plain sight. Like taunting me to press for more, yet I honestly dared not for I sensed the smoldering embers of something far more dangerous that lurked within, it frightened me."

She shook her head more confused than before.

"But Henry to write to Mrs. Dixon to express your disdain of this man would cause great pain to Emma and her family. Please, don't do this. She lost her husband and her only son. Emma only has her mother and sister Abby, now. You would send this kind of letter to her with Emma coming home finally, with someone she loves?"

He frowned deeper, listening.

"And pray tell: just who would you contact in the Government to tell of your suspicions? They believe they had the right man in the barn. His conspirators are going on trial. Surely death awaits them. And think Henry, think how this claim would appear. You could possibly feel the weight of the Government for uttering treason. All citizens are vulnerable now. What will this wild claim would do to Emma? She loves him. It's so hard to let go, but we must. Tear up that letter."

"Yes, you are right. I would never hurt Emma."

Louisa gave him a feigned smile.

"There now, it is settled. Come, let's go to breakfast. I would like to see Mr. Whitman, too. I believe he is still here. I only have to today to visit and want to hear of your plans."

The whole time she had been speaking to him, his hands covered hers as they held his tear-stained face. She searched his face, her fear that his broken heart and war weary soul could slip easily into a quagmire of helplessness and despair from which he might not recover.

The birth was surprisingly fast, the child a boy coming just before noon. Mrs. McLeary helped Asia through the birth, the pain that gripped her released upon the sight of her baby boy. She held the child, plump and pink next to her skin, the faint cries beckoning the beginnings of hunger.

Asia sat back on her bed pillow and gave the child her breast, feeling for that moment a sense of peace that had eluded her for these last several months. She kissed the top of his head feeling the silken strands of black hair on her lips. The child's eyelashes were black and thick and curled upward his features, all distinctly Booth.

Asia nuzzled the baby and said in a low whisper, "Your name shall be John, but only to me, for how deeply your Uncle loved you. All that you might hear in your life about your Uncle, I cannot nor will not understand. I only know the beautiful boy he was to us."

She gazed at the babe's innocent face.

"No, your father would not approve of his son being named after your Uncle. I should name you Joseph. My son, my child. Such joy and pain that live in my heart for you and for all of us."

Emma was up early already feeling the onslaught of the early spring heat. She made her toilette quickly. She distanced her thoughts and dressed quickly. She had packing to finish and good byes to say today. She shook her head trying to dispel the remembrances of those lost over the years, the hands she held, the letters she wrote, the constant moaning and screaming of those left to die in pain, sometimes no medication to ease their suffering.

Young and naïve, she was, when she first set foot on the hospital.

Coming to help ease the pain of the Confederate Southern soldiers, realizing her inadequacies for she was bred to be a great lady of the South.

"I'm going home," she smiled inwardly, "Going home to be married in the front parlor to handsome John Singer."

Just like she had always planned.

She wondered if her room still had the French blue accents, the duvet cover and the bed pillows and if the lace curtains still fluttered like a gentle wave when the late lazy afternoon sun danced through them. The giant four-poster bed where as young debutants, she and her girlfriends whispered about the marriage bed and giggled to hide their fear.

She thought of those girlfriends now and the lives they would lead so unlike what they had planned they would be.

And she thought again of John.

By some trick of fate this man she loves, whose life she helped save, who had given her his heart and body, is indeed the murderer John Wilkes Booth. She was risking her life and those lives she would bring John into, by accepting and helping to hide his identity.

What choice did she have? None. She loved him.

She thought of the diary and of John's sister Asia, the moving letter he wrote. It was not the heart of a murderer, referencing her pregnancy and the child to be named after him, should it be a boy. It was a brother and Uncle, a man who loved his family.

What had happened to her John? Was it a singular misguided idea or the inner secret workings of the Confederacy, with John as their champion? And what it said of her, falling in love and giving herself to him; thereby going against all she was brought up to believe.

"The most wanted man," she cursed herself, "is the same man who mysteriously bends my will with a look from those eyes. I burn from the fiery passion of his very soul."

She knew her deceit was complete, realizing they were both culpable now of this life commitment to deceive.

It was said he shouted *Sic Semper Tyrannis* from the stage after murdering the President. It meant *thus always to tyrants.* His misguided thoughts believed the President was the tyrant. But by his unholy act and some miserable twist of fate, it is John who became the tyrant.

She whispered into the night, "I know you are not John Singer. Your name is John Wilkes Booth." She repeated this over and over with the pain of his heinous deed now shared in her heart, yet still stirring within her a passion that only he could complete.

John limped into the corridor of the hospital. It was too early in the day to be regretting his former life as John Wilkes Booth.

But that regret never left.

He leaned upon the corridor wall, where unknowing to him, Emma had stood just a few weeks ago, exhausted and waiting for the last ambulance to bring in the dead and wounded, that very same ambulance that brought him to into her life and saved his.

He leaned his head upon the wall. The coolness did little to quell the fire burning up his thoughts this early morning. The circle around his deception was tightening. He could sense the suspicions and felt tired of the accusations. John hobbled on his crutch, able at last to put weight on his broken casted leg. He continued out of the hospital, outside to benches on either side of the entrance.

He sat down.

John closed his eyes and leaned forward forcing his mind to recount those twelve days on the run, trying to push past the swaps of Maryland to stay ahead of the Government troops, thinking all the time he would be lauded as a hero for assassinating the tyrant President. He was a fool who had been fooled. How many times in the last four years had he heard his fellow Southerns rail that Lincoln needed to be eliminated, only who to do it?

They claimed the one who did this heroic deed would be the glory of the South. In truth, he was not lauded, but hated. While on the run, he was turned away from homes of Southern Confederate sympathizers; refused a warm house, fire, food and rest.

No rest for his aching leg and tortured mind.

It was while at the Garrett's farm, the soldier James W. Boyd arrived, someone John knew from meetings late at night at Asia's home in Philadelphia. Boyd was a Confederate sympathizer and smuggler, a member of the Knights of the Golden Circle. It was a secret organization with the Confederacy that supported pro-slavery, the goal to increase the power of the Southern slaveholding upper class in such a manner it could never been broken.

Boyd was dispatched to take his place. He was older with red hair and freckles. He doubted Boyd could pass for him. But he followed instructions and fled. He slipped away from the barn and disappeared far into the woods. For a few hours he sat huddled in the thicket when he heard the pounding of horses and saw the Union Cavalry surround the barn.

A blaze of fire was set all around the walls.

There was shouting and such a commotion that even from my distance his ears were ringing from the unfolding events. Poor Davey Herold screamed as he surrendered to the waiting Calvary, "It is not Booth, his name is Boyd."

Then a shot pierced the night. He knew Boyd was dead. John made haste through the thicket, unsure of his next move, for no provisions were made for him to meet another operative once he escaped.

The government believed they had their killer. It was up to John to survive from there, alone. He came upon the corpse of a dead Confederate about his size and stole his uniform, ridding himself of the trademark black clothing he always wore.

With the name Singer embroidered upon the cuff with great care of embroidery, he continued to hobble out of the forest with no compass, no direction and passed out on the road and landed here.

He kept the diary tucked into that that threadbare uniform, the news clipping defaming him and wanted poster were like daggers to his heart. Nothing had gone as he expected. Not a hero, but the nation's most wanted man. Yet for all the agony it contained, he could not rid himself of the items.

It was the last piece of his life as John Wilkes Booth.

Then the diary disappeared as his illness raged. He was wrong to believe by ridding the South of Lincoln everything would be made right. Now he was forever vilified by the deed.

There were Northern supporters of this act; radical Republicans in the Senate. It was suggested members of Lincoln's own cabinet, an outspoken critic of the Lincoln administration was also a member of this Circle.

John pursed his lips at the thought. He would never get a chance to go to Washington and clear his name, to tell the whole truth of this event.

So now, he was leaving tomorrow to be married, to deceive his wife and her family, to hide in plain sight for the rest of his life.

He sighed deeply as he wondered why God has spared him twice from death, first in the Garrett's barn and later with malaria.

God would judge him, someday, he was sure.

He shifted his feet, turning his face towards the early morning sun feeling the heat already of this early spring.

He closed his eyes.

John recalled once again his home at Tudor Hall, a bedroom that faced east. He loved to catch the first part of the day, rather than west facing and watching the sun sink to night. He remembered the bare hard floors of his bedroom and books of Shakespeare upon the shelves where he first learned his craft as an actor, reveling in the great plays that they beheld. Remembering too dear sweet Asia, thinking she must have born that child and wondered if it was a boy or a girl.

He was mindful of her great sensitivity and great care she gave him through his boyhood and thereafter. She was his truest friend, his sister to love. As much as he missed her, he really had no idea what this deed has done to the family and to mother.

Regret was dark inside.

In anger then John raised his fists once again to the heavens crying to himself, "I am dead to you and all that knew me, yet I still have blood cursing through my veins and breath in my lungs. But I am unable to run to you to tell you I am alive. How can I exist without you?"

That knowledge broke his heart.

"Deceit is my constant companion now. What I would give for just one look at you, dearest sister, to show you I am alive. Then I could disappear forever, left to roam this earth in search of the forgiveness that will never come."

His rant spent, he bowed his head and thought of Emma, the one who saved him, who loves him and will marry him.

He remembered the five carte de visite also kept in the diary. The missing diary. The letter for Asia she would never read, know of his repentance for the crime which mankind would immortalize, Lincoln the martyr.

He would remain forever the villain, the cold murderer.

John Wilkes Booth; the mad misguided Booth brother.

CHAPTER FIFTEEN

"Booth"

~~ *Doctor Henry Bradley*

While John sat and resonated in these thoughts, he heard footsteps near him. He looked up blinking against the sun and heard his given name boldly spoken. "Booth," spouted Doctor Bradley.

John's head turned towards the Doctor and said calmly and evenly. "Why sir there is no one here with such a name. You are mistaken."

The Doctor's feelings for Emma were worn like a badge on his arm for all to see. It was sad, yet he held no remorse for winning the beauty's love. And Henry was a fool to believe he could catch him with a simple slip of the hated name.

Henry drew close to John's face and snarled at him, "It is such you may deny who you are, and those around me have oft said of me to abandon this idea, but I cannot for I know it is you, John Wilkes Booth."

"You are sadly mistaken, sir." John calmly denied.

But the jealous man was raging, shaking his fists. "I don't know how you escaped that burning hell of a barn that you deserved to die in, yet here you are at my hospital, a man I helped Emma save, as is my medical oath. She begged me to tend to your worthless life."

"For that, I am deeply grateful. But my name is John Singer."

Henry's face turned red. "I will prove it is you. Somehow, someway watch your back. You may think you can fool Emma and those closest to you, but it is not to be, and for hiding in plain sight will be your demise. I only hope it is I that will do it." The Doctor's face twisted with rage as he spat the words to John.

John then stood up, leveling a steely gaze to his aggressor, "So it is revenge you are really after, isn't it? Not to avenge the murder of the President, but to avenge a far deeper matter, one that is eating your insides as we speak, isn't that right?"

"Emma," he could only grind out her name.

"Yes, beautiful Emma never looked upon you as a potential husband or lover, but purely as the tending physician here at the hospital; a neighbor and a family friend. Yet I won her heart swiftly and completely. That fact alone is sending you on this mad course of beliefs."

"I swear," Henry's whole body shook with rage.

Seeing the other man too angry to speak, John calmly composed himself, proving he was in utter control. "You cannot stand it was me she chose to take her, and to love that sweet luscious body and promised to marry in the same front parlor that you thought was reserved for you."

His cool voice was perfect and cool yet cutting, making the other man pale. This was exactly the effect John wanted.

Fear, it would keep him safe, keep him alive.

"So you think you know me, call me Booth and rail against me. Then rail, dear Doctor, go ahead and rail. Contact the Government and send them to Emma's house to find me, and see what they say of you uttering such blasphemy at this most fearsome time. The wrath of the Government for speaking treason will be swift and just, with only your blithering wild beliefs to keep you company in the jail cell they will surely confine you to."

He started to push past the Doctor and yet could not resist one more remark, "I think I will go see Emma, as a matter of fact. My sweet fiance' should be warned of your madness. Her friendship with you is over. Your rantings will only bring her pain. Good day, sir."

He walked past the Doctor, using the crutch for balance, his shoulders squared in the indignant pose of a wrongfully accused man.

Glancing back, John saw Henry collapse in defeat on the bench.

It was a battle won, for now, an important battle, indeed.

Emma opened the door to her room, happy to see John. He pushed past her quickly and entered her room. "Good morning John, I see you are up early, I have lots to do, finish packing and such. I have new clothes for you, so you have proper clothes to ride in."

"A better lot than the used clothing of the dead I have been wearing?"

"Much better." She smiled at him yet his face remained without emotion. She stepped closer to him and looked at his face. "John, what is it? Has something upset you?"

"No my darling, I just wanted to see you. I love you so much. I cannot believe you love me. I don't deserve you."

Emma reached to touch his handsome face, the diamonds on her ring glinting in the early morning light. "You have nothing to fear, I will never leave you, ever."

John's face dropped as not to look at her, the confrontation with the Doctor and his accusations resonating within him. "I can offer you nothing Emma, no station, no status, just my heart."

"That is all I have ever wanted, your heart."

Emma placed both her hands on either side of John's face and pulled him gently to kiss her. John held her close, resting his head on her slim slight shoulder. She moved herself to her bed and sat on the edge and waited. He reached behind her and with skilled hands removed the bindings from her plaited braid. The hair fell about her like waves of corn silk gliding through summer breeze.

"John," she murmured his name.

He moved to face her and gently took the side of her face in his hand. He tilted her head slightly and gently kissed her full waiting lips. He waited for Emma to lean into his wanting kiss for he knew from experience any resistance would be gone. He played about her lips with his tongue until he felt her breath quicken.

"Oh, the things you do to me," she breathed.

John moved quickly.

He unbuttoned her dress and watched it fall from her slim but curvy body.

She stepped from it and he led her to the bed, where he removed the chemise from her shoulders and then enjoyed seeing her breasts, the skin so soft and smooth. Lingering a moment, he touching her breasts with his hands. It pleased her. Soon, he again went for clothing, fingering the restrictions with expert knowledge, removing the underpinning of female garments. Emma sat on her bed when he gently removed the chemise from her body. She was completely naked.

Her hands skimmed him, begging to touch his skin, too.

He reached for his light loose-fitting shirt and removed it, then the trousers as they fell from his body.

He too was completely naked.

John leaned toward her and let go of the crutch as he placed himself on top of her. He smiled to hear Emma breath words of approval. He kissed her fully swirling his tongue about her enveloping her completely so her breath mingled with his breath. He continued to kiss her full ripe breasts. He nestled them, caressed the soft skin and kissed and suckled the beautiful flesh until she whimpered with pure pleasure.

John then continued to move down her luscious body and moved her legs to open for his love. He continued to kiss her until she could no longer bear it, and cried out his name over and over as her body convulsed in passion reserved only for him. He swiftly and deliberately gave himself to her.

"Oh, yes." She wrapped her legs about him and pushed her heels into small of his back. He smiled at that and gently loosed her grasp so he could bring himself to full passion as he began to love her. He watched her beautiful face, her eyes half closed as she loved him with an open heart until he was nestled tightly against her and called her name to him.

Emma knew she was powerless against him. Whenever he called, whenever he wanted her, she knew she would acquiesce, his passion swift and complete there was nothing she would not give him. "*Even my deceit,*" she thought in the aftermath of his lovemaking. "*My deepest deceit is my greatest love for you,*" she rationalized.

Breathing heavy, his skin gleaming with a light sheen of sweat, he lifted himself carefully off of her. Emma reached for her clothing scattered about the small confines of the room.

She tried to cover herself with the chemise before stepping into it. He took it from her. "You are perfect, your body and your face God's perfection. Don't fear showing yourself for you are mine in my heart and through my passion. When I am near you darling it's like a man thirst, quenched for a time and becomes thirsty all over again."

"We have a lifetime to quench your thirst, dearest John."

She hastened into her dress as she went to the small trunk at the foot her bed. The package of clothes Emma had sent for arrived yesterday and wanted to surprise John with its contents. He watched silently as she pulled what looked like men's proper black trousers with a matching waistcoat and white shirt.

The shoes too she placed before him waiting for his reaction.

"Why Emma, such fine clothes are these."

Emma thought of how handsome he would look. Dressed all in black with a slouch hat to match, he would cut the most dashing of figures clothed in black with his inky black hair, his white skin and dark eyes.

"So you are pleased?"

"Ah yes, I am most certainly blessed, especially to never to have to wear these used garments again. You please me deeply, dear. You please me most of all."

He reared his head back and laughed deeply. She loved the sound of his voice. It was like a euphoric melody that played in the secret places of her heart playing chords that only he could answer.

Louisa and Old Sam found the Doctor sitting on the bench. He was upright but had his arm crossed in front of his face, sobbing and heaving deep and painful tears. Everyone passing the doorway entrance was a witness to his pain.

Old Sam steadied the Doctor in his large and expansive arms, "What is it, what has happened?"

He wiped his face with his sleeve, "It's ok, just a spell of sadness. I am fine, just let me catch my breath." He managed a weak smile to his friend.

"No suh, that ain't it. I know you. That kinda weepin' is not from sadness, but from grieving. That kinda crying was from your heart."

Louisa reached for her friend's hand and asked him gently, "Henry, I saw John Singer leaving. What was said between you?"

"I couldn't help myself. I just can't let go of my suspicion of this man, he was sitting on this very bench and was deep in thought, I thought then I could trick him, I called his name out Booth!"

Louisa's eyes grew big as he told her of his encounter. "Henry, you didn't."

"He is canny. He did not answer when I called his name, but rather he was cool and said that I was mistaken. He taunted me about Emma, said I was mad, that my rantings would only bring her pain, and that my friendship with her was over." His shoulders slumped at those words as if the utterance of them cut through his very insides, leaving them open with nothing to ease the pain.

Old Sam had held his tongue long enough, seeing his friend grieving was too much to bear even if it meant telling Miss Emma's secret. "I got sumptin' to say to ya'll. I promised Miss Emma not to tell, but now this here's man of Miss Emma's is causing too much upset." The Doctor and Louisa both looked at him. "Well," said Old Sam with a tilt of his head, "Remember the day Miss Emma done come back to the fire pit looking for a uniform?"

The Doctor knitted his eyebrows in recollection. "Yes, I remember. Did she find it?"

"Yes'sur, she did."

Now Henry was truly listening.

"I didn't know why she wanted this uniform, it was so worn you could see almost clean through in places, but I done pulled it out from the fire with long tree branch moving it away from the pit. I checked it and a small red colored book was in one pocket. Not the readin kind, cause stuff done fell out of it."

"What kind of stuff?" Louisa asked.

"It was a bunch of pictures of fancy women, not nice ladies like you Miss Louisa or Miss Emma, just well, fancy kinda ladies."

"I think I understand."

"There was also a bunch of paper clippins, pictures of that man who killed our President. Miss Emma grabbed all the pictures and stuffed em back into the book. Then she told me never to speak of it. I promised I wouldn't tell. You see there, Doc, youse is my family, you all I got. Seeing you so upset about Miss Emma and that man of hers, well, I just had to tell ya what I did. I is so sorry."

Old Sam hung his head in shame.

Henry said evenly, "Tis not that I hold any anger to you dear friend, you were only doing what Emma had asked you to do. For as much as you held the secret, you have now shared it with Louisa and I, so for that I am grateful that your fear was not greater than your good heart."

"Thank you. I'm getting back to work now."

They watched the big man walk away, his stance a little taller now for having spoken the truth. Henry turned towards Louisa, and with a sneer of a smile whispered to her, "Now I have evidence."

"What can it prove?"

"That I deserve her," he laughed, almost delirious now with joy, the look on his face both satisfied and disturbed. "You will see, Louisa. In the end, I will win."

"Henry, don't you understand there is nothing to win, the war is over."

"Not for me Louisa, not for me!"

Louisa thought it best to take Henry back to his quarters and to have breakfast brought to him.

She decided to stop by see Doctor Hendrix as he was the head administrator at the hospital to advise him of her worries about Henry and his delusions that were bordering on madness.

As John finished dressing, Emma thoughts went back to her her home in Richmond, a time right before the war, remembering her father as he stood at the head of their dining room table, telling his guests that although he was a Southerner through and through, he believed that indeed slavery was wrong. He had no slaves, that this great civil war must take place, for the life of nearby plantation owners was coming to an end. Emma wondered if her father imagined how mightily he would pay mightily for his beliefs, with his son fighting for his beloved South to prove his love and devotion of Virginia.

John sensed her change in mood, "Emma, what is it?"

"For a moment, pain strikes my heart. I was remembering father being at the head of the table in our dining room, trying to advise those in attendance their world would change as they knew it." She hung her head at the memory and then said in a rush to him, "I have lots to do today John, goodbyes to be said and to finish up packing. Our transportation, a buckboard driven by the stable boy Isaac leaves at dawn tomorrow. Then the train from Fredericksburg to Richmond and then we take my family's coach to home. Home, John, we are going home."

"That sounds wonderful."

"I have asked Mother to prepare with haste for our wedding. I want us to be married. The date of our wedding will be this Wednesday, May twenty-seventh; only two days away."

"Darlin," he smiled, "it can't be soon enough for me."

She stepped closer to him mindful the man she would marry was a murderer, yet was capable of such repentance and regret that she read in the heartfelt letter to his sister; it made no sense. "This has happened quickly with your illness, our declaration of love, and now a marriage just two days away."

"Yes love moves quickly, sometimes."

"I share this with you now so you know, when I was just eighteen and was busy with parties, and dances and the latest dresses from Paris, there was always talk of the marriage bed, my girlfriends and I giggled about it, yet feared it so. The older married women would tell us it was the wife's duty to succumb to the requests of her husband and not to deny them, and let him have his way to satisfy his needs."

"That was the husband's right in the marriage bed."

"But I have given my love to you before such time as we are man and wife, and although I was told I would not enjoy my husband's needs, I must be honest." She felt her cheeks grow hot, but told him honestly, "It is such a pleasure for me, an addiction, I fear. The love and desire I have for you will never be enough."

John rewarded her with a magnificent smile. "That you should have me as you did just now and speak so plainly of how it makes you feel, just fuels the fire within me."

"What I am trying to say is that it will never be enough, that I give myself to you and we are complete. Touching you completes me. Yet soon, I yearn for the next time. Such is my passion for you. It will never be enough. Our loving together is truly an addiction. You have awakened my body and that part of my soul will always and forever be yours."

John kissed her. "I love you darling. And no matter what may be said of me, please always remember that."

"What do you mean?" Emma feigned innocence, yet felt the deception in her heart, knowing she was culpable in hiding him in plain sight and for supporting his false name for the sake of his life.

She wondered what would happen when she saw Asia, hoping to convince her to come see the brother who was not murdered, but alive. She feared what John would do when he realized she had known all along his true identity and lied to him the whole time they were together. All she could give him was her love. She prayed it was enough.

John then broke the silence, "It is on great faith you have taken my body and soul, knowing that the question of what happened to me in the war and where I hail from will never be uttered even to you my darling."

She nodded to show she respected his silence.

"I arrived here filthy, starving, and ready to leave this earth. That you love me, have taken me unto yourself and now even at the marriage altar before God, is beyond all that I deserve or could have hoped to have in this life."

"It will be a good life," she hoped.

He drew in his breath, "Yes, together it will be." As if needing to reinforce the deception he added, "My name is John Singer, and soon we shall be as one."

John smiled.

But Emma thought: *Your name is John Wilkes Booth and soon, yes, we shall be as one.*

She watched as he fingered the glittering gold medal around his neck, the Agnus Dei, Lamb of God symbol and wondered of its meaning for John. Was this his faith or did someone give it to him? She sighed realizing once again her questions would go unanswered, at least until she found Asia.

CHAPTER SIXTEEN

But this one, he needs killin'

~~ Sergeant Beauregard Jackson

After helping Henry back to his quarters, Louisa went to the kitchen at the hospital and requested a full plate of breakfast foods for her friend. She urged them to deliver it quickly to him at his quarters where she knew Old Sam would stand sentry guarding his friend with all the reserve he had to give.

She then made her way over to the one building on the grounds that had a single occupant the hospital administrator, Doctor Jonas Hendrix.

His wise guidance over the years had kept the hospital funded and staffed an amazing feat during wartime. He kept the medical supplies stocked as best he could so Doctor Bradley as well as the other physicians could save lives. Occasionally he assisted with surgeries, helping when there were more injured men than physicians. He was an extremely talented surgeon, firm and candid. He had assembled an important and extraordinary team.

It was there Louisa found herself knocking on his door this early morn.

She knocked softly.

It was early.

She knew he might be reading. Doctor Hendrix was well known for his avid interest in books. It was distractions such as reading that kept men sane during war.

The door opened. The Doctor had aged poorly.

Was no one immune to the casualties of this war?

Before her stood a middle-aged man of medium height and weight, but his carriage was stooped and his face flushed and red. His eyes look beyond her as if they were eyes born from having seen too much death, the shine and luster a thing of the past. She had assumed him about forty or so, yet add twenty to that in the lines on his face.

He looked at Louisa quizzically, with no recollection of her.

"Yes, may I help you?"

"Doctor Hendrix, I am Louisa May Alcott from Massachusetts. I came here early on the war to work, but caught typhoid fever and was very ill. Since that time," she decided to appeal to his literary senses, "I have been writing under the pen names Flora Fairchild and A.M. Barnard. Some of my stories have been produced in plays in Boston."

As she had hoped, his eyes lit with recognition.

"Most recently I wrote of my civil war experiences in Hospital Sketches. Have you read my work?"

"Why yes of course most certainly, dear. What brings you to my door?"

"I have come back these few days, to say goodbye to the people that helped me while I was here and to wish them well on their journeys home, after this terrible civil war, but this morning I have come here to ask you for help for one of your physicians."

"Come in, let's talk."

The Doctor swung the door wide, and motioned for her to sit in a small but comfortable dining area, the breakfast for the physician already on his plate, the smell of coffee and biscuits permeating the air.

"Doctor my apologies; I have interrupted your breakfast."

He motioned to his housekeeper for another place setting and ordered coffee for Louisa. He leaned his elbows on the table revealing the deep lines in his face, ravages of worry to keep the hospital running and from the suffering he had witnessed during the war.

"Tell me please Miss Alcott; you say one of my physicians needs help. In what way and whom it is that brings your deep concern?"

Louisa's expression turned solemn. "It's Henry Bradley. He is my friend, a good and kind man. His compassion and kindness are well-known. It is with deep concern that I come here to ask you to please watch over him. The war has taken so much from Henry. He had big dreams for his life. All he has ever done is tend and work, these four long years."

Doctor Hendrix leaned closer.

"This seems more than just latent concern."

Louisa took a deep breath and began.

"You see Doctor Hendrix, there is case here of unrequited love. It seems our lovely devoted nurse Emma Dixon has fallen in love with a soldier and is planning to be married soon. His name is John Singer."

"And Henry has not taken kindly to this?"

"No. In fact he is deeply disturbed. Henry is a family friend of the Dixon's and at Emma's eighteenth birthday was given permission to court her, but then the war broke out. Emma volunteered to come here to tend the injured, Henry content that she was in his purview, perhaps hoping to state feelings he has long kept secret. But Emma's father and older brother were both killed in the First Battle of Manassas in July 1861, so any promises of Emma and Henry passed away with his death."

"Yes, I can see if she were promised to him, Henry would not accept her engagement to another man."

"Most certainly there is no fault here, for one cannot ever say who we fall in love with, but well," Louisa decided to trust, sharing all that she knew. "This John Singer has an uncanny resemble to John Wilkes Booth. I tell you Doctor Hendrix, it's his double. An unfortunate resemblance, but in Henry's pain of unrequited love he believes it actually is Booth. He is adamant and steadfast. I fear the situation is getting worse."

"It is impossible, of course."

"Yes, but he won't let go of his feelings for Emma nor his belief that Singer is Booth. I am worried for his safety. He is talking about going to the Government to tell them they have the wrong man, claiming the real killer is hiding right here in plain sight. I reminded him the Government has their killer and such talk will speak of treason. Doctor Hendrix, there are many people in jail, swept up in the conspiracy of the horrible event that has befallen our country. If Henry doesn't stop this I fear he will be next."

"My God," whispered Doctor Hendrix, "I knew he was exhausted as we all are, but this is madness. To hear of one so diligent and talented suffering from this delusion saddens me. And most certainly you are correct to worry. Such talk is treason. Has anyone else heard of this?"

Louisa nodded her head, "Old Sam witnessed much of it."

"Ah yes Old Sam; that man would go to the ends of the earth for Doctor Bradley," he too seemed to share grave concern for his friend. He rose from his chair, the coffee now cold and the breakfast uneaten, "I will get to the bottom of this Miss Alcott, and I will tread lightly on behalf of your friendship, but will most definitely get to the bottom of this."

He showed Louisa out and muttered to himself, "Madness, this is madness." The pain of unrequited love could break a man.

How painful to see the person you have loved day after day, never speaking of it, only to see that love given to another. It combined with unspeakable conditions, the screaming of men that would die waiting to be attended to, the ones screaming when told amputation was the only way to live and floorboards slippery with blood.

Doctor Hendrix made haste to Doctor Bradley's quarters.

Whatever their discussion, it will be heartbreaking.

Jonas knocked and was surprised when Old Sam appeared at the door, his large and expressive face downcast and worried.

"Good mornin' Doc Hendrix, youse come on in. I was trying to get Doc Bradley here to eat some, but he ain't feeling so good today. I just will set here a spell and make sure he gonna be ok." The large hulking man shifted his feet, the worry etched along his expansive face.

"Not to worry, I have stopped by to see how Doctor Bradley is feeling. Miss Alcott came to visit this morning, so I thought to come by."

Old Sam eyes grew wide.

"She's powerful worried, Doctor. She told me to set here, to keep him safe. She had them vittles fixed up, but he ain't eatin noffin."

"I am here now. I will sit with Henry, don't worry." Trying not to appear worried, he feigned a smile at Old Sam. "You know, is nearly time for those poor souls over at the hospital to have their breakfast. I am here now. You go ahead and help them out."

Old Sam was slow to move towards the door, as he did he said to the head physician, "Please try to help him, you see he's done all I got. He's my family. I don't have anyone else in this world just him. Please make him better," he cast his eyes downward to the floor and opened the door to take his leave.

Henry called out from the small dining area, "Old Sam, who is there?"

Doctor Hendrix walked into the room, "It is just me, Henry. Thought I would come see how things were going."

Henry's myopic eyes narrowed, "Why all is just fine, Jonas, no worries," as he forced a smile.

"Well now that is not exactly true, is it?" He looked over at the breakfast place, long since gone cold, not a morsel even tasted.

"I was asked to come to check on you as your friends have a growing concern over your well-being. Before you answer, understand I have come with only the best intentions for your care, that although the matter may be deeply personal, I only want to help. We have known each other since you first graduated medical school and came here to work, foregoing the start of your career to aid those poor soldiers that passed through these doors."

"Help," cried Henry, outraged as his voice raised even higher, "Help? You can't help me; you can't help any of this. No one can."

He drew his hand over his chest.

"My heart is broken. The only woman I have ever loved loves another. The pain is ripping me apart. She would have been my queen. I have waited for her for years, loving her in silence. With me, Emma would have the life of a great lady. Just as the war ends, this imposter, a murderer comes to our hospital, and she gives herself to him!"

Jonas listened to him rage.

"That which was mine was given away, I saw him coming out of her room last evening," he shook his head in disgust, "I know what is going on, it's killing me! They are leaving tomorrow to be married, in the front parlor that her father said would be for me."

His ranting became louder as he threw back his chair, whirled around to the visiting physician and shouted, "He is a dead ringer for John Wilkes Booth, that murdering conniving man that somehow has glommed the name of a real Confederate martyr, John Singer."

"It is impossible."

"I tell you Jonas, it's him. I know it's him. I'm going to get him one way or another. Emma will see I am the better man and leave him."

"How?" Jonas questioned, deeply worried now.

Henry's arms flailed around as he spoke, his motions as wild as his thoughts. "The Government must know they made a mistake at the barn. I am going to Washington. They will listen."

"Not without proof. They will think you mad, Henry."

"There is even evidence! Emma has it. Old Sam said he saw a diary fall out the uniform right before it was burnt. He told me and Louisa that there were five carte de visite of women, can you imagine, five?"

Jonas said nothing, but was stunned by the news.

"And that there was a news clipping of sorts along with a wanted poster, you remember the one posted for his capture?" Henry glanced as his friend, waiting until he nodded, then continued pacing the room.

"Why would he carry something like that?"

"Because it was Booth's personal property," Henry proclaimed, waving his hands with the words. "Perhaps Booth was not willing to give up the only evidence of who is really is."

Jonas pondered the scenario, "If Emma has his diary," he said evenly, "she must have shown it to John Singer and questioned his veracity as to who he really is."

"Perhaps they are counting on the sanctity of marriage to keep this secret hidden from the world," Henry snarled with contempt, "but I tell you Jonas, as long as I have breath, I will find out the truth."

"Henry," he tried to calm his friend, "Listen to me please. Miss Dixon has been a wonderful addition to this hospital. Her youth, care and compassionate nature have been a blessing. Who can say how or why we fall in love? From what I am hearing from you, she gave no indication of feelings other than of respect and friendship. She has made her choice. The heart makes its own choices in the matter of love."

Henry only made a gruff sound, but was listening.

"Does she not have the right to love?"

Stopping his pacing, he cast Jonas a regretful glance.

"Do you not wish her happiness?"

"Yes, of course. Her happiness is my greatest joy."

Jonas sighed, hoping they had finally found a source of reason, an end to the madness. "You must learn to let her go Henry, let her go. Let this frenzied talk that her fiancé is really John Wilkes Booth stay within your heart. It is not for others to hear."

"But it is true."

"No, you must realize this notion is beyond farfetched. Booth was murdered at Garrett's Farm on April 26, 1865. This is May 25, 1865. The man Singer simply bears an uncanny resemblance, no more no less. To continue on this path will most certainly cause treason to spread. Your safety will be at risk. Think of those soldiers who are counting on you Henry, the ones who cannot leave here whose last breath will be within those walls. Who will care for them should you be imprisoned for this talk?"

"You think this is farfetched and I speak treason," the younger physician grew angry again, "well Jonas let me assure you I speak the truth!"

Henry's face had contorted, changing his kind, reticent personality into a raging diatribe, bordering on hysteria. Even his blue eyes were wide with emotional turmoil too great for his mind to handle.

Doctor Hendrix shook his head realizing this colleague was completely exhausted mentally and physically.

He needed rest and care.

But Henry huffed at his colleague, clearly having enough of this conversation, finding no merit in it. Making a big display of leaving, he threw on his physician's jacket.

"Well I must get to my rounds, Jonas. I have some soldiers leaving this morning and I must see them off."

"Henry, please. You must think of getting some rest and eating, perhaps a few days off rounds will help. I shall see to your rounds. And again, let this notion go. It will do no good."

Henry remained annoyed and agitated.

He saw the head physician out and tried to shake off the morning's events.

"Booth," he said, shaking and railing his fists, "Go ahead and hide in plain sight. Go ahead. The sanctity of marriage will be no haven for the devil himself, your day of reckoning will be soon enough."

He smiled crookedly, "You just wait and see."

Doctor Bradley strode over to the hospital where earlier he had confronted John, and made his way through the sea of beds, finding some patients readying themselves for their journey home. He waded through the aisles stopping to say goodbye and wishing by God they were going home the way they left their home. He saw patient after patient missing an arm or leg, some with a disfigured face to take back home.

Men gave too much to war.

No cause was worth this much pain.

Henry wished he could have done more. As he continued his pace when a distinct Southern voice pierced the room and called over to him.

"Hey, Doc, stop over here."

He turned to see the burly Sergeant Beau Jackson, a lively yet fiercely dedicated soldier. His spirit and candor was a welcome sight and sound even in his deepest suffering. He saw the sleeves of his shirt and that there was just one arm, a sight hauntingly familiar.

The Doctor made his way over to his bedside; the bed next to him belonged to John Singer and was empty.

He cringed at seeing the empty bed for he knew whose bed the man was visiting.

But the Sergeant wasted no time as he shouted, "Hey lookey here, I am going home today. Thanks to you my wife and little girl will be meeting me this time tomorrow!"

Henry smiled at the exuberant man, "Why Sergeant Jackson, congratulations. It is a blessed day it is for you and your family. I really wish I could have saved that arm."

"Doc hey, I gots more than most that are going home. I don't blame you, I thank you. I have been lucky yes, but not as lucky as my bunkmate yonder," he motioned toward John's empty bed, "You see he done gots all his parts, and also got that sweet Miss Emma, I understand."

The Sergeant saw a veil of anger and hate fall over the smiling face of the Doctor with just the mention of this John Singer. He sensed something evil in that man. Perhaps the Doctor felt the same. Beau wasn't a wise man, but he did enjoy stirring up trouble.

And there was trouble a plenty, where John Singer was concerned.

"Why there Doc, I tell ya, he done got up in my face cause I said something about how lucky he was to have Miss Emma. He pushed his face into mine and them black eyes was like looking at the devil. I swear I saw flames in 'em!"

The physician was definitely listening.

"I told her friend that Miss Alcott the same thing. I just hope Miss Emma knows that side of him, is all. I seen and done lots of wicked things these last four years, none of which I am proud of, but that there look in his eyes, it done turned my blood ice cold."

The Doctor looked at the Sergeant in comradery and said evenly, "Why yes Beau, I have thought the same exact thing by the way." His eyes were narrow and his face tightened, his teeth pushed together tight like someone was squeezing the life out of him.

"You know doc, I would like to give you a gift for your care of me."

"I couldn't."

"Now now," he insisted as the Doctor shook this off, "You must take this, it was my father's and I want you to have it."

With that the Sergeant dug into his folded bag that held a handful of personal possessions and slid a small sleek derringer into the Doctor's hand. "Take this and use it well. The war maybe over, but this one, he needs killin."

Henry silently agreed.

The pistol in his hand felt like power, the power to change fate.

"See now, you use it well, Doc."

He smiled in solidarity, rose from his bed to go home and left the Doctor standing in the aisle. Beau make his way to the door, turned one last time, nodded his head then disappeared.

Henry slid the small pistol into his pocket, the weight of it hitting his thigh as he continued to walk through the hospital ward, with each step smiling inwardly as his tired mind began to justify the unthinkable.

John finished his dressing and kissed Emma as he took his leave. His passion for her was quelled for the moment.

He hobbled on his crutch as he thought about this encounter, that he had taken her knowing she would bend to his needs, yet she proved she needed him equally. Her words that it would never be enough, no matter what, she would always want him more showed how deep their attraction for one another ran.

Strong enough to last a lifetime.

She was so beautiful.

He imagined them in a real home together and looked forward to night after night of unbridled passion. Oh, to tell her of who is really is and what he did!

She must never find out.

All the suspicions in the world amounted to nothing. The Government has their man, James William Boyd.

He pondered this thought as he heard footsteps behind him and heard his name called, "John Singer!"

He turned to see his bunk mate fully dressed in homespun pants and shirt, and striding towards him, a tied up sack of possessions, holding it with the one arm he had left.

He had his fill of this one too.

John stood his ground and waited. The Sergeant stopped in front of John and said, "Well here look see, you heading out somewhere or just finishin' up from somewhere?"

John sneered at the burly man. He obviously knew he had just come from Emma's as he was just a few yards from her door.

"I believe that is just none of your damn business."

He proceeded to push past him when the Sergeant blocked his way. "Well now iffin I was you, I would watch my back. I ain't the only one round here that had enough of your smart talk and arrogant ways."

"Is that so?"

"You're hiding somptin ain't ya? I ain't one for fancy talk. Someone's asks me somptin, I just comes out and tells em. But not you. Damn near iffin I care, but you better be careful. You looking like that John Wilkes Booth is damn near a crazy twist of fate. But you keep talking smart, you just might get yourself killed."

"You dare threaten me, Sergeant?"

"Sure am. And rightfully so, I reckon. These days seem to me the Government ain't too picky who they are stringing up."

John had enough of this burly crass man, "Well, if you are man enough for the task, you just try it. Might prove difficult with just one arm."

"Rest assured, there is someone here who gonna kill ya."

John threw back his head and laughed.

"Good day, And goodbye," he nodded toward the buckboard that was waiting for Beau to take him away from the hospital and out of John's life.

"And good riddance."

The Sergeant smiled at his response.

"Watch yer' back."

John stood staring at the man as the Sergeant turned and walked towards his waiting stage, the heat of the early morning no match for the icy cold warning of his former hospital mate.

CHAPTER SEVENTEEN

Mama, do we have another baby brother?

~~ Jacob Junius Clarke

The young mother held her infant son sitting up in her bed, the noises outside her room unmistakable. It was Jacob and Joshua anxiously awaiting their newborn sibling. She called them into her room and smiled at wild abandon and innocent joy of how the boys raced to her side, anxious to see the newest addition to their family.

The dark-haired boys peered into her arms.

"Mama... mama," Jacob ran to her, "Do we have another brother?"

"Yes child, we do. Say hello to your brother Joseph."

The children peered into the blanket and whispered, "Hi Joseph, I am Jacob your brother."

Then the younger brother echoed, "Hi Joseph. I am Joshua, your brother."

They smiled with pride at their introduction and leaned in to gently touch the sleeping infant. The boy Jacob looked so much like his Uncle John. In his heart, too. The deep love for family resonated within both.

"Mama," Jacob asked after he had admired his new brother for a moment "I thought if this baby was a boy, you were naming him after Uncle John. How come you named him after Uncle Joe? Is that 'cause Uncle John did something bad?"

"What makes you think he did something wrong?"

"Because everybody says so."

Clearly he understood more than she realized. Jacob hung his head in remembrance of his favorite Uncle who cradled both boys and roughhoused with them on the floor, put them on his horse and walked them around the street, coddled them and adored them. That presence so greatly missed by the boys. The confusion of their Uncle's heinous deed was lost upon the young boys ability to comprehend such an act.

Asia saw the heartache the children's faces.

"Boys," she began, "I will tell you this, but you must never tell anyone, do you promise?" The boys nodded in agreement as they waited in anticipation for their mother to speak. "I have named your brother John Joseph. You see, I have kept that promise to your Uncle John, but right now let's keep it our secret."

"Why," Jacob needed to understand.

"Unfortunately, your Uncle John is not looked at too kindly right now, so only we shall call your baby brother John Joseph."

It was Jacob who spoke up once again, that defiance in his tone so like his Uncle John, "Ok, we understand, but when will everyone love Uncle John like before? People loved him on stage, wearing all those costumes. Is he ever coming back? When can we see him?"

Asia reached out to smooth the check of her oldest son. "I honestly don't know child, but we can love him just the same, no matter what."

The child stared at his mother and smiled gently, then whispered to his baby brother, "I love you John-Joseph," and softly kissed the sleeping infant.

Emma stood quietly in the center of her room, her skin still burning from where just moments ago John had touched her. She was taken aback by her unbridled passion for him. He was like an opiate for her, she felt satisfied for a short time then she wanted more, he always left her wanting more.

"Dearest God, what have I done," she lamented.

She was marrying a man whose name was false, who was a murderer as well. She had made love with him. Despite his crimes, she still loved him.

Emma shook her head. "How did this happen?"

Just a few weeks ago she was working in the hospital, tending to the sick, the last of the brave soldiers coming in. Then she saw him, those eyes following her, awakening needs and desires she never knew existed. Emma went over to her dresser, pulling out the well-worn petticoats and chemises, and reached for the red date book. She took it out and opened it, the carte de visite of the five women once again staring up at her.

Who were these women? They were all so beautiful.

How could he abandon such a famous acting career? Although she never saw him on stage, his name and talents spoke for itself. The sound of his voice is like a finely tuned instrument, his physical beauty captivating and relentless. He had it all and abandoned it all, not just the acting career, but his family and those who truly loved him.

Abandoned it to commit such a crime against the nation. It makes no sense, for the words penned to your sister Asia are wrought with love and devotion. John, why? For this unforgivable deed you committed against man, only God can judge.

Emma took the letter addressed to Asia and read it once again, the haunting words, of John saying ".... with every man's hand against me..." and ".... I must go to Washington to clear my name".... tells that John was chosen by Confederate secret operatives to commit this crime.

His beauty, fame, money, and his ease into the best houses both North and South, made him the perfect ally to commit this deed. And so where are they now? Abandoning him after the escape from the burning barn, giving him life, yet his only recourse was to live and hide in plain sight.

She unfolded the wanted poster with his handsome face and his flowing mustache, his face now completely clean shaven, his name changed.

Just having his book was an act of treason.

Her hands shook. There was so much at stake. She could keep this book forever and never expose the truth. She could defend his new identity. They could live together with their children and no one the wiser. But the book would be there, haunting her, calling to her, never giving her peace. Emma realized this sister Asia, to whom he loves so deeply, must be suffering. Clearly she loved John equally.

She must be told the truth.

"John, I love you so," she murmured, "so much so, I will risk it all to meet your sister Asia and somehow convince her to come and see that indeed you are alive. By this act my deception of knowing your true identity will be revealed. When Asia is brought to you and the lie exposed, what will you do to me?" She wondered aloud and hung her head. Squeezing the book tight to her heart, she hastened to finish her packing.

There were goodbyes to be said.

Emma heard another knock on her door and ran to answer it. Standing there was Louisa, her countenance tight and stressed. Emma beckoned her to enter, tidying up the piles of clothing on the bed that hadn't quite made it into her trunk and hiding the book under the pile.

Louisa welcomed her with a hug.

"Good morning. I came to say my farewells to you here in private. I know you are leaving very early tomorrow, I just wanted to say goodbye and wish you well on your upcoming marriage."

"You look so tired," Emma noticed, "is all well with you? Please come and sit. This early spring heat is so burdensome. If it like this now, what shall it bring in July?"

Emma smiled as she tried to keep the conversation light and easy, but Louisa was not fooled, she clearly wanted a moment of honesty with her friend, "Yes, I am tired. Not by this heat, but because I have been so worried about our friend Doctor Bradley."

"Oh? Is he unwell?"

"Yes, his heart is broken."

The abrupt truth made Emma feel bad.

"I had Doctor Hendrix stop by this morning to talk to him, to ease his heart and mind. The years of war with so much death, has paid a toll and his tired mind is now ranting about your fiancé and his unfortunate resemblance to John Wilkes Booth. I fear this ranting, if not quelled, will cause him great harm. You know his feelings for you. It is a strain he cannot bear. His mind is playing tricks on him."

"What can be done?"

"Doctor Hendrix is taking him off rotation for a few days. I will stay and watch over him."

Although Emma was concerned, it didn't seem fair that Louisa be held responsible or that Emma should carry the blame.

She had never misled him.

"I cannot help Henry's feelings about me. I think of him as a family friend as a gifted and talented surgeon."

"Yes, I know."

"I came here to work, harboring no alternative intentions." She shook her head, "I can't imagine his pain, nor can I help him. As for my John Singer resembling that man John Wilkes Booth; that is not Henry's concern. I love him, Louisa, and I will love him until I die. I never knew of this kind of love existed. I said to John and I say to you and all who would ask of me, having him is never enough for the moment the desire we feel is sated, then the need to be near him builds within me once again. If he were a drug, I would surely be addicted."

"It is serious, to be sure."

"From the moment I saw him arrive at the hospital no other man had a chance to win me."

She hugged her friend, feeling that perhaps this would be the last time they saw each other.

Louisa loosened her embrace. "Please be careful with this marriage. One can only hope that your John will soon recount fully where he is from and who his people are. I wish you a happy marriage, for I fear until such time as he can explain his past and clear his name from any resemblance of Booth, a shadow of suspicion will be cast over your John, and you as well. And yes I do understand the type of love you profess."

"Do you?"

Louisa nodded, "If my Jack had recovered I would have married him. I understand what has driven you, the uncontrolled passion to be with the man you love. It mocks all that we knew and grew up to believe. I wish you good luck in your future together. God bless you both."

Emma nodded her head, and watched as her friend left.

She sighed.

She still had to bid farewell to Old Sam and to Doctor Bradley.

She would remind Old Sam to keep his promise not to tell anyone about the diary that he saved from the smoldering hospital fire pit, the book that contained and subsequently signaled John Singer as a fake and points to the life of John Wilkes Booth.

CHAPTER EIGHTEEN

I know he is not John Singer.
I know he is Booth, and so do you.

~~ Doctor Henry Bradley

Although he had been relieved from duties, Doctor Bradley made his way through the many bedsides of those soldiers that were ambulatory, the ones that had remaining arms or legs enough to take them on their journey home and stood at the bedsides to tend those that would remain behind. The ones he knew might never recover.

As the Doctor continued his walk, he began to feel sated as the weight of the small derringer gently hit his upper leg with every step forward. It was while he continued on his rounds when he spotted his friend Walt.

The white haired gent sat quietly at an empty bedside, his heavy posture slumped, his head hung.

Henry stepped near, laying his hand gently on the poet's back, "It is early, dear old friend, are you too are biding our soldier's farewell?"

The older man turned to face Henry, his eyes red and swollen from weeping, it seemed they had been that way ever since President Lincoln was murdered.

"Good Doctor," he sadly greeted, "yes, I came to bade farewell to all our brethren, yet I have come too late for this one." He nodded his head towards the empty bed and once again the tears flowed from the red rimmed eyes onto the sad and grief stricken face.

"You knew this soldier?"

"His name was Josiah Lee Jones." He wept, "He was just eighteen and reveling in the fact the war is over and he was going home. Didn't even have far to go, just right down to Fredericksburg. Now he has gone to heaven."

"I'm sorry for your loss."

Walt could not be consoled.

"How is it such a fine young man with what appeared to be a small wound, grazed by the minie ball, that the wound would grow to consume him with fever and cause him to pass away? The world will never know the good he could have done. It is tragic we must bid farewell to one so young, and so many before him."

"It is a tragic loss, to be sure dear friend."

Walt nodded his white head to agree.

"We were friends, Josiah Lee and I. He had a gift he had for words, recited his poetry to me so visually beautiful I could literally see his words, a gift he had. Now he is silenced forever." His hands that were folded in front of him then released to wipe wet eyes to dry tears that would most certainly flow again.

"Walt, is not for us to understand why. We must accept His will and go on as best we can."

"It is difficult. We live in such desperate times. I cannot bear one more loss." Henry pulled up a chair so they could sit facing one another.

"Yes, I know what a true friend you were to the President. You told me you would see him on his horse, Bob, and nodding to you as he journeyed onto the Soldier's Home his summer retreat from Washington. I even remember what you told me about his face; you said there was a latent expression in his eyes that no artist could capture of him. I believe it was the pain of the nation he carried in those eyes, Walt, and knowing that he would not survive to see his second term fulfilled. He knew he would die."

Wiping his face again, the sensitive poet seemed to agree.

"And for your friend, young Josiah Lee, he has found favor with God and fear not the silence of his words and voice of his great gift. Take those words Walt, and create a piece in honor of his life. In this way he most certainly will not have died in vain."

The old man stopped weeping, clearly feeling the poetry of the young soldier ringing in his head. "Yes, so much wisdom you have spoken, dear friend," He patted Henry on the shoulder in gratitude, "such wisdom. I will most certainly consider your words. For this, I am most grateful," and with those words spoken he bowed his head politely to his friend, a gesture that touched the Doctor's heart.

"You are quite welcome."

Finally lifted from his own sorrow, Walt noticed Henry's exhausted face, "Doctor, forgive me but are you well? Have you been eating? You look so very tired."

Henry stood, placing his hand on his friend's shoulder to reassure him. "Those around me say I am fatigued in the mind and spirit, that rest is my cure. But let me tell you that rest will do little for what ails me, but rather justice will set me free."

The old shook his head in confusion. "I don't understand your desire for justice. What holds you hostage that freedom is not within your grasp?"

The Doctor bent to face his weary eyed friend and said with a steely voice, "Walt, you were right. That John Singer is a dead ringer for Booth. I can't put my finger on it, but it is more than mere suspicion driving me. I tell you this, so you know. I now believe that man in the barn was not Booth, for the devil is here among us, leaving tomorrow with Emma to be married in Richmond at her family's home."

Walt looked stunned, but kept listening.

'I was wrong. It is not by coincidence that the man we know as John Singer looks like Booth, by some trick or twist of fate. You were right. It is Booth. And he believes to get away from his most vicious crime by hiding in plain sight. No, it is not to be. For now I know it to be true."

The old gent suddenly rose up, "By what proof do you have this is Booth? For me it was only a sense and a feeling of familiarity from having seen him perform in Boston, yet I had nothing to prove it, you do?"

The Doctor leaned in, his voice hauntingly calm and steady. "John first came in wearing the uniform with the name Singer embroidered on the sleeve. It was in the burn pile where Old Sam was tending the fire pit. Emma came looking for his uniform. She too was questioning his inability to state where he hailed from. As luck would have it, Old Sam pulled out the bloodied uniform. It contained a diary with five carte de visite of God knows who and what kind of women," the Doctor spat, "along with the wanted poster of Booth and a few newspaper clippings damming his evil deed."

"That is evidence, indeed."

"That plus the broken left leg, the uncanny resemblance, the deep, rich and practiced tone of his voice, and his inability to say even where he fought just as to point to his true identity."

The old gent shook his head in disbelief, "You mean to tell me our dear Miss Emma knows of this and still plans to marry him? It cannot be, it just cannot."

"Emma asked Old Sam to swear never to speak of what they saw, but he is a loyal and dear friend to me and has voiced concern over my wellbeing, so much so that Doctor Hendrix has relieved me of rounds for the next few days."

"Perhaps rest would help."

"Like rest will cure what ails me. Only justice will set me free."

A strange look of calm spread over the Doctor's face, as he deliberately nodded his head in affirmation of the unthinkable deed running through his mind, and the solace of the derringer signaling its presence as he slowly walked away.

The next morning at the hospital found no relief from the early spring heat, the sun rising and blazing, warm even at the earliest of hours. Emma packed the remainder of her things in the two small suitcases she had arrived with in the beginning of the war.

She made her toilette with care knowing the one hundred miles to Richmond would be difficult to travel. The hospital buckboard to Fredericksburg was the halfway point to Richmond, and the train from there to Richmond proper would not be an easy journey.

And once in Richmond at her parents' house she would wed John and be forever involved in his deception. She wondered at the thought of standing in front of clergy, agreeing to marry a man whose name and identity she knew was false and what that really would mean.

It was too much to think about.

Her love for John ran deep and true. She would hold onto his secret, now her secret. But she must find her way to Asia's house and present her with the fact her brother is alive. Perhaps Asia could help them leave this country.

It is the only way to assure his safety.

But his family must be told he is alive. Emma knew she must use all her strength and evidence of the diary and the letter to convince Asia. It was monumental to consider, hoping and praying it would work. Otherwise, she feared he would be at the mercy of those doubting his guise, who feel justified in their motives of revenge against him.

It was in her power to help.

She could not allow John's second chance to be destroyed.

In her heart she knew only love could save him.

Emma went to the stables where the young black stable boy Isaac had agreed to lend John and Emma a buckboard. He would accompany them to Fredericksburg and then return.

It was a difficult way to travel for sure, riding over the rutted and rough spring roads, but modes of transportation were scarce. Even the railroad from Fredericksburg to Richmond was just now up and running again after the burning of Richmond over a month ago. She prayed for an uneventful trip home. With that thought she picked up her two suitcases and walked to find Isaac.

Just outside the stables Isaac greeted her, "Good morning Miss Emma. I just got this here buckboard all ready for your trip. I got this here nag to get us going," he patted the brown mare on the neck. "She is old, but steady and sure."

Emma smiled at the boy of about fourteen, slender and slight. His home and his family were the hospital and stables for these last several years. He ran away from his slaveholding master early in the war, found hiding in the hospital stables and stayed. He had a way with the horses and cared for them deeply. He even slept in the stables, calling the animals his family.

"Thank you, Isaac. We just have to see to Mr. John." She let Isaac hoist her bags into the back of the buckboard wagon. "I am going to say goodbye to Doctor Bradley and then we should be ready to depart.

"Yes'um, I will just set a spell here and wait for Massa John."

Emma smiled at the boy then walked to Doctor Bradley's quarters. She dreaded this moment and considered what to say. Hopefully he would relent and realize there was never anything between them. She needed him to accept her heart cared only as a friend and nothing more, ever.

She came upon his door and knocked gently, only slightly surprised to see Old Sam answer. The large hulking man stood in the doorway, filling it. But he gave her a welcoming smile. "Why good morning there Miss Emma. Today you leaving with Mr. John?"

She looked up at the towering man, "Yes Old Sam, we are leaving today. I shall say my goodbyes to you and then to Doctor Bradley. I heard Doctor Hendrix took him off rotation for a few days and that he was handling patients. Is this true?"

Old Sam nodded, "Ye'sum, its true, Doctor Bradley is some powerful tired is all. He just needs some rest. I'm taking care of him now. He wandered on over to the hospital for a walk. Can't seem to sit still. But I gonna sleeps here, making sure he eats and gets some rest. He'll be all right. He have to be, he my family. Where he goes I go."

"He is fortunate to have you."

Old Sam leaned down and said carefully, "Miss Emma, I heard you be getting married to that Mr. John."

"Yes, we marry in two days."

His head shook with disapproval.

"I don't know there. Ain't my place to be saying noffin, but I been hearing your Mr. John looks like that man that murdered the President. I saw them pictures that fell out of that book when we found his uniform. I might not know nothing about readin and writin, but I got good sense and a good set of eyes. Them pictures and papers look mighty powerful like that murderer. And what of all them fancy ladies? Those ladies not good, like how you is. I'm sorry Miss Emma, but that there man you marrying, he ain't who he says he is. Now I'm thinking you must'a read that book of his. Are you sure he is John Singer? Or is he someone else and he's hidin?"

Emma knew Old Sam was right, he had seen just enough of the evidence to question the existence of John Singer. He knew he was a fake. She only hoped he had not told Doctor Bradley of his findings.

There was nothing more to say.

"Old Sam, I love John Singer. We are leaving today and we are going back to Richmond to be married and start a life together."

"Miss Emma, I just wish you luck. I think you gonna need it."

She turned away from the doorway to see the slim figure of Henry walk towards her in the early morning light. His clothing was disheveled, his hair uncombed and his demeanor unsteady. She looked into his eyes, seeing exhaustion and pain, realizing too late that her coming to say goodbye would do no good.

"So Emma," he gruffly greeted, "today you are leaving for home, taking the imposter with you. I know he is not John Singer. I know he is Booth, and so do you."

"No Henry, please you are tired, you are mistaken."

"Of course I am tired. We all are. But I am not mistaken. When Old Sam was out burning the threadbare uniforms of our dear soldiers, you found something didn't you?"

Emma's eyes went wide as she realized Old Sam had divulged the discovery of the diary. No wonder Henry was so resolved in his diatribe about John.

She said nothing, standing firm.

"No need to tell me. Old Sam told me enough. I know I am right. You are now liable in this crime. You still have time, Emma. Leave him, let him go and be free of him. Then we can be together. We can go to the Government and explain they have the wrong man."

Emma backed away.

John was in grave and possibly mortal danger.

She spoke carefully as she bade him farewell. Her knowledge of John's true identity would today and every day henceforward be denied.

"Henry, please listen to me. This man I love is John Singer. The dairy was just a book filled with papers and a soldier's collection of daily events, nothing more. I know my father had promised you we could court after my eighteenth birthday, but the war broke out. Our life was torn apart. Now the war is over now, my father is dead. I choose who to love. It is John Singer. I am sorry."

She turned to take his leave, not waiting for him to reply.

But his eyes became a steely ice blue, they narrowed then widened and a strange look befell them.

It frightened her.

Emma hurried to the stables. The haunting stare of the Doctor was one of agony and what she feared the most, madness.

Emma found John standing in front of the buckboard, the old nag horse lightly stomping the ground in front of her, as if even in her old age was ready to start on the journey to Fredericksburg. He looked resplendent in a white shirt and black trousers.

The cast was removed. He was whole again.

He was clean-shaven, his jet-black hair in stark contrast to his white marble skin. His deep dark eyes met hers and she was once again struck by how handsome he was.

It was impossible not to look at him.

"Good mornin' darling," his deep and melodious voice welcomed. "I trust you have said your goodbyes and are ready to leave?" He smiled at her and she felt his powerful presence resonate through her.

Emma was slightly out of breath, "Yes, I am ready. Please can we leave right now?" She did not wait for anyone to help her into the buckboard, but climbed right in. "Issac, please help Mr. John, his leg is not completely healed yet."

Isaac nodded his head quickly. The young man placed first the crutch into the buckboard then he helped John in, who still favored the healing broken leg. As Doctor Bradley predicted, he would walk with a limp now. Once settled beside his fiancé and they began moving, John asked, "Emma tell me please what happened?"

"It's Henry. He won't let go of his incessant professed love for me. It's disconcerting."

Now John looked troubled too.

"Never mind, we are on our way now. Going home is all that matters. Only think of our new life together. In two days we will be married. I love you."

John sensed there was something more Emma was not revealing, but he was powerless to ask more. He loved her and wanted only to keep her from finding out who he truly was, for then certainly she would leave him.

He turned to her, "I love you too darling."

With that he reached for her hand the rutted roads beneath the old buckboard tossing them both with each mile they rode away from the hospital and towards their new life together.

CHAPTER NINETEEN

And this is Richmond.
~~ John Wilkes Booth

Mrs. Dixon walked the expansive foyer of her Richmond home, surveying the marble flooring that was scratched and dull beneath her shoes. She noticed the tiles below the great marble staircase had a horseshoe imprint dented into the creamy stone. She and Abby had only been home a few days. They felt shocked by the state of disrepair. She put her hand to her forehead not knowing how to fix it. The whole house was worn and dirty from fireplaces not properly drawn by the soldiers who borrowed their home during the war. Smoke and soot stained the French wall coverings and darkened the white marble fireplace mantles to a dirty steel grey.

The furniture too showed signs of neglect and heavy wear, as Southern Generals and their subordinates from the battlefield had used the parlor furniture, their dirty clothing staining the silken patterns with each soldier that rested upon them.

She paused, looking up the elegant staircase, remembering walking down the polished steps with her dear husband, William on her arm. They made a striking couple, descending into the sea of waiting guests that flooded their home with yet another dinner party.

Mrs. Dixon reminisced and closed her eyes, seeing herself resplendent in the newest silken gown from Paris, her golden mass of hair twined with heirloom pearls, the diamond broach glittering at her breast, a gift for the party from her dear husband. She recalled William had been so handsome in his white broadcloth shirt and black dress trousers, his coat black and classic cut. Tall, slim and fair haired like herself with deep set pale blue eyes, so like daughter Emma.

Her heart leapt.

Her dear sweet Emma was coming home, and with a fiancé.

They would be a family again. She yearned for her dearly departed husband and son, but at least she still had her girls. She heard the child's footsteps echo on the great marble floor. "Mother, where are you?"

"In here, dear." Mrs Dixon smiled as her young daughter came in from the back yard, Abigail just eleven years old full of life and energy looking strikingly like her mother, her long fair hair falling about her as she ran to her mother's side.

"When is Emma arriving?"

Mrs. Dixon wrapped one arm around Abigail's slim shoulders. In another year or two she would lose that fair youthful innocence in her face. Womanhood was coming. Like her older sister, Abigail would be a striking beauty. Emma returning was a great joy to them both. The excitement of the impending wedding was a celebration that would certainly be a blessing to their family.

"Your sister will be home tomorrow and she is coming with her fiancé, a Mr. John Singer. They will be married right here in the front parlor, exactly how she planned before the war."

"That's so romantic. Emma must love him."

"Yes, she wrote that she does."

"Is he handsome?"

"Without a doubt. He stole sweet Emma's heart." She smiled at that fact revealed, enjoying how it made Abby's eyes shine with girlish dreams of tender love. "Come, we must prepare the house and see about that trunk in the attic, the one that has my wedding dress. We must make it ready for Emma."

The younger sister looked in awe, "Oh Mother, it will truly be special. Can I help you? The gown is so lovely. I've always adored it. Emma will be a beautiful bride."

"She certainly will. Together we will make her wedding perfect."

"I'm so glad she is coming home. I have missed her."

Smiling, they held hands and trotted up the stairs to find the wedding dress, both laughing aloud for the first time in forever, feeling the weight of the war leave at last.

It was good to be happy.

Love was in the air, love would warm their hearts and fill their home with joy. Love was the happiness that all women dreamed of, the hope they kept alive when times were difficult. And Mrs. Dixon knew, if anyone deserved love, it was Emma.

The buckboard tilted and heaved along the rutted and damaged roads to Fredericksburg. Emma felt herself tossed about the buggy, wishing only to put as many miles as possible between her and Alexandria. She absently fingered the pearl and diamond engagement ring on her finger, lost in thought as she heard John ask, "Is it second thoughts you are having darling?"

He smiled as he teased her with that question, his lips parting to show perfectly even white teeth, she realized in that moment there is no part of him that is not desirable.

No part.

"Not I dearest, not I," she laughed, lightening their mood. "I have no second thoughts of my life with you. Know that it is now and forever."

"Yet a moment ago you were frowning, my love."

She shrugged, "Going home to see mother and my precious little sister Abby has me anxious. I haven't seen them n three years. I hope it will be the same, yet inside I know Richmond, our home, and the people I love are forever changed."

John heard Emma's words and remembered his own plight, no family to share anything with ever again, an acting career gone; all he loved and cared about destroyed. The life he believed so grand and thriving, full of high ideals and Causes he believed to be right were now his deepest regret. That life ended in the blazing fire at the barn at Garrett's Farm. If not for James W. Boyd sent to warn of the Union army nearby, he would have been the one murdered in that barn for certain.

He chose his words carefully to his soon to be wife, "Darlin, you are always hoping for things and those we love not to change, yet life moves forward, whether we want it to or not."

She nodded to agree.

"But one thing I do know," he tenderly continued, "is that no matter what, nothing will change between us, ever."

He reached over and held her close.

John kissed her deeply then pushing his tongue into her waiting mouth, her breath heavy and desirous from just that touch. He whispered into her ear, "Darling if not for that boy in the front of this buggy, I would take into the woods and would show you again, again and again, of how completely I love you."

"Perhaps tonight?"

"Yes. Tonight. He let the heated passion fade, pleased the young boy Isaac remained heedless to the scene of his two passengers behind him.

Emma sat back to try to get comfortable in the rickety buggy, once again knowing that whenever or whatever John wanted of her she would relent. He was impossible to resist, her desire to be near him maddening. They were complicit to each other's passion, a flame that burned deep and unending. Such a passion would never burn out, the need to be near him never be satisfied.

Their connection was for life.

Both in bed and out.

The weary passengers in the buckboard finally arrived at the outskirts of Fredericksburg. The picturesque town was now burned and partly destroyed from the battle that raged on December 11-15, 1862. Emma knew that the Union lost over twelve thousand men and the Confederates almost six thousand in attempting to cross the Rappahannock River and take Fredericksburg.

The young boy Isaac drove toward the station. He turned, telling his passengers, "Well here now is the train depot. I guess this here is where I leaves ya' both."

Emma was grateful their rough ride was over. Isaac helped him down and pulled her suitcases from the buggy. He then took out the crutch for Mister John as well, and helped him to the ground.

"Well Miss Emma, Massa John," He tipped his hat, giving a smile, "I wish ya'll good luck in getting to Richmond and then getting hitched and all. I need to see about getting this here nag some hay and water and rest before we head back to the hospital. I have a bunch of horses there that need me to tend to 'em."

Emma took the boy's hand, "Thank you Isaac. Be careful going back. Take care of yourself and the horses as well."

Isaac made his way to the local stables to care for his horse.

Emma and John went into the train station, learning the last train to Richmond would be leaving in another two hours. As Emma went to inquire about a room where she could tidy up, she noticed the Wanted Poster of John and his conspirators plastered on several walls.

Her heart plunged.

Evidently they had not as yet taken it down with the knowledge that Booth was killed and his conspirators caught. Emma tried not to look but the poster was glaring, almost mocking them.

John stood frozen as he looked at himself.

Emma noticed something about his hesitation and quickly dispelled the difficult moment, "In just four hours John, we shall be home." Whether she knew it or not, she was his saving grace, the only bright spot in his world. The sweetness on her face was pure adoration.

In that moment, he felt unworthy.

"You are like a star shining in the night, Emma. No," he decided, "more than a star. You are the sunlight in my life; the best second chance at life that any men could have. A second chance not just to live, but to love."

She laughed aloud at his romantic sentiment, spoken so freely in a public place where others could hear. "Why, John Singer, you flatter me. You do have a gift for words." But her blue eyes were sparkling with love.

He held her tight and buried his face in her neck, never wanting to look up again, feeling safe in the knowledge of their love. He desperately wanted to tell her everything.

No matter what, he never could.

They waited for two hours, quietly passing the time by eating lunch at a small near-by peddler's stand outside the depot that sold bread and cheese. They were fortunate to even find it as food was becoming scarce.

It wasn't fancy, but it satisfied their hunger.

Finally the great plume of black smoke from the engine heralded the train in advance of its coming into the station. It stopped to allow them both to enter the train. After finding their seats, the couple rested together, exhausted in their travels. Secretly, they were both equally exhausted from their unspoken deception of one another.

Secrets wore down their hearts.

Mrs. Dixon paced her home in Richmond, the preparation for the wedding almost at a standstill, for there was very little in the way to prepare for a proper feast. The foodstuffs were long since eaten, the flour and sugar almost to the bottom of the barrels, the flowers in the garden trampled from the prior occupants. Her wedding dress from those years ago was the only thing she could offer Emma, for it had been put away lovingly in the chest, the onslaught of the Confederacy not touching this one precious item.

It was all she had to give her daughter on her wedding day.

The tall and spare black house servant named Charles looked crisp and reserved despite his frayed clothing. He respectfully addressed the mistress of the house, "Excuse me, ma'dam, but it's time I head to the train depot. Miss Emma and her beau will be coming soon. She sent a telegram to the Richmond depot as to when to expect them. A telegraph runner brought it to me." With that news he bowed respectfully to his mistress, reminiscent of the former glory of the house and the civilized way of life they had once enjoyed.

"Yes thank you Charles," she nodded to her longtime house servant, "please see to the livery and have Miss Emma and her Mr. John brought here quickly. I can't imagine how exhausted they must be." She fussed with the lace on the dining room table, the last respectable piece they still had left.

"I will tend to them quickly."

Still at a loss about the house and their lack, Mrs Dixon raised her hands and exclaimed, "Charles, look at this house; a wedding in two days and all I have to offer my daughter is my wedding dress. We have no feast, no flowers, and no gifts. What shall I do?"

Wise and calm, he simply said, "Mrs. Dixon, after all this family's been through with strangers taking over this fine house, having the family scattered and lost to the war, I think we are blessed to have a home to live in."

"Yes, of course. But she deserves more."

Charles gave his regal head a slight shake, "I think Miss Emma is not concerned with her wedding feast or flowers or even gifts. She has a good heart. I know her. Our sweet Emma will just be happy that she is home to all of us, and bringing with her now is a man she loves. Yes indeed, I think we are blessed."

"Blessed," she repeated, trying to feel convinced. "Yes, we are blessed. But she deserves a beautiful wedding dress and a beautiful wedding cake."

"There is flour and sugar in the kitchen barrels for a sweet cake. There is only Esmeralda the cook and me left from the old days. As you know, the rest run away after Master Lincoln freed the black man, but me and Esmeralda couldn't leave for we was born here."

"I'm very grateful to you, Charles. Thank you."

"We got more than most Mistress, we got more than most."

He bowed then and took his leave, making his way to the stables to see about hitching up the workhorse Juniper to the carriage to fetch Miss Emma and Mr. John. With luck and good timing, they would arrive back home before the sun set on this long anxious day.

The train slowly chugged and heaved its way to Richmond, the view from the windows of the train of the ravaged City leaving the occupants speechless. John saw the leveled city that was still smoldering in places and said under his breath, "And this is Richmond, and this is Richmond."

Emma could barely recognize her childhood home, for there was only a smattering of structures that remained. In one piece the landscape was littered with debris with only the stone chimney stacks still standing. It was eerie. She looked for the millinery shop that brought in the latest fashions and materials from France, the confectioner's shop, the dry goods store, the theater, the primary school, the town hall for records and deeds.

It was gone, all gone, wiped clean.

"I recognize nothing here. It's as if I am coming home to a foreign city."

Compassionate as always, John understood her heartache. "Emma when you see your family home you will feel better. Try not to be so sad. Don't let this spoil our homecoming and our wedding tomorrow. Try to think of that, please."

Emma looked at John and could only nod and try to smile.

They departed the train to the waiting coach or what was left of it, driven by Charles the house servant of the Dixon household. She had known Charles every day of her life, he was family.

Emma noticed with dismay the family coach was battered and broken, a shadow of its former glory. The initial D scripted on the carriage door carriage was scratched. The richly appointed leather seats were worn. Her heart sank as she realized this would be the new norm, all that came before was truly gone.

"Miss Emma, you are a sight for sore eyes," said the impeccably dressed and well-mannered house servant, "it's been too long. Welcome home."

"Oh Charles, it is good to be home, but look at our beautiful Richmond. It's burned to the ground. There is nothing left, nothing." She tried not to cry as she stepped into the family coach remembering too its former glory of carriage rides with her parents, older brother and little sister.

"Now now Miss Emma," he softly chided as he stood in the open doorway, assisting John up the small step. "You listen. You saw hardship at that hospital in Alexandria. Now think of those poor souls having no home to come back to, no loved ones. The City, it will rebuild. It's just bricks and stone. I was just telling the Mistress, we got more than most, cause we got a house to live in and each other to call family."

"That is very wise, Charles. Thank you."

"You're welcome," he gave a gentlemanly bow of his head toward Emma, then his wise gaze lit on John's face. "Not to mention, you brought home your fiancé. We are rich, indeed, today." He smiled, politely closing the door and taking his seat as the driver of the carriage.

"He is right," John agreed as the carriage moved forward, taking them to the homes high upon the hill, houses spared from the destruction, "A wise man doesn't focus on the ashes, Emma. A wise person keeps their gaze upon the future. It will be all right."

"I hope so."

The coach rounded through the decimated City. The only sound it seemed was from the horse's hooves stamping upon the ground, and the wind whispering through the spires of stacks of blackened chimneys.

Approaching the entrance of Emma's home, the grand walkways that were once resplendent with dogwoods and rhododendrons had been trampled and neglected. The expansive lawn had pieces of sod torn up and littering the grass that had clearly been used as a walkway for the many visiting soldiers of the Confederacy. The brick paver driveway that formed a semicircle to the entrance of the great house had pieces pulled up from their mortar, broken and out of place, their design a mystery to their former glory.

Emma allowed herself to be assisted down from the coach.

She walked forward, then stood on the expansive stone stairs to her home.

Several steps were broken, in some instances they were dented as if being struck by something. She then turned her attention to the front of the house, the massive four columns of Greek revival architecture standing silent to what they must have witnessed these last few years. Their off white solid stone columns reached to the second level of the home, each one carved and chiseled with precise care.

The sun was setting on their long day, but she could still see the entire exterior of the whitewashed home was shadowed in black soot from the massive fires that had devastated Richmond. She looked at the impressive French double front door. This was her home.

"It's beautiful, Emma."

"It used to be."

Holding her hand, John assured, "It will be again."

She held her breath as they walked inside.

She crossed the threshold and entered the great foyer immediately feeling dismayed at the condition. The once shining and immaculate entrance foyer showed extensive signs of wear and neglect. She pushed the sight from her mind as she called out, "Mother, where are you? I am home, Abby, where is everyone?"

Mrs. Dixon came running, Abby trailing behind her.

"Emma!"

Both mother and daughter embraced at the sight of each other, the pain of their losses and the pain of separation evident without having to speak. They sobbed in each other's arms, as John stood behind and watched. Emma loosened her embrace and kissed her mother's cheek, then held her at arm's length. She looked into her mother's eyes and smiled, the blueness of them not dimmed from the pain and sadness that had invaded them since her husband and son's untimely death.

Her hair was twined tightly to sit on the nape of neck, the sun kissed strands fading with a sprinkling of grey. She was once the most sought after belle in Richmond, and was known for her countless beau's and ease on the dance floor. Her home hosted great dinner parties, the dining table festooned with fine china imported from Limoges of France, the finest crystal and the ornate silver service which was always the centerpiece of the table.

"I am finally home."

"Darling Emma," she said through the haze of now happy tears, "We have missed you."

John watched, thinking of his own lost family. It was difficult. Missing them was a constant ache inside, one he feared would never leave. Finished hugging her mother, Emma turned to grasp his hand again, where he stood silently behind her.

"Mother, I want you to meet my fiancé, John Singer."

Mrs. Dixon extended her hand in welcome. "It is a pleasure to meet you, Mr. Singer. I welcome you to our home and our family."

John stepped forward, took her soft hand and kissed it like a gentleman. "It's a pleasure to meet you, Mrs. Dixon," he bowed from his waist. He rose, giving his best charming smile.

Assessing him fully, she seemed extremely pleased. "Why Mr. Singer," she cooed in her most Southern drawl, "how very kind of you, and I might same the same of you. I should welcome you to our family, not just as Emma's husband, by my son as well."

John nodded to his soon to be mother in law, "It's with such kindness, dear madam, that I come to you, knowing fully of how very much I love Emma. Her happiness alone is my utmost concern. It is a blessing and a gift. I now have found not only Emma to love, but a family who is so generous with their love as well. I am eternally grateful."

As expected, Mrs. Dixon was struck by his speech, his diction and pitch strikingly perfect.

The moment was broken by the sound of a young voice, "My name is Abigail, but everyone calls me Abby."

John looked into the face of the youthful girl. This is how Emma must have looked as a child, golden, innocent and beautiful.

He took her hand and kissed it lightly, "It is wonderful to meet you, Abby. My name is John Singer." He released her hand. "You look very much like your beautiful sister."

"Thank you, sir," she giggled at the gesture and curtseyed slightly to John, then her cheeks flushed pink and she proceeded to run from the adult reunion happening in the grand foyer. He could still her sweet laughter as the great hall echoed her voice throughout the house.

"Well now," said Mrs. Dixon, "We should get you two settled. Emma, your room is ready upstairs, understand it is not in the same condition you left it. This house has seen great upheaval."

"Yes, but we are grateful to have it."

John gave his beloved a warm smile as she hid her shock at the condition of the home and had wisely adopted a positive attitude.

"Mr. Singer, there is room for you as well. I trust you will be comfortable in the extra room off of the kitchen. It is just for one night, as you will be wed tomorrow. Our cook Esmeralda has prepared it for this one night. I trust you understand the need for decorum." She nodded her head so that no further discussion could be had.

As Charles carried Emma's suitcases upstairs, Mrs. Dixon picked up her skirts and followed, expecting her daughter to come upstairs too.

Emma obediently followed her mother's orders. "I shall bid you goodnight here, John." She said loud enough for everyone to hear. "I am tired, dear husband to be. I must rest to be fresh and ready for our wedding, tomorrow eve."

John held her close and whispered only that which is meant for lovers, "Leave your door open a smidge, dear Emma, and I shall find you tonight."

She blessed him with a happy smile.

With that he bowed to take their leave and followed Esmeralda to a modest bedroom near the kitchen, apparently used only when the house had an overflow of guests, or rather when their maids or servants needed to stay. He imagined there were additional finer bedrooms upstairs available, but decorum must be followed.

He was not to sleep near Emma.

Heaven forbid he touch her beautiful body prior to taking marriage vows. Or taste her. Or enjoy the sweet sounds of her delicious pleasure.

The wicked images made him grin.

No matter. He would only be in there for a short time, just until he was assured the house was deep in sleep.

CHAPTER TWENTY

You left here a young wide eyed girl,
and have returned now as a woman.

~~ Mrs. Annabelle Dixon

Upstairs at Emma's room, her mother opened the door. The room was large and light but the white marble stone fireplace was smudged and covered in soot. The three large pane glass windows were covered in grime inside and out from the dirty air when Richmond burned and so many improperly ventilated fireplace fires. The French lace curtains had become faded and stained.

The four poster bed was intact, its linens recently washed.

The armoire was the only piece of furniture that sustained almost no damage or wear. The giant cherry-wood doors were slightly open revealing a space where gowns of the latest fashion once prevailed, only now it stood silent and empty.

Emma surveyed the room, "I dreamed of coming home, back home to my room, my refuge, my sanctuary." Her eyes stung with emotion. "Dearest Mother, is hard to see the house like this, not to mention our fallen City of Richmond and the loss of father and Caleb."

"It was a shock for Abby and I, too. We have only been home a short time, coming home from my cousin's after the end of the war. Repairs of the house will take time as will the mending of our hearts."

"Yes, I know." But it still made her sad.

Charles set down her suitcases and left them alone.

Now her mother chided, "Emma, listen to me. You left as a young girl excited about the war, believing like all Southerners it would end in a month or two. But the war stole not only your dear father and brother, but our way of life. Everything has changed. Even you are changed. You left here a young wide eyed girl, and have returned now as a woman, with a new life with your new husband."

"Yes, you are right. I have missed your wise counsel, Mother." It did lighten her heart. "Letters kept me going, but hearing your voice again erases so much pain."

That pleased her mother deeply. The smile she gave Emma was proud and adoring. "Mr. Singer is gracious and handsome, with the most elegant of manners. He will make a fine husband."

"I'm happy you like him."

"I do, indeed. But I must tell you there is not much left here for a fancy wedding. Some of the silver is still buried under the floorboards in the basement, but the china and the crystal is all chipped and in some instances either gone or broken all together."

"It is fine. A simple wedding will do. Later, maybe we will buy more, when stores in Richmond open again, or we will order from New York or Boston." She planned, wished in her heart that in time their lifestyle would be elegant again. "After all, father was a wealthy investment banker. His funds are secure, are they not?"

Her mother nodded, but worry etched her face.

"Yes, but none of that helps us today. You saw Richmond, there are no stores and I know very little of accounting. Your father handled our finances, yet I fear what money there was has turned into Confederate funds. Perhaps after the wedding your John can help us figure out everything. I know nothing of managing investments or business dealings, yet now I must."

Emma took her mother's hand.

"We will all learn together. But for tomorrow we shall only think of enjoying a wedding. It will be perfect no matter the size."

That brought a wide happy smile to her face.

"Dearest child, I have a surprise for you." With that Mrs. Dixon opened fully the big doors to the armoire and there on one side hung the wedding gown, pressed and repaired for the bride to be.

"Mother, your wedding gown!"

Emma squealed with delight as she ran to the armoire and lovingly fingered the gown. "Thank you. I am so happy, so truly happy!" She hugged her mother, "please help me try it on, it is scrumptious!"

Emma hurried out of her clothes and soon stood in the center of the room as she waited for help putting the dress on.

"Oh daughter, how very thin you are. I hope being home now and settled with John, you will fill out more."

The soft material descended down, lying upon her body.

She turned to look at her reflection in the interior mirror of the armoire. The gown was made of off white silk, the entire gown and bodice heavily beaded with seed pearls. The top of the gown had sweetheart design dipped low to reveal the subtle outline of her décolleté.

Her mother laced it up, tightening the stays. Her breasts ripe and full swelled beneath the fabric. "Emma," her mother sighed, one hand over her heart. "Such a beauty you are."

"Thank you. In your gown I feel beautiful."

"Wait, I have one more thing to give you."

With that she rushed into her own bedroom, returning with the string of pearls that were her mother's, the same set that once twined and decorated her thick blond locks of hair.

She put them in Emma's hand and smiled, "A gift to the bride my most beautiful daughter. You will wear them in your hair as I did on my wedding day."

"Oh mother, thank you. I love you."

"And I love you, my beautiful girl."

After admiring her reflection for a few moments, they carefully removed the gown and packed it away in the armoire again, ready for tomorrow.

"I will have Charles bring you a tray of food. You must rest now. It has been a long day. I shall see you in the morning. Welcome home."

After Charles had bought her dinner and later removed the tray from her room, the exhaustion of the day assaulted her. It was late. Her body and mind were weary. She slid into the cool sheets of her childhood bed and was almost instantly asleep when she remembered John's words as he said good night.

With that she gently opened her door a crack as to let him enter at will. She knew he would come to her as promised.

Emma eyes fluttered open. It seemed like she had been asleep for days, but was awakened by John lightly kissing her lips. He murmured, "Darlin' Emma, I must have you now. Please my love, please."

Emma surprised herself with her boldness with John, it's as if all decorum was nonexistent when he wanted her and called her name with that deep smoldering voice. She said nothing, but sat up and removed her night clothes. Exposed and naked to his eyes, her breasts were full, heavy and inviting.

She said simply, "My husband to be, for this you must never ask me, for surely as my heart is yours, my body doubly so if it pleases you."

"Emma," he cried gently to her, "my beautiful Emma."

He leaned into her then, his passion overwhelming as he kissed her full mouth then worked down her neck, caressed her breasts until she moaned with pleasure.

"Quiet now, dear," he playfully chuckled, enjoying the way she responded to his hands and mouth upon her skin. "We must not get caught. Decorum, you know."

Emma giggled feeling wild, young, and free. "To hell with decorum. Just take me, John. I need you, just as you need me."

He kissed her flat belly and loved along the sides of her supple hips. When she was melted beneath touch he pushed her legs apart with both his hands opening her up fully. He kissed and tasted until her body smoldered with building and pulsating need. Emma shivered beneath his touch.

He knew exactly when to give himself to her, bringing their passions to their fullest at the same time.

Her body bent and rocked in ecstasy as she bit her tongue not to cry out.

He loved her, fully and madly, loving her until he too exploded in ecstasy.

Sated and sleepy he turned to Emma, "Dear wife to be, tomorrow you will be forever mine." He lifted himself from her bed and kissed her good night, picked up his clothes from the floor and crept out silently to his room off the kitchen; a room that would never hold him as long as Emma was in the house.

At mid-morning Emma was still asleep; her mother peered into her room to check on her daughter, satisfied she was in need of much rest. Not wishing to disturb her, she crept out and went down the stairs.

In the kitchen the cook Esmeralda was preparing the cake for the late afternoon wedding. "Ah it will be a fine cake Esmeralda, with your talented hands I know it will be a wonderful treat for our Emma and John."

"Thank you, Ma'am."

"I will be going to town to see about some lamb and some fresh vegetables. What a shame my dear husband turned all our money into Confederate bonds, useless now."

"How can you buy food, then?"

She gestured to the cook and said in a low whisper, "I went to the basement last night after all were asleep." Annabelle pointed to a small uneven pile near the back door that was covered by a piece of tarp, "I have uncovered a few items of the silver tea set in which to sell to buy foodstuffs for the wedding feast. I am not even sure where to go. I know that the City of Richmond is starving as well, but I must try. Charles will help me, I'm sure."

Esmeralda's eyes went wide at the news, "No Mistress, that was your wedding silver. I remember polishing it for you and Mr. William and now you must sell it?" The heavyset black woman with lovely dark, the deepest and most compassionate eyes stared at her in disbelief.

Annabelle said simply, "Miss Emma is here with her Mr. John and she is happy. I don't care about these things that before the war had seemed so important; only that we are here and together. I will find a way to give my daughter a proper wedding feast."

"Yes," she agreed, "we should."

"Please have Charles get the coach ready and I must hurry. Plan only for seven for the wedding party: John and Emma, myself and Deacon Burns and of course Abby, you, and Charles."

She gathered the mismatched pieces of silver and left, riding away in the carriage with Charles who took her into Richmond in the hopes of selling her family's valuables to pay the wedding dinner.

Emma rose from her bed then stretched and relished being home for the first time in three years. She made her toilette quickly. The time for the wedding preparation would be later.

She dressed with haste.

As she then thought of last night with John, a slow smile crept across her face. She looked back at the bed that was witness to the smoldering passion she now enjoyed with complete abandon and remembered girlhood whispers of the marriage bed and the wifely duty therein. The giggles that hid the fear from tales that women were to bear it, but not enjoy it.

No. Sex was pleasurable, far from a duty.

Especially with John.

Emma shook her head and could not imagine what her life would have been like had they not met. She may have ended up with a man that she could love, who loved her, but it would have been without the deep and abiding passion of her John. Only he held the power to love her so completely.

As she descended the great staircase she saw her beloved at the bottom, clearly waiting for her.

"Why good morning, Miss Emma," he bowed his most gentlemanly bow as she face him.

"Why good morning Mr. John, I trust you slept well?"

He gave a sly smile, stepping close enough to whisper, "Why yes, I did rest a spell, especially after the visit I made to your bed last night."

He smiled his greatest smile, took her hand and kissed it.

Emma's heart was overflowing as she smiled back at him and said with a teasing lilt in her voice, "I would have to say the same thing, as well. But they claim it is bad luck for the bride and groom to see each other before the wedding, is it not?"

"It's a Puritan wive's tale. Is it also bad luck for the bride and groom to sleep together before the wedding?"

"No, 'tis very good luck, indeed."

With that said he threw his head back in deep and melodious laughter.

Emma stood on the bottom step, shook her head in exasperation and could only join in the laughter of two people utterly consumed by the sweetness of their love and yet equally consumed by the shadows of deception that surrounded them.

After eating, Emma retreated back to her room and began the preparations of her wedding day. She was told by Esmeralda that mother had left on a few errands and would be back in plenty of time to help her dress.

She wished she was here now.

Emma made her way over to the imposing barren armoire fingering the white silk wedding dress she would be wearing in just a few hours. She then opened the last drawer and fingered the pieces of clothing until her hands fell upon the small red diary.

It was like a drug to her, intriguing and tempting; its presence a reminder of her complicity of John's true identity.

She opened the book gingerly and stared at the wanted poster.

It glared up at her, the handsome face of her John with the news clipping of his cowardly act. She also looked at the five carte de visite of unknown yet strikingly beautiful women, the letter to sister Asia which nagged at her.

She must return it to Asia in person.

Somehow she would find secretly a way to Philadelphia to convince her John was alive. Emma decided to bring her to Richmond.

The two must meet.

She needed Asia's help to get him out of the country safely out of the United States. It was a wild scheme at best but there was no option. Saving John was all that mattered. She had to see Asia, as soon after the wedding as possible.

It was midafternoon when Annabelle Dixon returned, the large pile of silver pieces now diminished. She gave the slaughtered lamb and vegetables to Esmeralda with instructions to make haste with the dinner preparations all the while not looking at her left hand, barren now without her large engagement ring and her single gold wedding band. She gave that too, even though it was inscribed from her precious husband, William.

Staying fed and keeping the house in order would be a monumental task every single day. Neighbors that were once friends had turned ugly with their own desperation.

She knocked on Emma's door, inside finding both daughters sitting together on the large four poster bed visiting and laughing.

It was a beautiful sight.

Abby jumped up and ran to the armoire, "Mother look, we found one of Emma's first fancy dresses. May I please wear it to the wedding?"

"Of course. Does it fit proper?"

Abby smiled and jumped about the room with joy, "Oh yes it does, see Emma and I have been mending it to fit me!" She ran and squeezed her sister tightly, then hugged her mother too. "Thank you, my first party dress!"

She bounded from the room to prepare for the wedding, leaving mother and the bride alone.

"Emma," she began, sitting near her on the bed. "We have missed so much sharing and talking, these past years. I know now you are a woman, yet as you go into your wedding night, the physical love of the marriage bed need not be just for duty to your husband. Do you understand?"

"Yes."

"The physical love you share is the extension of your heart. Never fear it, never be shy of it. The right man will bring passion out of you and together you will experience a lasting and loving relationship. Marriage is to be entered into with no fear or hesitation between husband and wife, for it cannot survive otherwise."

Emma held her breath, realizing her mother had known all along. "I love John deeply. Yes, I want our love to be passionate."

"As it should be daughter. You will be happy. Like your father and I."

Mrs. Dixon smiled at her daughter and then walked with her to the armoire. It was time to get ready. She helped Emma into the underpinnings of the dress, the chemise, pantalettes, the crinoline and corset were all adorned before the dress was finally slipped over her head.

The white silk and satin offset her milky white skin. Her slim shoulders and arms were bare. The dress covered with seed pearls throughout and a bustier top tied tightly at the waist. The skirt flared with yards and yards of Parisian silk. The upper mounds of Emma's full breasts were visible at the neckline of the dress, the bust-line a bit too snug as they strained against the fabric that fought to hold them.

Emma turned to look in the mirror and instead of euphoria at the thought of her wedding she suddenly realized what was truly happening. Her blood ran cold. The room seemed to spin. She feared she would faint.

She was marrying was the most wanted man in the United States.

In marrying John, she was now an accomplice in his deception.

Not only this, but when she stood before the Deacon and declared her wedding vows to John Singer, it would be a lie. To keep him safe, in marrying a murderer, it would set her on a lifetime of being on the run. If they left the United States, she might never see her family ever again.

For one brief moment, she nearly shouted his secrets.

Then she glanced at the bed they had shared last night. No, she could not betray him. Her love for John overpowered all else.

"Are you well, dear," her mother asked, "You look pale."

"Yes, just a little nervous. It is a big day."

"One of the biggest days of your life."

Emma nodded, giving gave her mother the pearls to twine in her hair in a family tradition, just as Annabelle had worn them on her wedding day. But instead of twining them into Emma's hair, her mother laid the pearl necklace around her head as a crown across her golden strands of hair.

"There. I believe that style suits you best."

She turned to look in the mirror. The effect was that of a Parisian princess. Emma hugged her mother as she waited for the time to descend the stairs to take her place beside John. She noticed her mother's left hand glaring empty, without her large engagement ring.

"Where is your diamond ring, you never take it off?"

Mrs. Dixon looked at her hand and said simply, "Not to worry. I was just cleaning up some and took it off, all is fine. God bless you, precious daughter."

John was finishing the last of his toilette, he was fresh shaved, the formal suit of Mr. Dixon was a good fit, only slightly snug. He looked in the small mirror above the ancient dresser that served as the only decoration in the stark spare bedroom.

Was it possible to be really be happy, to live here with Emma and her family, and to hide in plain sight as John Singer? Surely fate would not let him live, giving a taste of perfection, only to take it away.

Love made his life worth living.

Emma brought him back to life, giving a second chance to live for her and only her. He wanted that more than anything.

He shook his head at the worries and grasped the gold medal around his neck for just a moment, as he remembered Asia placing it on him, to help him heal from an injury, *The Lamb of God will save you dear John, He will.*

"Oh Asia," he lamented, "how I miss you so."

She should be with him now.

She should smile and see how love had found him at last. With that thought he bowed his head and sobbed for the deception that surrounded his life and how the lies would soon encompass be Emma's world, as well.

His sister should be here today, to witness him marry the woman he loved. It pained him that on a day that should be filled with joy, his heart was heavy with the loss of his own family. Oh, to see them again, just one last time. The things he would say.

Such regret.

But one could never go back. A man must move forward.

It was time for the wedding.

John made his way to the great parlor and slid the ornately carved cherry double doors open. The house servant Charles and the cook Esmeralda were present in their finest clothes, as was Emma's little sister Abby, smiling and looking very lady like in her proper party dress.

Also present was Deacon Burns, a tall, older and spare man dressed in an ill-fitting suit and holding a tattered bible in his hands. John approached the Deacon to greet him, with Abby trailing behind him, looking like a young Southern belle as she stayed at his side, not wishing to miss anything of the great occasion.

John shook his hand, "Hello sir. Thank you for joining us today. My name is John Singer."

"Ah yes Mr. Singer, it's a pleasure to meet you. It is an honor to be here under such happy circumstances, the wedding of our dear Emma. I have known her since birth. You see, I married Mr. and Mrs. Dixon. This is doubly a blessing."

"A memorable occasion, indeed."

John felt his coat tugged on, he turned to see the young sister Abby. Her blonde hair was neatly styled in a young lady upswept style and her milky white skin was lightly flushed across the cheeks from excitement.

"John, see my dress," she indicated the pale blue silk, "it's my first party dress. It was Emma's, but we altered it so I could be pretty and grown up today, too!"

She was a delightful young girl, so full of enthusiasm and life.

He smiled. "Darling child, how beautiful you are. Why in no time for sure there will be lots of beaux coming to court you, and you will only have to choose with your heart."

Abby's blue eyes turned wide and large, "I will choose someone handsome and kind, like you, Uncle John. Is it proper to call you that, since you are marrying Emma?"

"Yes, I would like that, very much."

Just then Esmeralda called to her, "Abby child, it is time. Your sister is coming. You come here and stand with us now."

She obeyed.

There was no music to announce her arrival, but his heart knew his beloved was drawing near. From his place in front beside the Deacon, his pulse began to race when the double doors opened again and in walked Emma's mother, looking lovely in a blue satin dress, albeit slightly faded from years of unattended storage.

She left the doors open.

John watched as his lovely bride slowly descended the grand staircase and made her entrance into the great parlor. She walked in with the ease and grace of a queen, her gown of silk rustling as she moved towards John and the Deacon.

She carried only a few sprigs of hydrangea as most of the flowering plants in the garden had been trampled by the multitude of soldiers on horseback. The deep set lavender and blue color of the flowers set off Emma's eyes, as they were shining and full of wonder.

Her gaze never left his face.

She is my second chance to live and to love.

She drifted closer and took his hand.

"I love you, darling Emma." He said before the Deacon could speak.

She gave his hand a squeeze and smiled. "And I love you. Now and forever, John Singer."

He could not recall a single moment in his life when he had been happier.

"Are you ready to take me as your wife?" She sweetly asked.

"I am, indeed."

It was late in the evening, after enjoying the wedding feast of lamb and vegetables, cake and wine that John and Emma found themselves alone, back in Emma's room. It was now their room since they were joined as husband and wife, now known as John and Emma Singer.

"Emma darlin' come here," John cooed to her, "Beauty like yours, I have never ever seen. So pure and golden. The fact that you and your heart are mine is a miracle that I will not understand, but am eternally grateful for."

He kissed her softly, showing his devotion.

"Your love brought me back to life when I did not want to live, and your love now sustains me in a life that will be only lived for you. I am humbled by this twist of fate, and now will forever fight to hold onto to it, and never let you go."

Those seemed to be words she needed to hear.

The joy in her lovely face lit his world.

Emma turned in her husband's arms so he could unfasten the buttons on her bustier and then slip off the wedding gown.

He did so quickly and deftly as she stood silent and seemed to enjoy letting him help her remove the crinoline. Then came the chemise and the pantalets until she was naked, quivering with excitement and waiting for his love.

The sight of his beautiful wife standing before him, waiting for him, trusting him with his deception became too much.

Emma deserved better.

She deserved goodness and truth.

John sank to his knees before her, his legs tangled up in the sea of crinoline and lace at her feet.

Overwhelmed with regret for his crimes, he covered his eyes and cried to her, "Darlin' what I have done? What have I done? I did it for my country. I had to do it, but you see it wasn't just me, it wasn't. It was..."

His voice trailed off as Emma bent down to gather up her husband.

Her hands caressed his face.

Coaxing him to stand, he dare not touch her. She was naked and he felt unworthy of such perfection. But she gently kissed his brow and wiped his cheeks with her soft hand.

"Dearest John, have no fear for whatever came before us has no meaning in this moment now. Life is beginning anew. You are safe with me."

"But Emma, I..."

"Shh. It is in the past. Love me John, just please love me."

With that plead in her voice he gathered her up and laid her on their bed. He divested himself of his suit and joined his wife on the soft covers.

Her body welcomed him and he loved her, loving her with his body and giving her all of his heart, thinking that at all costs Emma must never ever know his truth.

The morning found the newlyweds the last to arise. Emma marveled in the newness of their marriage, yet having heard John's almost confession to her the previous night, she realized there was no time to waste.

The lies ate at him.

The deception could not last.

She thought also her last encounter with Doctor Bradley, his tirades about John. Yes most certainly, there was no time to waste. She must lay out plans to travel to Philadelphia, alone.

"Good morning, dear husband."

He smiled, still sleepy and content. "And good morning, dear wife."

Emma's mood suddenly became serious, "John, I have to tell you something. Please try to understand when I tell you what I must do."

John's mood equally became serious. "I'm listening."

"I received word that a dear nurse friend of mine is seriously ill. She resides in Philadelphia. Her mother contacted me and has asked me to come to see her."

John scoffed and Emma knew he must be thinking of his sister and the deceptions he was trying to hide from, all of it originating in Philadelphia. "Emma darling, no. We cannot go there. I am sorry for your friend, but no."

"I was not asking your permission," she sternly insisted, sitting up so he could see she was serious, "nor do you need to come with me. I must go to her today, I must."

John jumped up from the bed, "We have only been married less than a day, and my bride leaves her husband?"

"It is as it has to be. I cannot help the timing."

"You knew of this already and did not share your concern for your friend with me?"

"John do you not trust me? How would it be if my friend should die without my being there? The burden and guilt of it I would forever have in my heart, knowing that I could have gone but did not."

She could tell he didn't like it, but her reasoning softened his intense gaze. "Now come here, darling," she turned the quilt down so he could see her naked and lush body, "come here and show me now how much you will miss me."

John crept back into the bed and held her close.

"Dearest wife, please if you must go without me, make haste to your journey and return here to me."

"I promise."

"I will see to your travel today, if that so pleases you," his voice spoke the words of acquiescence but his tone was heavy with worry.

John would not win this battle.

CHAPTER TWENTY-ONE

Get out, take that book with you,
you are not welcome here.

~~Asia Booth Clarke

The coach taking Emma from the train depot in Philadelphia to her destination turned onto a lovely residential area towards Race Street. The chestnut tree-lined streets stood as shade to the wide and expansive front lawns of the several large mansions. Each one was more impressive than the next. The driver stopped in front of a two-story imposing structure, whitewashed with two large Grecian adorned columns that held up the portico to the second floor.

The front entrance walkway was an elaborate design of brick pavers, creating a path that invited one toward the home.

Somehow she didn't feel welcome.

She felt anxious and worried.

The driver helped Emma stepped from the coach and unloaded her small suitcase to the platform near the street and then onto the ground. Gathering courage, she straightened her shoulders and walked along the brick pathway towards the large and impressive home, drinking in the beauty of such a stately place.

"My God, what am I doing?"

Too late to turn back now.

Her legs felt heavy as she forced herself to climb up one, then two, then three brick paved steps to the large, white washed, double door entrance decorated with elaborate brass fittings. Her blood turned to ice as she reached for the brass bell. She hesitated and turned the brass fitting, hearing it ring. It was then she heard the faint cry of infant from the upstairs window. She waited and heard the echo of footsteps approach the door.

She held her breath.

The door opened slightly but only on one side, revealing a middle-aged woman peering at Emma from around the corner of the door. Her deep-set eyes darted across her face not seeing any familiarity. Her gaze became suspicious.

Emma righted herself and spoke firmly to the woman at the door, "I have come to see Mrs. Clarke. Is she at home?"

The woman stood her ground.

Clearly, the last few weeks of the Clarke household had been torn apart by the family's association with John Wilkes Booth. Emma had heard the Government descended on the home in a frenzy, rummaging through the house looking for evidence that the family had connection with this maddening act.

Finding none they took Asia's husband, John Sleeper Clarke into custody for his affiliation by marriage, and for the connection of his management of the Winter Garden Theater in New York where the famous actor had performed. The Booth brothers Edwin and Junius were also arrested in New York. There they all sat in the old Federal prison in Washington DC, their only crime in being related to John Wilkes Booth.

The woman sharply commanded, "State your business with Mrs. Clarke."

Emma realized the fear of treason and conspiracy was never more real than right now. Her knowledge of John's existence could bring about her own death. But she regained her composure, lifting her head, "I will state my business to Mrs. Clarke when I see her and only when I see her. I have something I must give her personally."

The woman still kept the one side of the door barely open. "You wait here."

She closed the door and heard it latch, fearing she would be turned away. Emma began to shake and feel woozy, and whether it was the long journey or the fear of being turned away she did not know. If she did not sit and take water she feared she would faint.

But the door reopened, "Come this way."

Emma stepped into a large and gracious foyer with a marble floor of a black and white pattern; the entrance table in the foyer was a lovely Louis IV round design, its cherry wood glistening and shining in varying rich and deep tones. The vase upon the large tabletop was decorative with inlaid glass and filled with the flowers of the season; hydrangea, rhododendron, dogwood and lilies. Their scent, while normally fragrant and appealing, today it seemed a bit overwhelming to Emma.

How odd. Perhaps it was just her nerves.

The woman showed Emma into the parlor, and equally expansive room the large and imposing fireplace silent now due to the late May heat. The horsehair couch and wing chairs were perfect compliments to the room, the lamp shades edged in brocade and tasseled, the floor to ceiling windows on each side of the fireplace lined in French lace. The wall covering was a patterned deep red rich with a carpet from Brussels. It was a stunning room. Emma stood admiring the expansive room where the woman instructed her to wait.

It was then a small boy of about five bounded toward her holding a toy horse. The boy saw Emma and smiled wide, but she froze.

The child looked just like John. It was like seeing her husband as a little boy. She realized she was seeing the first inclinations of his family. And what if Asia didn't believe her about John, then what? Would his sister call the government to have her arrested too?

"And what is your name?"

The little boy smiled up at Emma, his innocent face making her heart flutter in recognition of the man she loved. "My name is Jacob. And what is yours?"

"Why my name is Emma, nice to meet you."

She held out her hand. He slipped his chubby fingers into hers, "Nice to meet you, Miss Emma." His Baltic black eyes were framed by thick black eyelashes. Emma was astounded at the resemblance of the boy to his Uncle. He was a beautiful child.

Jacob stood near Emma and asked as only an innocent child could ask, "Are you friends with Mama?"

"No, I am friends with your Uncle John." It was daring, but sharing the truth with Jacob gave her courage.

"You are pretty. My mama says Uncle John did something bad, but we love him anyways. See, he gave me this horse."

"It's a very special present."

He nodded. "I miss him. He used to come up to visit mama and would take me and Joshua for a ride on his real horse. Last time he visited it was too late. Me and Joshua were asleep. He left us each a toy."

The child hugged the horse to his chest. "Mama is upstairs. We just got another baby brother. Mama says his name is Joseph, after Uncle Joseph, but she promised Uncle John she would name him John after him, so she told us his name was John Joseph. It's a secret we can't tell nobody."

He smiled at Emma in utter innocence.

"I won't tell."

He giggled. They heard his mother call out, "Jacob, where are you?"

"I am in the parlor, Mama, with this pretty lady. She came to visit you."

With that said an attractive woman of average height and weight walked into the parlor. Her day dress was watered silk of pale violet, her medium brown hair was plated in braids and twined over each side of head. On her ears were violet amethyst earrings. Her eyes were wide set and hazel, her countenance pretty but her expression was exhausted and guarded.

She approached Emma, looking her up and down and with an icy stare.

"Mrs. McLeary said you have something for me, state your business quickly, and then leave." Asia then directed her attention to her oldest child and said sternly, "Jacob go into the kitchen now. Mrs. McLeary has bread with jam for you and your brother."

"Yes, Mama." he reluctantly left the parlor.

Asia stood facing Emma, her tone curt, "Well what say you? What is your name and what do you want?"

"My name is Emma Dixon. I have something for you." But she felt faint and woozy. "Please may I sit?" Emma did not wait for the invitation as the realization of her circumstances and fear combined with the woozy uneasiness in her stomach. Odd nausea once again was building within her, forced her to sit on one of the wing chairs.

"You look pale." Asia's tone was only slightly concerned.

"Please may I have some water? I have come from Richmond to see you." She wiped her face with one hand tried to calm herself. This was not the time to fall apart. "I have something of great importance I must give you."

Asia rang for Mrs. McLeary to bring water to Emma, her patience for the young woman at an end. Her frustration was evident in her tight lips and stern face.

"Thank you," Emma gratefully sipped the water as she felt herself return from the dizzying place of nausea, and stated simply. "I have a letter for you," Asia stood solid and unmoved as she watched Emma reached under her skirts to her petticoat and pulled out a small red datebook. Before Emma could even open it, Asia eyes narrowed in recognition and she stepped back from the young woman.

She recognized the date book. It was John's.

Gripped with fear and anger, Asia lashed out at the young woman, "Get out, take that book with you, you are not welcome here. You dare to bring this sorcery to my house. I have two small children here and a newborn infant. My husband and brothers are imprisoned in Washington DC for no reason other than they are related to John. My family is destroyed, my heart broken, and you come to me saying you have something for me. Is this trickery of the Government? Did they send you here to try to destroy us further by producing a fake book similar to his? A misguided notion. Did you think we knew of the conspiracy? We did not. They send a woman to trick us, so they can now justify hanging us all. Is that your purpose?"

Emma then stood up, her body shaking and opened the book. She knew her time was short. She had to act quickly. "Mrs. Clarke, I assure you the Government did not send me. I also risk hanging and treason for bringing this to you. Please just take this."

Emma opened the book carefully.

Asia saw the carte de visite of several lovely young women, the one she recognized as Lucy Hale, John's secret fiancé. Her heart began to pound so intently she thought it would explode. The beautiful blonde then pulled an envelope from with the book and extended it to Asia.

"Please," she softly begged. "Just look at it."

Asia stood just out of reach. Overcome by curiosity, she leaned forward and grabbed the envelope, looking at the address scrawled on the outside envelope.

Mrs. Asia Booth Clarke, Race Street, Philadelphia, PA.

The script was unmistakably John's.

Asia's hands began to shake. She lovingly touched the outside of the envelope thinking of the hand that wrote this to her. The tears welled up in her eyes, still uncertain of the young guest who stood in her parlor, wary of her intentions. Yet the compulsion to believe her was too compelling to dismiss.

She gently opened the letter, it was dated April 25, 1865 the day before John was killed. Fingers trembled as she read her dead brother's words:

Dearest Asia, it is with great sadness I write to you, the end is near for me dear sister, I cannot believe the deed I committed is not heralded and lauded as they told me it would be, but rather condemned to be hunted down with every man's hand against me, for the destruction of the tyrant.

They told me dear sister, I would be a hero to the South and to the nation, vindication for the six hundred thousand dead and wounded these four long years. I believed in the cause the cause of the South , my convictions as you know unyielding and steadfast. I was the only one brave enough to commit this act. And yet the words I read of news clippings brought to me here in the deep and dark forest are of treason and tyranny.

Davey Herold is here with me now, we are fugitives with no friends or family to help us, cold, wet and in such pain from my broken leg. Every Confederate door closed to us, so the end is near. Tell mother I did it for my country and that if some trick of fate should happen, and I can escape I will go to Washington and tell the government of those behind the plan, to help clear my name. Fear not dear sister, for the prophesy of that old gypsy looks to be coming true, a lauded life, a short life and brilliant life snuffed out in a blaze of fire. Let God judge me, not man.

Asia cried unchecked, letting tears stream down her face. The information that her brother was somehow convinced to commit this horrific act broke her heart all over again. Those Confederate operatives whose voices she heard in the many weeks before the assassination had been right here in her own house.

John did not act on his own, he did not!

While it was new information, it changed nothing. Asia knew this letter must never be published, must never see the light of day. It must stay hidden for the safety of her family and for this young woman who bravely delivered it.

Asia wiped the tears and sighed deeply. She looked at Emma who was pale and worried. She softened her tone.

"Miss Dixon, please tell me, who you are and how did you come by this book."

"I have been working in a field hospital in Alexandria since the 1st battle of Bull Run in July of 1861, after both my father and brother were killed. I was almost nineteen then. Now that the war is over, I have returned to my parent's home in Richmond. Today I have come north to give you this letter. I had the book stitched into my petticoats for fear of being detained or worse. The book is evidence of treason, but I needed to see you. It is important."

"May I have the book?"

Emma shook her head, "No Mrs. Clarke. It's John's, it belongs to him. You may look at the letter but I must return the book to John."

"What do you mean return to John," Asia demanded, "Return where, to a grave under the floorboards of the Old Federal penitentiary? We are still trying to get his body home to be buried with father."

"Mrs. Clarke, you don't understand," Emma stood close to Asia and extended her left hand. On her ring finger was a small pearl ring circled with diamonds.

"I married John."

Asia shook her head, remembering the heartbroken Lucy Hale and the dozens of others bewitched by John's beauty and charm. A wife. This truly was madness. It was again too much for the broken hearted mother, "I can't help you."

Emma took a deep breath, "I married John on May 27, 1865 in the front parlor of my parent's home in Richmond, Virginia. You are now my sister-in-law. Asia, I have come here to tell you, John is alive."

Asia's eyes grew wide with disbelief, and began to shout, "Get out, get out of my house, never come here again. He is dead, John was murdered in that barn shot and killed through the neck."

She was furious.

"You have brought evil into this house, a house that has seen such pain and agony. Yet you stand there and tell me you married John on May 27, thirty-one days after he was killed? If it weren't for the letter you have brought me, I should call the Government and have them arrest you and that imposter you married. You will tried and hung for the blasphemous talk that he is alive."

"No, please. It is true."

"What is it you are after, money, fame, who put you up to concocting this ridiculous lie? Get out now, never darken my door. Go back to Richmond and spew your lies there."

Asia grabbed Emma by the arm, pushing her toward the door. "No, please listen. He is alive, I tell you he is alive. Please, you must come with me. You must come and see for yourself, he is alive, he's alive!"

The pleading in Emma's voice stopped Asia for the moment.

"What proof do you have he is alive?"

Asia raised her head in defiance and the young woman trembled as her resolve began to ebb. "He wears the Agnus Dei."

"What do you mean?"

Emma rambled on quickly, "It is a gold medal on a gold chain he wears. It has the words Agnus Dei inscribed on it. He always wears it and never takes it off. Its Latin I believe, for Lamb of God, and I also believe it is a Christian symbol of some kind. But I am not familiar with it."

Asia shook her head, "No it's a Catholic emblem. I gave him the gold medal last year when he was severely injured during one of his acting performances. We didn't know if he would live. I put that on his neck and since that time I have converted to Catholicism and he attended Mass with me whenever he came to Philadelphia."

"Do you believe me now?"

"Perhaps," Asia allowed, "You must tell me everything you know and right now."

Emma sighed deeply in relief, "Yes, I will."

They returned to the parlor, sitting together on the horsehair couch. Emma took a deep breath and looked directly into Asia's eyes, noticing the strong resemblance between brother and sister. Asia was as beautiful as John was handsome.

"So much has happened. I hardly know where to begin."

"Emma, just take your time. I will listen. Please, tell me everything."

"It was several weeks ago at the end of the war, after the surrender at Appomattox when the last of our dear fallen soldiers arrived at the hospital, when I first saw him."

"John was in the hospital?"

"Yes. I stood at the doorway as the last of the soldiers were being carried inside. He was the very last one arriving on a stretcher from the ambulance wagon. Unlike the others, he was sitting up on the stretcher. I could see his left leg had been casted, but it was filthy and he was covered with grime."

"Was he in pain?"

"Certainly, but he bore it with incredible courage. His face had no expression. He never cried out, like the other men. But as I worked his eyes followed me, black and bottomless, with dark lashes that curled up, much like little Jacob. The expression in those eyes haunted me. The Confederate uniform he wore had the Singer embroidered on the cuff in an elaborate script. He told me his name was John Singer."

"John Singer?"

"Yes. And I was captivated. From the time his eyes followed me, from the time I put my hand into his, it was already too late for me. His voice was like a melody to me, deep rich and perfect. The attraction from the moment I saw him, was swift and compete. Never have I encountered such a beautiful man, he is magnetic and deeply intense. We had our surgeon Doctor Henry Bradley look at his leg. It was only by divine providence the leg was not gangrene, he would fully recover from the leg, only a slight limp would remain."

Asia sat motionless and continued to listen intently.

"Very soon after his leg was re-cast, John contracted malaria and was quarantined, Doctor Bradley was not hopeful as to his recovery, there was so very little quinine left. But I begged him to save John. He gave me what he had. I sat and nursed John for three straight days as his fever raged through his body."

"Your devotion is heartwarming, Emma."

"He had won my heart. I sponged him and kept him comfortable. I noticed the medal and wondered if it was a clue as to who he was and where he was from. John just kept saying he was from the South, that he had no family. He still remains vague and silent about his past. It was just by accident I found the diary. I asked Doctor Bradley about the uniform John wore when he was brought in. Normally those are burned to prevent the spread of vermin and disease."

"I hoped to find a letter or a note that might tell me more about him. Behind the hospital our freed black hospital worker Old Sam stood over the fire pit burning uniforms. I saw the embroidered cuff with the name Singer and directed Old Sam to pull it from the pit. When he did, he found the red book with the carte de visite of the five women, newspaper clippings and a wanted poster for John Wilkes Booth and his conspirators. I hid the book for several days, not reading it. Finally, I could stand it no more. It changed everything."

"What happened to make you read it?"

"You see, he was being noticed by hospital personnel and by visitors all saying he had a remarkable resemblance to John Wilkes Booth. It worried me. Although he claimed to love me, John remained so mysterious about himself. It worried me. One night I opened the book and was astounded by what I saw and read."

"You were not sure of his true identity?

"He did look like this John Wilkes Booth, I could readily agree to that, but we all knew he was murdered at Garrett's Farm on April 26, 1865. But I opened the book. The poster, his writings of his time trying to escape to his beloved South, and the letter to you -- I read it Asia, and I just knew, I just knew. I was already deeply in love and committed to him by the time I discovered the man I love, slept with, and given my life and love to, is John Wilkes Booth."

His sister let out a faint gasp. Her skin had paled.

"Asia, I know this is unbelievable, but it is the truth. Somehow he escaped the barn and someone else was murdered instead. Please, come back to Richmond with me. Come see that your brother John is alive. Please help him to leave the country. I fear for his safety, for he is hiding in plain sight, yet the suspicions of his deception are coming to a crescendo. I fear for his life. Please Asia, help me."

Emma was weeping, begging for her husband's life.

"This is inconceivable," Asia refused to believe. "This just cannot be, it cannot." She continued to shake her head in disbelief.

Emma boldly asked, "I heard the body was on the USS Montauk, and an autopsy performed there. Were there no Booth family members or friends there to identify the body?"

The pain in Asia's heart began to overwhelm her.

It was true. No Booth relative or friend was allowed to see the body the Government claimed was John's. Just his physician Doctor May who removed a fibroid from John's neck a few years ago was allowed, yet the physician claimed the specimen on the slab to be autopsied was not Wilkes Booth.

Asia heard rumors that the man autopsied was red haired and freckled while John's skin was marble white and without blemish. The man also was of slight build and was much older while John's youth of twenty-six and years of physical activity had built a solid rock-hard physical body.

Yes there were rumors, but just rumors.

She also knew Doctor May recanted his earlier observation and finally positively identified the body as being John; as did all the participants present at the autopsy who were associated with the Government.

To oppose the official identity of the man on the slab was paramount to treason.

"No family members were allowed on the Montauk," she confessed to Emma, "and well we heard rumors that the man they autopsied bore no real resemblance to our John. But the Government said it was him, so what were we supposed to believe?" She shrugged her shoulders, the story of John possibly being alive felt too unbelievable to be true.

But if he had somehow survived?

A cold shiver went through Asia despite the spring heat, fearing the answer.

"You came here of your own accord. John did not ask you to come?"

Emma dropped her gaze and hung her head in shame, shaking it from side to side, "No, he did not ask me to come here. He knows I am in Philadelphia. But my husband believes I am visiting a sick friend. John does not know I actually came to see you."

"Why would you lie?"

"You see, he does not know that I am aware of his true identity. When we were married at my parents' house, I took the name Singer, fully knowing it was really Booth. My life is forever twined in helping to hide him and I vow to love him until I die."

Asia's eyes flew wide open. "You must realize, should I come to Richmond to see him, he will know of your deception. You are willing to risk your relationship to bring me to him?"

"Yes, I love him that much. How could I live knowing his family thinks him dead, and yet I did nothing to tell you? When John sees you, my deception will reveal itself. I have no idea what he will do. Yes, I worry. I only know those words to you in his letter and his love for you has compelled me to come here, to make you believe me and understand we must get him out of this country."

"You say this with such passion. How can you be so sure?"

"I have no choice, I love him more than my life."

Asia had never seen such intense devotion.

"You mentioned there were those who had suspicions of his true identity. How is this possible without proof that this John Singer is not who he says he is? Who Emma, who is suspicious enough for you to leave your new husband, come here and enlist me to help you?"

"It is a long story."

"I will listen."

"Well you see, right before the war broke out, I had my coming out party. My father had promised a young medical student he could court me. I told my father I only had friendship feelings for the young man, nothing more, yet he thought Henry could provide me with a wonderful and happy life."

"Father's always wish for a prosperous match for their daughters." Asia agreed, thinking of her own marriage a match that promised wealth, but proved less for love.

"Then as fate would have it," Emma continued, "this young medical student graduated and began working at the field hospital in Alexandria, VA. After losing my father and brother, I too wanted to help our soldiers. I stayed for three years. I knew Doctor Henry Bradley carried feelings in his heart for me, but I never encouraged it. Once I saw John, my heart was his. There will never ever be anyone else for me."

Asia leaned in closer, her worried voice nearly a whisper, "Is this doctor the one who has the deep suspicions of John?"

"Yes, he is. I fear Doctor Bradley, in his loss of me has also lost his mind. Combined with the carnage he had seen over these last four years, he is spiraling out of control. He told me right before we left for Richmond that somehow he would reveal my John to the world and that his death would surely follow."

"Oh no God help us, please!"

Emma nodded, "This gentle kind man is mired in madness, believing he is the better man for me, thinking I will realize this once John is out of the picture. I fear for his life in so many ways. I fear his ruse as John Singer will soon be discovered. This time he will be murdered for sure."

Asia reached out to grasp Emma's hand.

"Do you not fear of your life as well?"

"My life would not be worth living should John be parted from me. Perhaps this is my own madness, but I love him deeply. Just being away from him this short time, fearing something may happen while I am here while trying to enlist your help causes pain inside my heart. He is like an opiate to me, for I am surely addicted. Nothing could stop me from coming here today. You are my only chance to save him. Please, I beg you to come with me. See for yourself. Look into his face and judge if this man is your brother."

Asia's heart lurched.

"I know nothing of you, yet you're brave to come here to bring me the letter and to tell me that John did not die in the barn, but is alive and married to you. From what I see, you are driven by your love for him. You see, I love him deeply too."

Asia reached under the collar of her dress and pulled up a chain. On the end hung a small photo of John. "This was hung over my boys beds. John used to run into their room when they were asleep and say Pray for me babies. I saved it when we heard of what John had done. I have kept it on my neck ever since. I feared the government would have ripped it down and taken it as evidence against the family. They came and tore apart our home. What they did not take, they burned in front of me."

"How awful."

In that moment the faint cries of the infant John Joseph drifted down the great stairway into the front parlor. Asia stood up suddenly to tend to the infant, as did Emma, expecting Asia to instruct her to leave. The mother was already ascending the marble staircase.

"Wait, I will come back down."

Emma waited. At least Asia had asked her to stay.

Perhaps there was hope.

Asia returned with her infant and sat upon the great wing chair with the child settled within her arms. Emma peered into the blankets that held the baby. Her heart fluttered with joy to see dark hair and the familiar facial features that were so much like John.

The Booth family traits were strong.

"He is a beautiful boy, so much like your son Jacob."

Asia smiled her expression kind and open now, no longer suspicious and hostile. Emma did not blame her for being suspicious. Even to herself the truth had been difficult to swallow. "Yes, Jacob is so like his Uncle, resembles him and loves mischief like him." She snuggled the infant closer as he fell asleep in his mother's arms. "I have much to think about, Emma. The mere hope John lives is still too unbelieving, yet you are so very convincing. I ask you, kindly, to please let me see the book again."

Grateful Asia was considering the truth, weighing it in her mind, this time Emma handed the book over to her without hesitation. She was a loving mother. Perched in the chair like a true lady, Asia opened it carefully, while skillfully balancing the infant on her lap as not to waken him. Handling a baby so well clearly took practice. The boy looked loved and at peace.

She watched Asia flick her thumb across the photos of the ladies who had haunted her mind. The sister to her handsome husband frowned, in apparent disapproval of the collection of beautiful faces. Emma could no longer hold her tongue as to inquire about those five carte de visite, and who they were they to John. She braced herself as she asked Asia, "Please, do you know who the women are, whose faces John was carrying with him? They are all so beautiful."

Asia sighed with clear regret. "There is but one here I know of, this one," she pointed to a lovely young women who soft dark hair was wound about her head in a stylish knot to fall at the nape of the neck, her features strong and refined. She looked wealthy and proud.

"Who is she?"

"This one is Lucy Hale, the daughter of the senator from New Hampshire. I know of her only because of the letter that came to my brother Edwin, who said that she and John were secretly engaged and had pledged marriage."

Those words tore Emma apart. A pain stabbed her chest, like her heart really was wounded. Unchecked, a single tear rolled down her cheek.

"I am so sorry dear, but it is the truth. The letter Lucy wrote was of such agony over what John had done and her sorrow over his death as well, such that she said she would have gladly gone to the gallows with him. Such were her feelings for him, even at the darkest moment. I heard that her father accepted an ambassadorship to Spain. He took Lucy with him. They sailed weeks ago. These others look to be actresses that John worked with on stage."

Emma bowed over then, the pain inside becoming increasingly real. Her heart ached. Clearly John inspired devotion and passion in all women. She had known he was a practiced and skilled lover, having fallen to his charms. But it seemed her inability to resist him was like so many before her.

"Lucy loved him then?"

"Perhaps it seemed that way."

"He does bring that out in women," Emma breathed, sitting upright again. "He is my passion too. Yet, I do love him beyond my own life."

Asia saw the distress in Emma and said to her simply, "When he chose to marry Emma, it was you he chose. The others he never truly loved. What came before should not matter, only how he feels about you now. He married you, he loves you."

"Oh yes, he truly does."

"Then understand dearest Emma, even though he may have given a part of his heart to Lucy he has given you more, in marrying you, he has given you his love and his life."

She turned the pages of the book, "This is John's handwriting. I would know it, beyond a doubt." The time was upon Asia to decide if she would follow Emma to Richmond to face the man Emma claimed is John Wilkes Booth. "I will go with you. We leave tomorrow."

Relief rushed through Emma. "Thank you." She stood to take her leave. "What time should I call on you tomorrow?"

To her shock, Asia laughed aloud. "No dearest. You will stay here."

"I am grateful."

"And I believe, if your claim is true," the sister added with a smile, "I will be eternally grateful to you."

Asia then rang for Mrs. McLeary, to give her John Joseph to put bed and to escort Emma to the upstairs guest room. She gave orders for her to be as comfortable as possible and that dinner be brought to her room, as to give Emma the benefit of rest and care after not only a long journey, but of the emotional toll of their conversation.

After Emma was settle upstairs, Asia also asked to have Jacob brought to her in the parlor. She was pacing and thinking when she heard the running steps of her oldest boy.

"Mama, mama." He ran in, "The pretty lady is staying with us?" He wore his effervescent smile and the ever present toy horse was gripped in one of his chubby hands.

"Yes, child. Emma is our guest. You must let her rest. She has made a difficult journey today." He nodded and seemed to understand. "Come here. I want to tell you something very, very important."

Jacob stood close to his mother, lifting his face as to see her fully.

"What is it, Mama?"

Asia walked over to the horsehair couch and took Jacob's hand, the same couch where just moments ago while sitting with Emma, Asia's life took a dangerous turn. "Jacob, I am going to tell you something very important. I am telling you this as a young man, not a little boy. Do you understand, son?"

Jacob's countenance became very still as the gravity of his mother's words resonated through his small body.

"Yes. I do."

"I must go away for a few days. I am leaving with Emma."

"Why?"

"All I can tell you son, is that I will be going somewhere important with Emma, but I won't be gone long."

"I don't want you to leave." He whimpered.

"Listen carefully to me. You need to be a big boy to Joshua and help Mrs. McLeary with John Joseph. I will make arrangements for his feedings. My trip is a secret. Like John Joseph's name, remember?" He nodded. "You must say nothing to anyone about this." The boy's eyes were wet. "You must not cry, Jacob. You must be strong. Your mother loves you, do you understand?"

Jacob began to quiver as he forced back the tears.

"Mama, why do you have to leave with Emma?"

"Son, I know this very difficult, but I have to go. I must leave as soon as I can."

The boy took a deep breath, steading himself inside.

"That's good. I'm proud of you."

With innocence of a child's heart Jacob tried to be brave.

"Mama, are you going to try to find Uncle John?"

Asia was too shocked for a moment to respond. But Jacob looked at her in earnest, those dark eyes so much like the brother she loved.

"Child, whatever are you talking about?"

"Mama, I didn't tell you this because everyone is angry at Uncle John, but one night I woke up and I thought I heard Uncle John crying and saying he was alive and come find him. You are going to find him, right? He's crying, Mama. He's crying, saying come find me."

Asia remembered that same night, the one where she also thought she heard John's voice echoing the night, crying out for help.

"You kept it a secret?"

Jacob nodded. "I won't say anything Mama, I won't say anything, I promise."

Asia gathered her son in her arms as both mother and son wept together, the pain of their secret binding them forever on a course set with only their love of the Uncle and brother John as their guide.

CHAPTER TWENTY-TWO

You knew all along, Emma you knew.

~~John Wilkes Booth

John anxiously paced around the bedroom he and Emma now shared. He missed Emma these last two days, waiting now for the sounds of the coach to bring her home. He had wanted to go to the train depot and pick her up himself, anticipation of being without her was riveting for him. He needed his wife, needed to hold her close and smell the softness of her skin.

But she was a stubborn, headstrong woman.

In her telegraph she insisted to come herself.

He went to the mirror, taking stock of his appearance. A clean-shaven face stared back at him, without the mustache he had adorned for years. His creamy complexion was changing. He now had lightly tanned skin from the daily work of repairing the length of fence trampled from the former occupants of the house. He enjoyed the physical work, putting his muscles to good use remembering his days on the stage and the exertion of some of his more physical roles.

Those days were over.

This new life would make him even stronger, not just physically but emotionally as well. He embraced his new role as husband and provider to Emma.

He pondered the fact that he was living next door to the house where Jeff Davis spent his years of the war, directing the great leader General Lee from the very office where the tyrant came and sat, reveling in his victory of the South. Jeff Davis had fled just as his beloved Richmond fell, fires set by our Southerners to leave nothing for the Yankees to plunder.

His eyes gazing back at him in the mirror were black like coal without expression, his lips firm and set. His face was familiar, but the man inside had changed dramatically.

He was no longer an actor living high on grand ideas and wild schemes.

He was a husband, a grateful one; for the woman he loved meant everything. As he stood staring into the looking glass, he remembered when Emma announced she needed to go to Philadelphia, just a day after being married.

She told him a former nurse she had worked with was ill and dying, needing to see Emma. Still he did not understand why he was not allowed to go with her. Of all places, he agonized. Philadelphia; the city where Asia lived, he visited and performed numerous times.

Such a coincidence!

"Asia," he spoke to his reflection, "What must you think of me. And mother? Did I break her heart? Did mother know I did it for my country?" Regret once again burned deep into his soul, the agony of his horrific deed that could never be undone.

The Knights claimed he was the only one who could strike against tyranny to slay Lincoln. In his mind, he had envisioned a triumphant ending. Not this.

Hunted. Wanted. A murderer, not a hero.

He had been so wrong.

John chastised his reflection, wishing he could explain to his sister, who he mourned more every day. "I did it for my country, Asia. I did it believing my actions were for the better good of all. Now here I live without my name, hiding, yet living in plain sight, married and suspicious of anyone and all I meet. Those who aided me in my escape helped me survive the burning barn, but not the burning of my soul."

Regret was tearing him apart. It was difficult for a man to bear.

He hung his head, letting those feeling scorch his heart.

If only he could explain.

John heard the distant sounds of the coach approaching the house. His heart leapt, hoping it was his wife. Yet in the next instant his insides grew cold with fear, wondering if the Government had found him. He went to the window and saw the coach coming down the length of driveway toward the front of the house. It was Emma!

He bolted down the stairs and waited in the foyer to greet Emma, but decided at the last minute to run to garden to welcome her with fresh flowers. He had noticed the hydrangea had a few fresh blooms and loved how those blooms complimented her ice-blue eyes on their wedding day. He hurried to the garden unaware of the visitor his wife had brought with her.

The coachman from the train depot helped his two passengers exit the paid carriage and placed their traveling bags next to them. It had been a trying journey, having to leave her children and Asia was nervous over the outcome. She looked up at the tall pillars of the Dixon home seeing the damage the war had wrought on Richmond. The house man Charles came out of the house to greet the mistress and her guest.

"Why welcome home, Miss Emma," the tall and elegant black man smiled, "I see you brought a guest with you." He politely inclined his head to Asia. Then without being asked, he automatically picked up their traveling bags. "I will have a room ready to receive your guest shortly, Miss Emma." With that he bowed from his waist and welcomed Emma's friend.

"Thank you, Charles. You are very kind to prepare a room. This is my friend Mrs. Clarke from Philadelphia," Emma looked at Asia and smiled slightly, looking a little nervous too. She then asked the faithful house man who must have served the Dixon's all his life. Although free now, he chose to stay, proving his loyalty. "Where is Mister John? Is he in the house?"

"Why now Miss Emma," he looked around as they walked into the house and carried the luggage through the great foyer, "I think I saw him run out into the garden. Would you like me to see about that?"

"Yes, that would be nice. We will wait for him in the parlor." Emma glanced at Asia who nodded that some privacy would be nice. "And see we're not disturbed, Charles."

"Yes ma'am," he bowed respectfully to Emma and excused himself.

Charles hesitated, "Miss Emma, so as not to worry you I thought you should know, Mrs. Dixon and Abby will be back day after next. They heard of some neighbors who needed help. The Mistress took a supply of food and clothes and set off to visit."

"Oh Charles, thank you. I wondered where they were. That is so like my dear mother."

"Yes, ma'am. Help where we can, that's the best way to live."

Inclining his head, he left them alone.

Asia's heart stopped and started, feeling unable to draw breath as they both waited for the sounds of his footsteps. She stood on the far side of the parlor with her back to the closed set of double wood French doors. The interior of the front parlor showed signs of its prior stature, however after serving as part of the Confederate quarters the room had become sullen and dark.

She quickly scanned from her view, seeing the large floor to ceiling windows were uncovered and undecorated, the marble fireplace mantel was blackened from overuse. The rug upon which she stood was stained and pulled from the soldiers treading on it with their spurs still on their rough boots.

The once beautiful French wallpaper, Asia recognized it as similar to her parlor, special ordered from France from a catalogue from Philadelphia. It too was blackened by fireplace soot. The furniture was bowed and dirty from their ruffian temporary occupants. Such a great sacrifice it was for the Dixon family to give over their home, to help the cause, only to return and find it in such disrepair.

She heard the sound of the doors opening and stood transfixed as she waited. Her throat was dry her head spinning her fear rampant, her heart pounding.

A man appeared.

She whispered, "John."

John bounded into the room carrying a large bouquet he picked especially for his bride. He did not notice the outline of the figure across the room. He only had eyes for his beloved.

Seeing his joy made her heart race.

He ran to Emma and exclaimed in his perfectly pitched voice that she adored, "Emma dear wife, I have missed you so." In his handsome face, she saw truest love. "Only two days seemed like a lifetime." He noted the blue hydrangea blooms, "perfection from the garden for you," he handed her the flowers. "For the perfection of you, in God's creation."

He smiled at her, his teeth perfect and dazzling, the message behind them sensual and desirous.

"John, darling. I missed you, too."

Then he captured her in his arms.

With that touch she trembled as the realization hit of all she might lose over the exposure of his true identity. She might lose him. The fear of his reaction, of losing his overflowing love after he learned she knew of his deed was frightening. Courage fled. Her breath became labored, her hands ice cold.

John leaned into his wife and asked in his most concerned voice, "Emma, what is it? Are you well? The trip must have been difficult. Come dear, sit and rest."

He led her over to the closest wing chair when Emma suddenly stopped.

"John, we are not alone. I have brought someone back with me."

Asia stood by the window across the great parlor, too anxious to move. The tone and tenor of the man was so hauntingly familiar, her knees quivered in anticipation.

"My God," she whispered, "It sounds just like John."

John suddenly turned, jerking his head around toward the silhouette of a female standing there watching him. Asia felt frozen to the spot by the intensity of his gaze.

John cleared his throat, unhappy with the intrusion upon his reunion with his beautiful wife. "Emma, I did not realize you were bringing your friend back to for a visit."

From where she stood by the curtainless window, Asia realized the bright sunlight prevented him from seeing her face. She was just a dark outline, in his eyes. But as his penetrating gaze swept over her Asia saw a small shudder run up his spine. He controlled it well, but she knew him.

This was her John, alive and well.

He knew something was amiss.

Fearful of his reaction, she remained silent.

He addressed Emma, demanding an explanation. "But I thought your purpose to Philadelphia was visiting a dear friend from the hospital who was dying." With authority that only John could wield, he knitted his handsome brow in confusion and inquired, "Who is it then you have brought with you?"

Emma simply said, "My friend."

Shaking and trembling violently, Asia felt drawn toward his familiar voice. Even she, who knew him so well, was powerless to resist being near John. From the time of their childhood, his natural charisma was soothing and safe to her. She turned to face him fully and walked across the room.

Asia knew with each step closer, the familiarity of the stranger came into view.

She witnessed that shocking moment of recognition. His skin blanched and his eyes grew wide. He blinked, as if in disbelief. His head shook. No, this was real.

The brother she dearly loved let out a cry of pain and anguish. It was the sound that reminded Asia of a wounded animal. The howl of John's voice resounded in the room. He fell to his knees and covered his face with his hands.

"Asia, no please. It can't be you, it can't."

He rocked back and forth on this knees the disbelief of seeing her was a deviant trick of fate. Emma's blue eyes were wide. She looked ready to cry over her husband's distraught reaction. The young wife stepped away from both brother and sister as the unbelievable was unfolding for all of them.

Asia knelt in front of John. She placed her hands over his and gently pulled them down as to see his face. Her heart leapt with joy at knowing he really was alive, even while tears streamed down his face in disbelief of what he was seeing.

He shook his head, "No no, this cannot be. No no!"

Asia remained silent as she reached into the collar of her dress and pulled the locket from its hiding place. John saw the picture of himself, the locket he had hung over her baby's bed, was now around her neck.

She reached then to touch his face, stroking her fingers lovingly across his perfect skin. No longer trembling, she smiled carefully and waited as he too reached into his shirt and pulled out the gold medal she gave him when he was injured during one of his performances and the family thought he might die.

"The Agnus Dei." He whispered through his tears, "The Lamb of God."

"Yes, it kept you safe." Asia finally spoke.

She watched with joy as the sound of her voice brought a light of love to her brother's intense gaze. It made him all the more handsome. She studied his face, drinking in every feature as if seeing him for the first time.

"She was right John, you are alive. Thank God, you are alive!"

He studied Asia's face as well, his dark brows knit in wonder. Together, still touching, they rose from the floor. She couldn't keep her hands off him. Love filled her heart. But her distraught brother was still at a loss. She knew him so well. The sorrow he had suffered, believing they would never meet again was clear in his eyes.

"You are the friend my sweet Emma went to see?"

"Yes."

His hands clasped hers, holding them tight. "How Asia, how has this trick of fate happened? I can't understand." Rapt in her every movement, his dark gaze followed her hands as she reached into her dress pocket and handed him the letter he had written to her when he thought was he lost forever.

Now it was returned to his own hands and she stood in front of him as proof.

John looked awestruck and incredulous to be holding it. "I don't understand."

Asia gave him the kindest smile. His mind was racing so fast, she knew he needed a moment to catch up. "Where was this letter, John?"

"It was in my red diary, along with new clippings and," he hesitated as she placed the leather book in his hands, returning it to its rightful owner. He continued in wide-eyed amazement, "This is the diary I had with me. I spent hours writing in while with Davey Herold in the swamps and in the forests, and boat crossings with only a faint candle and compass to guide us. For twelve days I was hunted by the Government with every man's hand against me, dear sister. All for the cause for my beloved South and a mission I had so loftily agreed to complete," his head shook in dismay and regret, "As with that belief burning inside my heart, the surrender of General Lee and the burning of Richmond, it all found inside me the perfect storm to act on their behalf."

"Yes," she gently replied, "I read it. How did you escape death, dear brother?"

Still gripping the book and letter, he visibly relaxed, relieved she did not judge his crimes, but only cared for his safety.

"The last entry was not finished, for it was interrupted by fellow sympathizer James W. Boyd who told me the Sixteenth New York Cavalry were closing in and he was sent to take my place in the barn. It was not a moment too soon. I made haste through the broken slats in the back of the barn and ran into the forest."

He drew a deep breath, the color returning to his face as he seemed to accept that his sister still loved him. Asia felt relieved. His initial shocked outburst was over. They were reunited, as it should be.

"I hid in the brush but from there I saw everything. Davey Herold was screaming to surrender. I heard the shot that felled Boyd. All the while Davey was screaming, 'it's not Booth, it's not Booth.' The Cavalry did not listen. Boyd was part of the conspiracy; he was one of those late night visitors to your home in Philadelphia. I kept those meetings secret as not to involve you, dear sister."

"And yet, in the aftermath, I knew."

Taking her in with a look of warm affection, John glanced to Asia's belly, flat now since the birth of her child. Her brother eyed this with a smile, "I trust the birth went well. Pray, tell me of the boys and of your new arrival. Do I have a new pretty niece or another clever tyke to rumble with?"

For the first time John released a playful smile.

It made Asia feel deeply loved. "I had another boy, a beautiful boy born May 8, with black hair and your black eyelashes that curl up at the ends."

"Our Booth traits are strong,"

"Yes, he is a joy to my heart and adored. I left all the boys with Mrs. McLeary and a wet nurse for the baby. I named him Joseph after our youngest brother."

"Ah yes." John shrugged. "It was probably best for the child and our family for him not to be named after their wild brained Uncle."

John chuckled at that name. The "wild brained boy" was older brother's Edwin's doing, a family name that seemed to stick with John's impulsive and intense nature.

Asia, leaned into John, sharing her secret.

"Well actually I named him John Joseph. The boys knew if they had a brother I would name him John, no matter what. They are sworn to secrecy," she gave a light chuckle at her children's open nature, "so of course it is so regularly discussed. I believe Jacob felt compelled to tell your sweet Emma the moment they met. No secret is safe in my household," she tucked her chin and frowned at her brother, "Except for your secret, of course. Your secret will be forever safe with me."

John felt amazed.

Needing to tell Asia everything, he hurried to share the events that kept him alive. They sat together on the couch. His bewilderment that Asia was actually here, listening and holding his hand still captivating his thoughts.

He explained how the original plan had been to capture the President and hold him for prisoner exchange. Then when hearing Lincoln wanted to give the freed slaves black citizenship, the plan changed. The President had to die. All the Southern supporters decreed it. Without asking forgiveness for his actions, taking full responsibility, John told Asia how he was cajoled into committing the murderous act, how he felt the death would vindicate the thousands of brave boys in Northern prisons and how it was right to protect the Southern way of life.

"Perhaps they should have left me to die in that barn," he solemnly confessed, "although I was saved from the barn burning, the life I have now ignites the burning within my soul for the heinous crime I committed. Killing Lincoln changed nothing. I was mad to believe it would. Now I must live the rest of my life in masquerade, using another's name to survive."

"This is your only choice, John. I would rather you live as another man than to have you dead." Asia's understanding and compassion were a gift. Telling her the truth was freeing. John felt the great sorrow from deep inside his heart disappear. He shook his head in regret, looking at his long-lost sister and then at his beautiful wife.

"The diary," he sighed, "the diary. I had thought of it when I woke up from the delirium of malaria, only to see the sweet and loving face of Emma there, willing me to live. Although I had no right to live, no right to love her, because of her devotion I thought perhaps I could embrace this second chance."

"The Government had their man and buried the truth with him. My only evidence against me was the diary. I feared I would soon be exposed. But I had no family, credentials and no comrades to speak of. I thought it fell out of my pocket. How did you come by this Asia?"

Asia only looked at his lovely wife.

John noticed her face was pale and she could see Emma was trembling. Her flowers lay scattered across the floor where her shaking hands dropped them.

"John, it was me," she quietly confessed. "I found the letter and brought it to her."

"You? Emma, you had my diary, all this time?"

She nodded. The truth of her deception weighed heavy in the air. For a moment, confusion and anger flashed through him. John rose to his feet, the disbelief in him steadying his anger until he heard her explanation.

Emma faced him with her head tilted upwards to look into his eyes. He saw courage there in her face, but great depths of love too. "John, yes it is true. I found the diary when you were delirious with fever. I had hoped to find something in your uniform to help explain your vague explanations of your life. Don't you see, I was falling in love with a man with no past, who only offered a present that was mysterious and compelling."

He wasn't sure how this made him feel.

"Doctor Bradley said Old Sam was out by the wood pile burning uniforms as to prevent the spread of lice and vile disease. I saw the name Singer on the sleeve. Old Sam retrieved it. The diary was inside. I saw all the news clippings, the wanted posters and the carte de visite. I grabbed them and told Old Sam to say nothing. It took me days to open the diary. I heard rumblings and suspicions around the hospital from people who kept saying how much you looked like the President's' assassin. Until I saw the letter to Asia, I dismissed it. But then, I knew the truth."

"Yet you agreed to marry me?"

"Yes, I did. I knew the man I married was really John Wilkes Booth not John Singer. I also knew I had to go to Philadelphia to convince Asia to see you. Your family deserved to know you were alive. I saw the sorrow you carried in your heart. It tore at mine. I brought her here John, not only as a reunion, but to help find a way to get you to leave the country. I felt the love between the both of you in the letter you wrote. Yes, I risked much in bringing her here, for if I were caught I surely would be accused of treason. But I risked more by not trying to enlist her help in your escape."

He was stunned.

For once in his life, he had no words.

"It is too dangerous for you to be here," his intelligent wife calmly explained. "I fear there are those who do not believe your disguise, who feel you must pay for your deadly actions. So in aiding you, dear husband, I am now as culpable as if I had pulled the derringer myself that night."

John steadied his voice as he realized what Emma had done. How could she put herself in harm's way like this? Didn't she understand how much her safety meant to him?

"Emma, you are the most precious, most perfect person to me. I am humbled by your devotion and love. You were so innocent of all the evil I had wrought. I wanted it to stay that way, never wanted you to know the truth of my identity. Because yes, now you are helping me hide, with clear knowledge. You are liable and responsible in the Government's eyes, as you are now aiding me in my destiny."

He shook his head.

"This is nothing I would have wanted for you, ever."

She stood firm, "I chose in clear conscience. My love for you is true. Is truth not better than believing a lie?"

Her reasoning was frustrating. But Emma, oh his sweet Emma was now in the worst kind of danger. "I hid the truth from you to keep you safe. You must understand that I lied to you for that very reason and that reason only."

John's anger began to rise, "Why is it you could not tell me you knew who I truly was when you found my diary, and read the letter to Asia? Even after our marriage you lied again to bring Asia here, knowing full well once I saw her, I would know the truth."

"Yes all you have said is true. I could have kept quiet about my discovery, and never travelled to find Asia. Yes, I could have stayed silent, but it was my love for you, and the desire to enlist her help in getting you to leave the country that drove me. She leaned in closer to her husband, "There are those who are plotting against you, John. Men who doubt your false identity, who would want you dead."

"You mean, Doctor Bradley."

"Yes. He is dangerous. I cannot risk your life. You have become my world. I must preserve it, all costs. It was for this reason I never revealed my knowledge of who you really are and chose instead to go to Asia's house and asked her to come."

Asia could stand it no longer as she ran to her brother's side.

"John please listen to her. Emma acted out of pure love. You are in danger. You must leave the country. Brothers Edwin and Junius were in prison, arrested with my husband John. It happened one day after the assassination. They were swept up by the Government simply for having the name Booth and being married to one. I had a Federal guard in my house for several weeks. Finally he was dismissed when they decided I posed no threat. The men are still being held at the Old Federal penitentiary in Washington DC. I received word from Edwin just before I left Philadelphia, the inquisition was over and they were being released soon. John, I won't lie to you. You must know what your act has done to our family. Mother is bereft that her favorite child committed such a crime and cries at the thought you were murdered at Garrett's Farm. I must tell Edwin and Junius. They will help you, we all will."

John stared at Asia, his black eyes drinking in the sight of her.

"And what of your husband?"

The pain of her marriage felt like a stake through her heart. "Ever since that fateful night, he has distanced himself from all Booth's. The name which gave him entry into the theatrical world has become the name most hated to him. You were right about him. He wanders around town without a thought for his wife or children."

She lowered her head in hurt, shaking it as if to dispel the pain that welled up inside her.

John reached to touch her arm, compassion in his face. She clearly recalled his warning not to marry Clarke that the Booth name was dowry enough and to be careful of those who would use it to advance their own destiny. Painfully, her brother had been right.

"Yes, I remember what I said to you, but I also saw the love in your eyes for him nonetheless."

"I love too easily, dearest John," she admitted, "look how deeply I love you."

His mouth curved in that clever smile that had often graced his handsome face in easier and gentler times. "As I love you, Asia. I can't believe I am seeing you again. I never thought to see my family again. I thought it best they think I am dead, for the crime I committed against man is too great for forgiveness."

She nodded, not forgiving the crime, but loving the man just the same. His survival was a miracle. Surely life had plans for him yet. They had to keep him safe.

"John, we must act quickly. Emma has explained there are those who would want you dead, even while you live as John Singer for suspicion breeds hate. Hiding in plain sight will not work. We can't risk that. Our brothers will help us, I am sure of it. They love you. Edwin told me he was at home in New York when the news broke the newsboys out on the streets bombarded him by the news. He said his heart broke for the deed committed by his Johnny. And mother screamed and fell to her knees crying out My bright beautiful boy, my boy Absalom; over and over again."

Aisa watched him swallow the guilt for the pain he had caused his loved ones. The truth was not kind, but his crime had brought hardship to all. He needed to see it.

"The Federals came and pulled Edwin out into the street, convinced he was guilty just because of the Booth name, and they came to my house too John, came and pulled the house apart, the boys crying too as they dragged off their father, his guilt only because he married a Booth."

"The boys saw their father dragged out of the house?"

"Yes, John."

"And they saw the Government search their house for evidence of a family conspiracy?"

"Yes, Jacob kept asking why is everyone mad at Uncle John?"

It angered him, knowing his innocent nephews witnessed such a scene. "Who plots against me, without knowledge of who I truly am?"

"Doctor Bradley is convinced you are not John Singer," Emma explained, finally speaking again. "but rather by some twist of fate, John Wilkes Booth. He is descending into madness. My fear is real and true. His unrequited love drives him. He intends to avenge his loss. He said it the day we left for Richmond."

"This is why you were upset when we left the hospital?"

She nodded. "He knows about the diary. Old Sam promised his silence but his love and devotion is too great for Doctor Bradley. He told him I had the diary. Right before we left Henry cornered me. He was convinced of your deception and mine as well. He rants to anyone who will listen. His ranting could cause the wrath of the Government to fall not only upon him for treason, but upon us as well."

Her husband was not convinced.

His jaw was tight and Emma knew he was angry.

"So what if he rants? What proof is there? He tried to trick me one morning as I sat outside the hospital ward, by calling me Booth. I told him he was sadly mistaken and laughed at his rantings. We have the diary. The ravings of an insane Doctor who never saw the diary, going on blind faith of the words of his uneducated black hospital orderly will hold no weight, none whatsoever."

"John, you don't understand. I was standing there with Sam when all the news clippings and posters and carte de visite fell out from the diary. You see the broken left leg, your cryptic past, and having no regiment to speak of only added to this suspicion."

John shook his head, "there may be a few men who might be unlucky enough to resemble the notorious John Wilkes Booth," he insisted, saying his own name with a tone of disdain. "The Doctor's rantings will certainly be the end of him. He spews against the government who claims they have their murderer. It won't be long before the long arm of the law reaches out to swat dear Doctor Bradley. If this madman is the cause of your fear for my life, then I have no fear of him. The good Doctor's oath to save lives will overtake any desire he has to hunt me down."

"No, it goes further than that." Emma argued, "He cannot accept it is you I love, that I never thought of him as anything more than a family friend. He's still convinced he is the better man. That if you were gone I would see that fact and would fall in love with him and marry."

John was listening now.

"The years of unspeakable deaths and dying from the war have addled his mind, the pain of unrequited love pressing him further into an abyss of madness. We must fear him, dear husband. Who knows what anyone is capable of when one's heart and mind are tortured."

"Yes, I too know the pain of a tortured heart and mind. I have felt the agony of a mind torn, the madness that comes from what I thought was a righteous act, but became an abhorrent one. They knew I was working as a Confederate spy and blockade runner. I truly believed the President was a tyrant and the South would be better off with him."

"Right and wrong became twisted inside," she softly summarized.

"Yes, very. And the torture continued for me both physically and emotionally while on the run from Washington that night, even after fellow Confederate sympathizer Doctor Samuel Mudd set my broken leg. I spent four days in the Zehiah Swamps in Charles County, Maryland with Davey Herold. It is a most ghoulish and miserable place. I was cold, wet and in pain. Then another member Thomas Jones aided us with food and the news accounts of my deed. I could not believe what I was reading, the loss of the beloved President, at the hands of a tyrant."

He spat the word, hatred darkening his voice.

"Me a tyrant!" He was exasperated by the claim, "It was there I wrote the letter to Asia, fearing I neared my end. Finally we crossed the Rappahannock River to Port Royal, guided by a small group of former Confederate soldiers to Garrett's Farm, and now you know the rest."

Emma reached out to stroke the lightly tanned cheek of her husband, "Yes my darling, I know the rest. Yet it truly matters not, for my love for you will never be broken. Never in my life have I felt this strongly or gone against all principals I was brought up to believe, but all I see is you and you must go on, John. We will help you leave this country, with or without me."

The pain of that possibility bowed her over with fear.

"Whatever do you mean, with or without you?" His eyes widened, "I will never leave you behind dear wife, never, for to be without you would be like certain death to me."

Emma stroked his cheek and moved closer to her husband, Asia stood back from the newly married couple who were obviously deeply in love and stayed silent. "John, you think I want to be parted from you? Never. The two days away to see Asia was like an eternity to me. But we must secure your safe passage immediately. I can't risk losing you. I will follow after we know you are safely hidden away."

He kissed her lightly on the lips, knowing she was right, that she had risked much in bringing Asia to him, so that his family could help secure his passage. She remained selfless of her own happiness, thinking only of him.

He owed her everything.

"Aye my sweet dearest Emma," he murmured, "For you and for my family, and my dear and equally brave sister Asia, I will do as you ask of me."

Asia promptly decided, "We must waste no time."

Everyone seemed to agree.

"I will travel back to Philadelphia forthwith. My husband and our brothers must have now arrived home from jail. I will convince Edwin and Junius to stay a few days before heading back to New York. I will speak to our brothers alone. I wish I could take you back with me so they can see you alive as I have!"

"It is impossible. At least you came. For that, I am grateful."

"Dearest John, we love you and we will take care of you and Emma. To the world it will appear you perished in that barn at Garrett's Farm. Only your family and dear wife will know otherwise."

John stared at his sister, so much more beautiful since becoming a mother, a fact that still astounded him even after giving birth to three beautiful boys. He eyed the locket around her neck, the picture of him.

"Dearest sister, is of a great risk that you came. You too are now accountable in this family tragedy of my making. Yes, I saw your worry on your face when I came to your house late at night, sleeping on the couch, and meeting with those who believed in the cause. I wanted you never to be touched by my egregious crime. Now here you are, risking much again to help aid me. I don't know how to accept what you are doing for me."

"John, please let us help you leave the country. We will help take care of Emma until we can secure her passage too."

He picked up Asia's hand and kissed it, "Thank you."

Emma moved closer to both brother and sister, addressing her sister-in-law, "Asia, may I persuade you to take rest now? Please let me see to your comfort as it has been a long few days."

Asia looked at her beautiful sister-in-law, who was so brave and selfless to travel alone to reunite her with John. There was nothing she would ever deny her. "I appreciate that, Emma. Thank you."

She went to John and held his face in her hands.

"You are alive and you will stay alive."

She kissed his cheek. They held each other, holding on as if each moment together would never be enough.

Emma motioned Asia to follow her upstairs after she called for the houseman Charles to bring Asia's small reticule of possessions. They walked the great winding staircase toward the second-floor guest bedroom.

The great Dixon house seemed even more silent as Asia realized Emma's mother and little sister Abby were still away having taken the coach to visit upon less fortunate neighbors and friends with food and the like to share.

They were good people.

Asia walked behind Charles, his demeanor of the greatest reserve, his clothes showing signs of wear like all of those who survived the onslaught of this great civil war.

She marveled at the curving stone staircase as she climbed up. The home was elegant, in its former glory. In time it would be again. The Dixon's had lost much to the soldiers who had occupied their home.

The once beautiful wall covering had scenes of the French countryside, but it was faded and gashed in areas. Outlines of where artwork had hung stood out like large empty rectangles upon the wall, now blank and empty.

Charles opened the guest room door.

"Here you are, Madam."

The women followed him inside. The four poster bed was devoid of the canopy top, the bed covering was worn but clean in a country blue pattern. The wall papering matched the same French blue, yet great portions of it had faded from the sun, from the soldiers never having had drawn the drapes.

Asia looked at the large ceiling to floor windows, two of them of either side of a grey marble fireplace, noticing the windows remained without covering. On closer inspection the marble was actually white, this too showing signs of hard use and neglect.

It would take time to repair all the misuse the Dixon's suffered while allowing the army use of their home. At least they had a home.

Most in Richmond did not.

Emma excused Charles, leaving them alone. "I hope you find comfort here, for you must rest. Later there will be time for you to travel back to Philadelphia. I can't imagine your sacrifice, dear Asia, in coming here and leaving your small boys behind and your beautiful infant son John. There are dangers I have now exposed you too, but I had to tell his family he was alive. It was the right thing to do."

"Finding my brother John happy with you and healthy is worthwhile. With all the breath I have, promise to help him leave the country and live safely. These are perilous times, but those we love become more precious to us, especially now."

"Yes," Emma agreed, "My mother and Abby are very precious, indeed."

"I am bursting with the news of our John, yet I know of the grave dangers. We must work to find him safe passage, perhaps the Far East would be far enough from the perils of the United States."

Emma touched her cheek gently and bowed slightly to her new found in law, "God Bless you, Asia. Rest well. I will instruct Charles to bring your dinner upstairs later, to give you as much rest as possible."

Asia felt exhausted and nodded in agreement. After Emma existed the room she sat upon the bed, leaned down on the pillows and fell quickly asleep.

Emma closed the door and made her way down the hallway to her bedroom, making no sounds as her footsteps were silenced by the faded red Brussels carpet runner that spanned the great length of the second floor.

She opened the door and saw John standing across the room, his eyes staring at her as she entered, black and deep.

Whatever he felt, he hid it well.

That gaze was fathomless.

He walked towards her slowly, his ebony stare never leaving her face. She shivered recalling the first time those eyes focused upon her.

"You knew all along Emma, you knew," he snapped. "Now you are part of this murderous act, by knowing who I am and aiding in my lies. Why did you not admit you knew my true identity, rather than risk everything to bring Asia here?"

"Because I love you."

"And I love you, but this risk is too great. I don't deserve it."

Emma kindly smiled, realizing the reason for his anger.

He was furious at himself.

His horrific deed endangered them all.

"Dearest John, from the moment they brought you to the hospital and our gazes met, I knew I am only yours. Everything about you drew me. The depth of my love for you holds no explanation."

He let out a deep sigh. Confusion and anger left his eyes.

"After I found the diary I was bereft and yes frightened, as well. Yet upon reading your letter to Asia, I knew your heart was kind and good. The picture of hate that was spread by the government was wrong, for it was spread without truly knowing the man who loves his family, nephews, and me."

"So you chose silence."

"Yes. Nonetheless, those around us at the hospital questioned your true identity. I saw this become more of a dangerous threat with each passing day. I married you knowing you not as John Singer, but as John Wilkes Booth.

Saying his name aloud felt surreal.

"I did that fully intending to bring Asia here to reunite with you. My love for you and your safety was and is, all I could think about. For all that, yes I have risked in loving you and now being complicit for the rest of our days. I do it of my own free will."

"My dearest Emma, you are a gift that heaven has sent." He reached to take her in his arms, but she stepped back, needing answers.

"There but one thing that I have not dared to ask you," she looked him square in the face, hoping he would search her eyes in yearning to know, "yet I must ask because the questions rip at my heart until I hear it from you, dear husband."

John steadied himself.

"In your diary were five female carte de visite."

His skin paled. His jaw remained firm and his stance was tight.

"Asia guessed four were actresses you worked with."

He nodded, affirming the guess.

"But one young woman was Lucy Hale. Asia said you were secretly engaged. Was there someone else you pledged your heart to just before we met? If this is the truth, how could you give your heart so easily? Am I just another carte de visite to be added to your collection?"

Tears welled up in her eyes.

This was difficult, but she must know. Emma feared her heart might shatter as she waited to hear another woman's name cross his sensuous lips.

"After all that you have done for me, from the time you saved my life and made me want to live, if only for you, to the risk you assumed by reuniting me with Asia; it is the knowledge of a prior love that is your greatest fear?"

"Yes."

John reached over to Emma and wiped the tears that were falling and held her cheek in his hand, caressing it gently.

"A woman's heart is deep, and yours, my love is a miracle."

He reached his hand and placed it on the nape of her neck, all at once loosening the pins that held her silken strands of her golden hair.

Emma felt the stirring within her as he touched her knowing she was helpless to his desires.

"Dearest Emma, fear not of anyone before you, for there is none who can compare with you. I saw you at the hospital and knew at that moment I had to have you, not as a fleeting affair, but as my one true love. I would awaken from delirium to see you by my bedside, willing me to live and comforting me."

"You are the greatest gift, to me. My second chance my reason for living. How could anyone else compare? Ease your mind, dear wife, for perhaps I did fancy myself in love for a time and did in fact become engaged, but do you really think any woman can compare to you?"

Emma stood riveted as John moved closer to his bride.

He leaned in gently and kissed her, tender at first, then as always was the need to be together soon had them both wanting more. There were no words, just naked desire.

Emma felt the buttons on the back of her dress slowly and deliberately unloosen. John skillfully moved her closer to their bed as the dress dropped from her slim supple body. It fell to the floor like in a soft rippling puddle as he lifted her and then carried her to their bed to consummate their love once more.

She needed this, needed his hands upon her soft and desirous body, knowing it was her and her alone would drive him to feel such fine pleasures. He leaned over her, unfastening the chemise with delft precision, until her perfectly supple and lush curves were exposed for his taking. He kissed her fully as his passion became inflamed, her waiting full and wanting lips thirsty for the pleasure only he could give.

He kissed her again, toying with the splendid heat until her breathing became labored and deep, taking that as his signal she was ready for his love.

"So beautiful," he whispered, his breath warming her skin. He trailed kisses from her lips to her neck and stopped then at her round and white breasts, savoring the places on her body that only he had ever been allowed to touch. "My Emma, only mine."

Emma threw her head back as she felt the heat of him against her, the weight of his muscular body against hers felt so right. She laced her fingers through his thick jet black hair, pushing it back from his face as the loose thick waves twined within her hands.

She felt herself moving beneath him, awaiting for John to make love to her. She held her breath as his fingers played and caressed across the curves of her silky white skin, pulling her desire into a frenzy that was both beautiful and wild, at the same time.

Emma awaited him.

She could take it no more as she cried to her husband, "please John, make love to me. I need us together. I am aching for you."

With these words he slowly and deliberately nibbled and licked from her lips to her smooth belly.

It was the purest torture.

Emma arched her back and threw her head back, eyes closed as she gave herself to this moment. She felt alive, loved and sinfully hot with passion as John tasted her body until the ache became an explosion of pleasure.

Then, only when her body quivered beneath his, extremely sensitive now from the rush of her climax, John gave himself to her, as gently as his passion would allow.

The union was perfect, unforgettable in intensity. Her magnificently aroused body was moving against him, crying out for more.

John loved her completely, feeling himself within her until he too felt the burning ache of passion smoldering.

He completely gave himself over to her in that moment, loving her deeply, heedless of anything except giving her all of him.

He only stopped for a moment as she reached up and caressed his face and then lifted her head to kiss him greedily, and then said to him breathlessly, "Dearest John, I am forever yours."

John heard her gasp with sublime pleasure as she cried out his name as she once again felt the tightening of muscles within her, at the same time he too released, pulling on her slim hips to complete the satisfaction of their love.

She reached to kiss him fully, her tongue playing havoc within his mouth, as they rode out the wildly intimate moment together.

They were as one, body and souls.

Their passions quelled for the moment, John moved from his wife, the both of them breathing deeply and quietly. He pulled Emma next to him beneath the covers and laid her head on his chest, her long blond hair falling about them. "Emma darling, my love for you overwhelms me, at times. You are my dear wife. Ease your mind of the past. Know that nothing will ever come between us."

She lifted her head to face him and was once again riveted by his beauty.

"I will never again ask. You chose me and it is I who have you now."

With that said, she pulled her legs over his naked hips and gently begin to move back and forth on top of him, slowly building up his passion once again.

Emma lifted herself up from his hips and began to caress him.

"Are you sure?"

She said nothing as she continued to caress him.

She straddled him, keeping him flat on the bed. He then tried to sit up and pull her down, but Emma stopped him.

In this moment, she was in charge.

She knew what she wanted and gave herself over to him. Her head tossed back in pleasure, sighing with passion as she imprisoned him with her love. John pulled her hips and gave himself into her, all the while Emma not letting him raise up from his prone position.

Emma smiled slyly. "You have taught me well, dear husband."

"Indeed, I have."

When they were both satisfied, she smiled then and slid beside him as they held each other, both slaves to the passions they ignited in one another, not knowing how long they would be together, for they both knew it would soon be time for him to leave.

In the room down the long hallway from John and Emma's, later that afternoon Asia awoke from her deep slumber.

She rose up from the four poster bed and walked over to the window.

From her second story height she could see the burned-out buildings that littered the City of Richmond. There were only a few scattered homes not wholly burned. Most were brutally reduced to only the outlines of chimneys that survived the onslaught as the residents themselves set fires to leave nothing for the advancing Union at the end of the war.

She ran her hand over her forehead trying to smooth her wrinkled brow from the impossible thoughts that assailed her.

John is alive, he is alive, and he is going to stay alive.

She needed make haste back to Philadelphia and speak to brothers Edwin, and Junius. The heinous act committed by John would not defeat the Booth family. As a family they would rise above this somehow, reclaim their good name and go on.

Asia remembered her mother's words, "*My boy my dear boy, Absalom.*" This was from the Bible as Absalom was the third son of King David, the handsomest man in the kingdom who met an untimely and tragic end.

John was also the third son, the handsomest man in America, but whose tragic end was not in death, but for the life he was spared.

She rang for Charles to bring dinner to her room and began to make plans to leave the next morning. There is no time to waste.

Impending danger loomed much too close.

CHAPTER TWENTY-THREE

Some people just need killin'
~~ Doctor Henry Bradley

Doctor Bradley awoke earlier than usual the next day. He opened the door to his room and peered into the parlor, squinting his eyes until they rested on the sleeping form of Old Sam. Doctor Hendrix had relieved him of his duties for a few days and asked Old Sam to stay and watch over him.

"It's such utter nonsense," muttered Henry.

All those poor soldiers in need of care and Doctor Hendrix pulls him off rotation to rest. He returned to his room, feeling like a prisoner.

"Why I feel fine," he declared to no one at all, arms waving in wild motions. "I barely need to eat and sleep. So what if I am not hungry, for this and for my belief that animal John Singer is really Booth and is by now certainly married to my Emma," he let out a pained outcry "I have been deemed in need of rest and that I am overwrought with exhaustion!"

He paced in his small room back and forth, from corner to corner, stopping for a moment at the small chest of drawers on the far wall nearest the window. Henry opened the last drawer, rummaging through the pile of well-worn clothes, until his hand felt the hard cold piece of metal.

Smiling, he pulled it out and reveled in the perfection of the small derringer. He drew in several deep breaths to curb his growing excitement as he extended the gun out from his hand and pointed it at the window. He dry fired the weapon.

It was time to find his real target, John Singer.

Henry remembered the words of the Confederate Sergeant Beauregard Jackson, who gave him the gun and the ease at which he said them as they parted, that 'some people just need killin'."

"It was like he had read my mind," declared the Doctor, feeling triumphant, invincible, and strong, "just like he read my mind."

Henry dressed quickly and quietly, packing a change of clothes in a soft bag, all the while scattering pieces of clothing on the floor as he made haste.

He must leave, right now.

Henry opened the window above the chest of drawers. It was too high to simply step out of. Using the chair from his desk, he climbed up and slid out through the window.

His shoes met the ground outside and the Doctor grinned.

He crept quietly around the far side of the hospital to find a horse. The stables would be quiet, holding only a few horses tended by the stable boy, Issac. While opening the door to the stables, a few of the horses whinnied and lowered their heads over the paddock doors when Henry came past them.

He made his way to a small pallet on the floor next to the tack room, and saw the small boy Isaac sleeping peacefully. He crept over to him and shook him old gently, "Isaac, wake up!"

The boy started, shocked into wakefulness to see Doctor Bradley had come into the stables, a place he never came before. The young boy sprang up from the pallet, his eyes wide and shiny in the pre-dawn hour.

"I's awake now Doc, what is it you needin' so early?"

Henry looked at the boy with a steely gaze.

"Isaac, I need you to saddle a horse for me the swiftest one here and you must do this quickly and quietly my boy."

The boy's eyes widened.

He shook his head. "The fastest one here is the one that belongs to Doctor Hendrix."

"It's ok my boy, just do it, we don't want to wake Doctor Hendrix, now do we? Beside I'll be back by tomorrow night most certain, and it is only for such a short time. He is my friend. He won't mind boy, he won't mind."

He looked into the Doctor's eyes and shivered with fear, even in the early morning heat. Isaac ran to the paddock where Doctor Hendrix kept his prized colt, Shiloh. The black colt with a star spot between his eyes whinnied and stamped the ground with nervous energy as Isaac approached.

"See here," the boy instructed as he led the horse from the secure paddock, "this horse got some spirit in him. Go easy on him, Shiloh could bolt from under ya'."

Henry nodded curtly at the advice and began to saddle and bridle the beautiful black horse for their journey.

He stood close to his head and stroked the horse, murmuring, "Easy boy, easy boy, be swift and sure for me today, for today is the day we avenge what is rightfully mine. Be swift boy, be swift. Bring me to Richmond quickly so I can eliminate him."

His words were for the horse, but the young boy heard too.

Isaac held the bridle to keep the saddled horse standing still while the Doctor hoisted himself up and grabbed the reigns, flung his bag over one side of the saddle. Isaac stood motionless as the Doctor spurred the anxious colt and they flew out of the stable in a wild pounding gallop.

The wide-eyed boy immediately ran to wake the good Doctor Hendrix.

Doctor Bradley had to be stopped.

Isaac pounded on the door, "Doc Hendrix, open up. I need your help." He kept on pounding until he saw the lamp light in the far window of the house. He stepped back, waiting for the door to open.

"Why Isaac, what emergency brings you to the door at this hour? It is barely sunrise." Wrapped in a robe, he was disheveled and stunned, but the physician swung the door wider, inviting the boy inside. "Well speak up boy, what say you?"

Isaac followed the Doctor into his quarters and waited until he closed the door behind him before he spoke.

"Doc, it's Doc Bradley, he done come into the stables, he had with him a small bag, he insisted on saddling up Shiloh and off he went! Said he would be back tomorrow night. I told him Shiloh was your horse, but he just said he would bring him back. I don't know Doc, there's sumptin just ain't right. He had this look in his eyes, crazy wild, done turned my blood cold it did, done turn my blood cold."

"Isaac, where he was going?"

"Well I heard him mumble sumptin about Shiloh being swift to take him to Richmond. Don't know why." Then he recalled, "Ain't that where Miss Emma and Massa John went?"

The Doctor stood riveted as the boy recounted everything that had just transpired in the barn. "Isaac, wait here I will get dressed. We must awaken Old Sam. He and I will go to Emma and John's to stop Doctor Bradley. I only hope it's not too late."

"Yassa, I sure hope so too."

The colt was skittish just as the stable boy had warned. Henry galloped at a frantic pace. He hoped to ride fifty miles today, rest at the halfway point of Fredericksburg and then continue the next day until he arrived at Emma's.

His mind was now battered and his soul was broken hearted as he again and again recounted Emma's leaving the hospital and their final conversation as she left with her fiancé.

He saw her face in his mind's eye. She was perfectly beautiful with long silken golden hair, hair he yearned to touch and stroke. That slim yet curvy body he ached to claim as his own.

Yet she betrayed him.

She chose to lay with this criminal before marriage.

At the hospital he slept just a few doors away night after night. He waited three years for her to knock on his door late at night. He always believed she would see his fine qualities.

He is the better man. And to think she gave her heart and perfection to this man, this imposter.

The murderer John Wilkes Booth.

Worse, she knew of his true identity and pretended his name was John Singer.

Doctor Bradley was convinced something happened in that barn at Garrett's Farm, and the Government is covering up the fact that they got the wrong man.

"What the Government failed to do right the first time, I am compelled to finish now." With that lingering thought, the Doctor spurred the colt and raced along the road to Fredericksburg.

Asia awoke just after dawn, for although she enjoyed a restful and deep sleep the knowledge of John being alive and the need to tell Edwin and Junius was all-consuming to her, not to mention the ache of missing her infant son she left and her two small boys.

She made her toilette quickly, twisting her hair in the traditional large braided knots on either side of her head. She packed her bag and left it waiting on the velveteen chair nearest the bed. She ran her hand over the side of the chair. The white cushions were hopelessly stained to gray, thinking once again of the faded glory of this magnificent house.

It would be fine and lovely again.

Her John would make sure of it.

She then walked down the marble staircase, her footsteps echoing throughout the house. At the bottom step, there she encountered Charles.

"I trust you rested well. It is very early, madam. May I assist you?"

"Good morning Charles, I am preparing to leave right after breakfast. I was looking for Miss Emma and Mr. John. Are they perhaps up at such an early hour?"

The tall elegant houseman bowed slightly at the waist to Asia.

"Come this way, ma'dam."

She followed him past the impressive foyer and further past the expansive parlor where just yesterday she learned of John being alive. Her heart began to beat faster, again realizing the danger of this situation, feeling anxious to see the face of her dear brother once more.

The house servant Charles stopped at a set of French doors, ornate and carved from cherry wood.

He slid them open revealing John and Emma, sitting close together at the dining table, holding hands as they spoke, their voice low and intimate. Charles bowed at the waist and took leave of them as Asia made her way over the newlyweds.

Emma inquired, "Asia, it is very early. Have you rested well, were you comfortable?"

"Yes, it was just fine. But I must return to Philadelphia right after breakfast."

"My mother and Abby are returning today. Wouldn't you like to meet them?"

Asia's head shook, "Not this time, Emma. The men will be home now. I must get back to infant John Joseph, not to mention the boys. I miss them. They are my world. They have been so confused about everything. John, they miss and love you so."

John arose from his chair, his white shirt in stark contrast to his rich black hair and dark eyed features.

"My affection for those boys is deep. You must always tell them of my love. Assure them that nothing can change that."

"Of course. They will know you love them. Remember the last time you came to my house? It was so very late. I heard you approach. You were so very troubled. I felt distraught with worry. I asked you not to go South again, for I felt there was something terrible coming that would keep you from me. I knew that night, I would never be happy again until I saw your face. It was true."

"Yes. I should have listened to you."

"And so now here I am, the happiness warm within me again to see you alive. Yet it is paled by the danger you are in, dear brother. My boys adore their Uncle, little Jacob carries that toy horse you brought him constantly. He resembles you in so many ways, it's like seeing you all over again as a young boy, and remembering our times out at Tudor Hall."

John head bowed down as he too remembered his former life; a life lost. This second one must be lived now as another man.

All that came before would never be again.

"Sit and eat dear Asia, I will take you to the depot and I pray that Edwin and Junius will be as forgiving as you when you tell them I am alive."

Asia smiled briefly and nodded her head, "They will dearest Johnny, they most assuredly will."

It was just turning dusk with the coming evening after their long day when John made his way to the stables. He had left Emma inside the great house to rest before dinner. She felt unusually fatigued today, claiming the past few weeks' activity and stress must be catching up to her.

Mrs. Dixon and Abby had recently returned from their trip and were in the library, quietly reading, so he decided to check on the mare he noticed had developed a decisive limp when he watched the carriage arrive home with the ladies.

His departure from Asia at the depot early this morning had been deeply tearful and heartbreaking. He searched Asia's eyes and tried to force a smile through the haze of her tears, trying to reassure her that he would be fine.

Asia would not be convinced.

She feared he was in mortal danger.

Her instincts were usually quite strong and surprisingly accurate. He hoped this time she was wrong.

John sighed.

He tried to shake off the pain of separation from Asia and the fear he felt and uncertainly of his family's reaction of hearing that he was alive. He focused his attention on the old mare, a workhorse that survived the war. He was concerned over the limp, for horses were in great demand and equally scarce.

The old mare was in the stable, leaving her head over the paddock gate and whinnied at the sight of John, "Easy does it there Juniper, easy does it," he cooed to the horse, stepping inside with her, "let me see your sore leg."

John gently touched the animal and stroked her neck, hands smoothing down her body in a trustful motion as he proceeded to bend and lift the right front left leg of the great mare to check the animal's shoe.

As he investigated he noticed a stone wedged in the hoof, causing the horse to favor the leg. "Well now Juniper looks like I can pull this out for you. I'll be right back to fix you up. You'll be good as new."

The horse neighed at John's words and nuzzled closer.

He stroked the horse gently then proceeded to look for the tool in the tack room with all the other gear. He found the steel curved pick that would remove the stone and returned, but Juniper suddenly began to pound the ground with her front legs.

"What is it girl, what has you so spooked?"

John looked around, searching for what could have shaken the animal, surveyed the interior of the stable. He saw nothing.

He again stroked the animal's side to calm her.

John loved animals, especially horses.

From the time as a young man, he enjoyed riding his horse Cola through the deep forest that surrounded his farm. The time on horseback was freeing, as he became an expert rider. Riding was one of his favorite skills to practice, besides acting. Often he combined the two, reciting memorized lines from various plays as he galloped wildly through the heavy blanket of trees.

A time spent preparing himself to follow in his father's and brother's footsteps in the theater was important to continue the famous Booth acting legacy. Standing in the thicket of trees all alone, with only the grass as his stage and birds as an audience, he remembered feeling grand, reciting the great lines of Shakespeare, preparing and honing his voice for the stage, the only witness to his recital was the forest and animals within.

John leaned into the horse feeling the animal finally relax enough he was able to lift the injured hoof and flick free the lodged stone.

"There you go, old girl." He patted the mare on the neck. "In a day or two you'll be good as new."

Stepping out of the paddock and latching the gate to keep the mare inside, the quiet of the moment was broken by the sound that was eerily familiar to him.

It was the click-click sound of a gun being pulled to cock the firing pin.

John slowly turned away from the animal and took a step toward the open stable doorway. He saw the outline of the haggard and shadowy figure of a man standing near the stable doors, his arm extended towards him.

"Who is it, who is there?"

But even as he spoke a chill ran up his spine.

John squinted his eyes, trying to recognize the man, but in that moment the stranger shouted, "Booth! I have you now." The derringer in his hand was pointed directly at him.

"My God," whispered John, as he then recognized him, "Doctor Bradley?"

Henry leaned in, shaking and pointing the derringer at John and shouted out to him, "I should have left you to die when you had malaria. I wasted the last precious drops of quinine on you, a murderer."

John said nothing, but cautiously stepped a safe distance away from the mare he had just helped.

He moved to the center of the stable.

"You are a murderer Booth, and what the Government failed to do I will," Henry raged in a wild dangerous voice.

"Not only will you pay for your crime, but I will take Emma from you, as well. You think you are the better man. But she will see the truth. Once you are gone, she will come to her senses and Emma will be mine. You stole her from me, just as you stole the life of our President."

"But you forget, my name is John Singer."

This solid denial enraged Henry further.

His voice roared, "You can claim all you want that you are this John Singer, but Old Sam told me of the diary that he and Emma found before that uniform was burned."

"He was sadly mistaken."

"No, lies! All you say are lies." He yelled, waving the gun around, but still keeping it aimed at John.

"Emma swore Old Sam to secrecy, but he told me of the wanted posters, the news clippings, and the carte de visite of God knows how many illicit women you kept in your social life. He grew suspicious. Booth, now my innocent Emma is complicit in this cover-up as well. Whether she knew who you are matters not to me now. Once your poisonous charm is extinguished, it will be as if you were murdered in that barn."

He let out a haunting evil laugh, "only I will have the pleasure of killing you. Then I will take my Emma to be my wife."

John held his hand out in a gesture he knew was fruitless, noticing the Doctor was unsteady on his feet, his thin frame even thinner. He was close enough now to view his eyes. The blueness of them was deep and frightening, wide and cold, touched by madness.

His heart lurched as the sound of Emma's lovely voice carried into the stables, drawing nearer as she walked toward the doorway.

"John darling, what is taking so long? Please come into the house. Dinner will be served."

When Henry heard Emma's voice his stance became rigid.

He stepped from the doorway, closer to John. In one swift move he extended his arm and pointed the derringer towards John's head. His words were eerily calm, "So Booth," he grinned with malevolent glee, "how will it feel to be murdered by the same type of gun you murdered the President with, divine justice don't you think?"

"Don't come in here, Emma," he yelled.

It was too late.

As he prepared to pull the trigger, it was Emma's scream that permeated the barn. "Henry, no," she screamed out again as she entered the violent scene, seeing John standing with the gun pointed at his head. "No Henry! No, you must not do this. Please you must stop."

"He is an evil man, Emma. Booth must pay."

"But you are a healer not a killer," she tried to reason. "You save lives, not destroy them. Please don't do this. Don't kill him."

John looked at Emma, the pain and fear of the moment evident on her beautiful face.

He stood still as he begged his wife, "Emma stay back. Please stay back. Go back into the house. I will be ok. Please, you must leave."

Henry, however was enamored by the sight of his beloved.

His gaze grew misty and his mind appeared to wander.

"Emma, remember at your eighteenth birthday and that beautiful blue gown you wore?"

"Ye--yes," she stammered.

The bereft Doctor's expression was a dangerous mixture of joy and delirium. "Oh my precious Emma. That night I held you in my arms we danced in the great parlor of your father's house. You looked so lovely. He promised me you would be mine, that I could court you. Remember that?"

He waited, focused intently upon her face.

"Henry, please stop," was all she could say.

"And after the war broke out and you came to my hospital," he continued, "I thought you would see what a wonderful husband I would make and that after the war we could be together."

"Yes, I know, but..."

She was silenced as his rage was revealed again.

Like flipping a switch he was once again wild and deadly, eyes wide and his voice thundered.

"But this murderer came to our hospital Emma, a liar and a philanderer. God knows how many women he has had," his face twisted in disgust and John noticed the hand holding the gun was shaking.

He had to do something, but the nearness of Henry to Emma and the threat of a bullet from that gun limited his options. If Emma would just leave the barn, once she was safely outside he hoped to overpower Henry. It wouldn't be too difficult.

In his delirium the Doctor looked weak and unsteady.

But John refused to risk his beautiful wife.

"Emma," he begged, "please go inside. For me, please?"

Clearly he chose the wrong words for it infuriated Henry.

"For you, a murderer and a liar?" He scoffed, "You deserve to be with me Emma, for I am the better man, and it is time I show you how. I will now take back what he took from me." He looked at John and shouted, "say your prayers, Booth and prepare to die."

Emma screamed as the Doctor's shaking hand fired the derringer in John's direction, but it was not foreseen by either of the men, Emma ran toward her husband, flinging herself between John and Henry.

The bullet found her, instead.

The air rang with the explosion of the gun and the echo of her scream.

She fell to the ground as the bullet went through her, crumpling up at the feet of her husband.

"Emma!" John screamed as he dropped to his knees to her side, "Emma, no please no."

He tore his white shirt off his body, the gold medal of the Agnus Dei tangling up with it for a moment, but he quickly freed it. He saw the blood oozing from near her shoulder and began to compress the area that was bleeding.

He watched his stark white shirt turn bloody red.

"Emma, Emma my love," he begged, "please don't leave me. You are all that I care about in this life. If not for you and the love I have for you, death would have been welcome. But you made me want to live, as you must live Emma, you must, please."

Her hand weakly reached to touch his face as the life seemed to be draining from her.

"Darling husband," she whispered, I love you."

Her eyes could not stay open.

John steadied himself and cried out, "My God please, please do not take her. Please let her live," he bowed his head in a wash of tears then remembered the medal he had on his neck, the Agnus Dei medal Asia believed saved his life from an almost fatal injury during one of his performances last year.

He had never taken it off since.

He reached behind his neck, unclasped the chain, and placed it around his wife's neck and began to pray.

It was the most heartfelt prayer any man ever uttered. His words became a jumble of begging and pleading with the almighty Heaven's above to save his innocent wife.

John did not think, he just poured out his aching heart.

She was everything good and perfect in life.

Surely the angels would hear his prayer.

He then felt the familiar touch of her hand stroking his cheek, wiping the tears from his distraught face.

"John."

He opened his eyes. She smiled weakly.

He grasped her hand to his cheek and bend low to whisper to her, "Emma, please don't leave me, I love you darlin'. Now and forever, I will love you."

Her eyes fluttered as if fighting to stay awake. But as she drew a breath to speak, her entire body went completely limp and her ice-blue eyes closed.

"Nooo!" John shouted, clutching her lifeless form against his bare chest.

The Doctor stood frozen as the scene unfolded in front of him, the gun still in his hand.

A wave of confusion flooded his senses. He could not process that Emma was shot instead of John. He watched the two of them as if in slow motion, Emma reaching to her husband the shirt pressed against her changing the white cloth to bloody red.

It was unfathomable what he was seeing.

It could not be. This is not happening.

"Oh Emma," he whispered.

The reality of what he had done came to Henry like a cold hand of death that chilled his soul. The woman he loved was dying, yet he stood unmovable and incredulous to the bloodbath.

He was now a murderer too.

He murdered Emma.

All those men he had saved in the war, thousands and thousands. Now in one rash moment of madness and rage, he betrayed everything he knew to murder a man who deserved to be dead.

Yet in a twist of fate that bullet killed the only person who ever truly mattered. She was the only woman he ever loved, or could ever love.

His devotion was eternal.

Henry began to shake.

His mind raced. His instinct to run and tend to her wound was immediate, but the thought of his heinous act was too great to bear.

He listened to John wail and cry, holding the limp body of his bloody wife to his chest. The anguish in that sound cut deep into Henry's fractured mind.

"Nooo!" John cried.

Inside, deep in the brokenness, Doctor Bradley cried too.

Without another lucid thought, only trying to end the abysmal ache inside his heart, Henry reached into his pocket and found another ball to load the Derringer.

He loaded it and pulled back the firing pin, this time not aiming at John.

It was the sound of the discharging gun that John heard when he raised his head at the loud noise. He didn't move from holding Emma as he watched the body of the Doctor fall to the ground in a thud as the bullet pierced through his brain.

John's only concern was Emma. He scooped her up easily.

Ignoring the slight pain in his leg that was still healing, he ran past the body of the Doctor towards the house to find help for his wife, praying that her heart still beat within her beautiful body.

She couldn't be dead. He couldn't accept it.

Even as she lay limp in his arms, he was determined her life must be spared.

As he ran past the courtyard he thought of how his life was made worth living because of the simple pure love that Emma gave him.

She had asked for nothing except his heart.

That love was rare and deep, binding their hearts into one. That love consumed him. And he knew it had consumed her. Together a lifetime of love and passion had been lived and cherished in a just a few weeks. His second chance belonged with her.

It was a life he knew would be not worth living without Emma.

As he ran, he heard the approaching horses galloping hard towards the house. He glanced briefly but continued to charge up the front steps of the great house. He felt enormous relief to see two men rush to his side, recognizing them as the head physician of the hospital in Alexandria and the black giant of the man he knew as Old Sam.

John said nothing as they came upon the still and bloodied body of Emma in her husband's arms. Her dress was stained crimson down her chest and the deadly wound was torn in her shoulder. Her long blonde hair had fallen loose, hanging in a golden bloodied cascade.

Doctor Hendricks already held his black medical bag. Placing two fingers along her neck, all three men were silent.

"Her heart still beats."

Without another word, they followed him into the house.

CHAPTER TWENTY-FOUR

Come back to me Emma, come back to me.

~~ John Wilkes Booth

Mrs. Dixon's screams broke the dead silence of the horrific scene. She and Abby had heard the noise and ran outside. John was shirtless, holding Emma tightly in his arms, running through the house along with two men she had never seen before: a slightly stooped older man carrying a leather medical bag and a large black man who looked worried and scared. They ran beside John as he charged up the grand staircase to their bedroom.

She cried out to her son-in-law, "John what has happened to Emma, what is going on?"

John turned, his handsome face twisted in grief, his black eyes clouded in pain, as his voice remained gentle yet agonized. "I am sorry dear Mother, but there was a terrible accident. Emma has been shot."

Her face contorted in horror, "No, not my beautiful daughter," she breathed, feeling the Mother's love she'd fostered since Emma's birth burn in her chest.

Meeting her strickened gaze, John struggled to confess, "You see," he held Emma's limp body a little tighter, clutching her to his heart, "The bullet was meant for me. I told her to return into the house, but she refused. Emma saw the gun pointed at me and jumped in front of that madman when it went off."

Mrs. Dixon picked up her skirts and ran up the stairs, following John and the worried men into the bedroom.

John then laid Emma's still form on the bed that the young husband and wife shared. The Doctor rushed to tend to the wounded woman, pushing John out of the way.

Seeing her daughter's entire upper body drenched in blood, Mrs. Dixon was prostrate with grief. The Doctor gently removed John's bundled shirt off from the seeping wound, the shirt's white color unrecognizable now, as it had become saturated with the crimson lifeblood of her beautiful daughter.

"No, Emma," she hissed, "not Emma."

Doctor Hendrix suddenly turned to John and Mrs. Dixon, drawing a deep breath, "It's a shoulder wound. I need to probe the path of the bullet to insure it went cleanly through. It will not be an easy sight, Mrs. Dixon. Perhaps you should wait outside while I proceed."

She immediately tried to argue, but the Doctor ignored her pleas. He nodded at the large black man standing at the foot of the bed, his large palm nervously circling around the oak corner bedpost, his ancient and well-worn hat tipped sideways on his graying head. "Old Sam, stay with Mrs. Dixon."

The giant hulking man nodded in agreement, "Yes Sir," he gripped the bedpost so tight his dark skin had actually paled, "You take good care of Miss Emma. She's my friend and a good lady. She don't deserve this bad hurt."

Old Sam turned to the grieving mother. He simply swallowed hard, suddenly realizing he stood uninvited in her home.

"See here now ma'am, this here Doc Hendrix," he gently introduced the man who was already hard at work, using his medical skills to save her bleeding daughter, "We need to give him some room to help our Miss Emma. I knows her from the hospital she done worked at, and this here Doc Hendrix, he done worked there too. We all knows Miss Emma. We love her."

Mrs. Dixon turned as Old Sam walked with her to the door.

She was crying aloud, "I don't understand who has done this. John please," she begged, but her son-in-law was busy helping the good Doctor, "please tell me what has happened." Her cries were muffled as the bedroom door closed behind them.

Inside, working frantically on Emma's wound, the Doctor shook his head wishing for silence, but Mrs. Dixon's pleading screams continued calling out John's name, a grievous sound that echoed through the newlywed's bedroom.

The Doctor then turned to John, "I must probe the wound for the bullet. Once I have completed that, then I will be able to determine the extent of her injury. I need an assistant. So steady yourself, young man."

John's voice was tight with grief.

"Anything you need. I'll do anything to save her."

The Doctor cut away the sleeve and upper portion of Emma's dress, politely peeling the material down to keep her breasts modestly covered; yet revealing the angry red wound. He then produced a long slender metal wand from the medical bag he habitually carried.

"Hold her down, if she moves. This will hurt. But it is necessary."

John watched, both hands carefully placed on his wife's limp body to restrain her, if need be, as Doc Hendrix gently placed the wand inside the bleeding wound that pierced Emma left shoulder. The sight made John's heart contract and clench.

Emma never moved, the shock of the blood loss and the painful wound rendering her unconscious. He slowly pushed the wand through the wound, gently prodding to see if the metal hit the bullet.

It was terrible to watch.

John kept his hands on her other shoulder and hip, just in case she moved, his gaze riveted on Emma's pale beautiful face, wishing it was him in that bed not her. He closed his eyes wishing this wasn't happening. But it was. That bullet meant to kill him had hit his wife, instead. His beautiful sweet Emma had saved his life, possibly sacrificing her own.

John could not imagine a life without her. She had become the center of his life, the object of his love, and his most trustworthy friend. She was his second chance. She had kept his secrets, loving him with all her heart. John knew her faithful devotion had changed him. Forever they were entwined in his terrible secret, yet she loved him unconditionally, never doubting that goodness lived inside his heart.

A second chance meant nothing without her.

He needed Emma his life. Without her, it would not be worth living.

The Doctor finally removed the metal probe from the wound, immediately putting a clean cloth on the shoulder, applying pressure to the bleeding hole. At his request for assistance, John helped lift Emma gently upright as the Doctor wrapped the shoulder tightly, pulling the cloth around her back and under her arm, then over the bullet hole again in a tightly bound circle intended to stop bleeding and to keep it clean.

When the Doctor was finished with the thick bandage, John reverently laid his wife back onto the bed. She still had not moved. Her breathing was shallow, and her dark lashes laying on her pale cheeks never fluttered open.

"There is no bullet or fragment inside the wound, it went clear through." The Doctor declared. "I cannot say for sure if she will recover. I am sorry, for she lost a lot of blood. Only time will tell. She needs many days of rest, but let's pray she soon regains consciousness."

"Is there any medicine you can give her?"

"No, until she regains consciousness I dare not give her anything for the pain. She needs to wake first. Then we will determine her medical needs."

Feeling at a loss, John simply offered his gratitude. "Thank you."

Doctor Hendrix looked pale and worried, too. "I will see to her mother and Old Sam, now. I fear Emma's mother is in shock. The rest is up to Emma, and to you, John." the exhausted physician advised, meeting his gaze with compassionate honesty. "It was said she brought you back to life, gave you a second chance. Now it's your turn."

John had sat on the edge of their bed, cradling Emma's hand in his. It felt cool and lifeless. His entire body ached to see his beautiful wife take a deep breath and open her lovely blue-green eyes.

The Doctor turned to exit the bedroom, but with his hand on the doorknob, he turned to John, as if suddenly recalling the important quest that had brought him to Richmond.

John saw deep regret etch the physician's care-worn face. "Yes, sir?"

The Doctor sighed and his shoulders slumped. "Where is he, John?"

"In the barn where it happened. He shot himself in the head after the bullet meant for me, found its way to Emma."

Doctor Hendrix hung his head.

"I should have seen this coming, I knew he wasn't well. He had endured too much death, too much suffering, too much pain for anyone to bear these four long years."

"That doesn't make his obsession for Emma right, nor his rantings against me. He may have been promised as a suitor to Emma, right here in this very house, but that promise died with her father on that Manassas battlefield. Emma remained a friend to the Doctor, but that was all her heart would allow. She loved him, not. He seemed to believe his skill as a surgeon and a healer would sway her heart, but it never did."

"No, it just proves the depth of his madness. He was another casualty of this war. It may be over, yet the scars of it still burn, still raging inside the hearts of the living." The Doctor still hesitated with his hand on the door, murmuring other thoughts to himself as he realized he had to tell Old Sam about the death of his close and dear friend, but John wasn't listening.

He only cared about Emma.

Finally, the door softly closed, and they were alone.

In the distance, lower in the house he could hear Emma's mother loudly questioning the Doctor, demanding answers to the terrible bloody fate that had befallen her daughter. Her voice made John cringe with guilt, but the agonizing cries of the Doctor's faithful friend Old Sam that pierced his heart the deepest. He heard the front door slam and the walls shook as Sam yelled loud denials of the mad Doctor's demise and ran from the house and towards the barn.

The pain and heartache rising from the horrified voices below brought a sting to his eyes.

His mother-in-law's heartbroken voice was for John, the emotional unleashing of all that had transpired. His stoic strength fled. He turned, dropping to his knees upon the floor beside the bed where he had loved Emma, where they had smiled and laughed, promising to love one another forever.

The pain of seeing her unmoving injured body gathered inside and burned deep in his soul. He fought the helpless feelings, but the heartache rose like an inferno through his chest and burst free into an agonized cry. Fearing others would hear, John gathered the edges of the comforter in his fists, burying his face in the cotton and his hands to muffle his devastated cries.

No one disturbed the grieving husband.

When John finally stopped yelling into his fists, he realized the entire house had grown quiet. Even Mrs. Dixon's sorrow had been subdued. A man's heartache is rarely expressed. The sound of it must have been shocking. Still, Emma lay pale and silent, her beautiful golden hair fanned out around her face.

"Darlin', never have I ever seen such a pure beauty," he softly admired, stroking one pale cheek with his fingertips. Her skin was cool and smooth. "You are as lovely and as perfect as one of God's angels."

She never stirred, never moved except those slow shallow, even breaths.

He held her still hand and spoke to her; softly at first, but soon gaining intensity as she continued to sleep. John poured his heart out to Emma. It became a heart wrenching plea from a young husband, whose wife married him knowing his dark truths, a wife who risked her life to bring his family back together, a woman he felt unworthy to love, yet she was his. Now, just when their life together was beginning, he was on the very brink of losing her.

This heartache was worse than anything John knew a man could feel.

He rocked back and forth on the floor, whispering to her, "Dearest Emma, what for life has given you to me and now it could so cruelly take you away? I cannot allow it to be true. And for what reason, other than a madman who you so greatly feared, has made his presence known to us. In an attempt to kill me, he has reached out to take you. No, my love, I cannot believe life would be so cruel. Not to you. Never to you."

John stroked her hand and rose to the edge of the bed, letting his voice come close to her ear. "Emma, listen to me, it's John. Come back to me Emma. You must live," he pled, yet she remained still and silent.

"Remember how you told me to live at the hospital? I had given up and did not want to go on. You willed me back to life, Emma. You loved me, offered me a second chance, and brought me back from the dead. Even after you knew my truth, who I really was and what I had done, you still risked everything to be with me, knowing that life with me would be that of vagabond, living in far-off countries and never again seeing your family's faces. You did it all for love, and all for being Mrs. John Wilkes Booth."

Saying it aloud put a lump in his throat.

For several moments, the words that normally came so easily to his lips fled. John lay a hand on her ribs, just below the swell of her left breast, relieved to feel her heart beat beneath his hand.

She was alive, but drifting in the dark of unconsciousness.

"You risked so much for me, so now my dearest Emma you must listen to me. Open your eyes and look at me. I beg you to see me, I beg you." John's voice staggered and broke as he slid from her side, kneeling once again on the floor.

His sobs emanating from his body were those of a lost soul, a wounded and grievous heart. He no longer cared who heard. Nothing mattered but Emma. His cries were wrenching and soulful, pleading with his wife to open her eyes.

While he sobbed uncontrollably, he felt a light touch on his hand, a caress like the silky touch of a feather. John gasped, as hope froze in his chest. He looked up and saw Emma's hand instinctively move to touch his.

"Emma!"

Rising to her side, he watched in breathless wonder as she fluttered her eyes. Her breath deepened, forcing life back into her pale skin as the cries of her beloved husband awoke her from unconsciousness. John knelt over her, gently stroking her face, whispering and waiting for her to come back to him.

She fought the darkened veil of death, yet did not entirely wake.

"Please," he begged. "Come back to me, my love."

The hand clutched in his gave a tiny squeeze.

"Yes, Emma. I'm here."

He touched the medal that hung on her neck, golden and gleaming in the afternoon light, and cried out pleading to all who might hear, "Lamb of God, you saved my unworthy soul three times, once from an injury on the stage, then from the burning barn that assured my death, and then from the fevered state of malaria. I never asked for your mercy. Yet now I beg of you to heal my wife. Bring her back to me, I beg of you!"

The blue-green eyes he adored fluttered.

Then they miraculously opened.

Her gaze was confused at first, but quickly she focused on her husband's face. Emma sweetly smiled at him and slowly drew a strengthening breath. "My darling John," she whispered, "you must not weep so. I am here. I love you. I will not leave you."

John thought his heart would burst with joy. Instead, it overflowed until that love glistened with wet tears that cascaded down his handsome face. "Emma, you have come back to me; just as I came back to you," he smiled through the joyful tears, "my heart is yours; willing you to live for me, and only me."

A lazy satisfied smile spread across her beautiful face. It was sly, almost as if Emma had a secret. "Well now John, tis not just you I live for now, dear husband."

John suddenly felt confused. "Darling, I don't understand."

Emma opened her eyes fully, the blue in them shining with life and love for him. With a graceful movement, she waved her hand across her body. Her right hand settled low on her belly, at the place where a woman's body held the miracle of life.

"I hope he has your eyes," she smiled, "I hope our baby has your eyes."

It was June, 1865.

Thank you for reading

"My Name is John Singer."

The Author, Lisa G. Samia invites you to enjoy reading the historical biographies and her research on the following pages that explain her personal experience writing this fictional tale that includes historical photos of John Wilkes Booth, his sister Asia Booth, Clarke, the writer Lousia May Alcott, and the talented poet Walt Whitman.

Biographies and Author Insights

Louisa May Alcott

The inspiration for "My Name is John Singer" truly came from an unlikely source. I was completely and pleasantly surprised to discover in my research of all things Civil War, I discovered that Louisa May Alcott, the author of "Little Women", had worked as a Civil War nurse for about six weeks in Georgetown in Washington DC.

This information availed itself to me in a book penned by Ms. Alcott called "Hospital Sketches". This book or collection of sketches are actually four letters written to Louisa's father while Louisa worked at the Hospital. They are a collection of the author's feelings and observations while working as a duty nurse.

While the sketches detailed her journey to Washington DC and the dismal appearance of our Nation's Capital during the war, there were several descriptions of some of the patients that she nursed that I believe was the center piece of her letters.

There is one sketch however that has stayed with me since the first time I read it and still continues to compel me. It was in my mind the inspiration for "My Name is John Singer."

In this sketch Louisa describes her interaction with a vital and handsome Virginia man named John, with bonny brown hair and eyes like a child.

She quickly realizes her initial observation that his wound was not serious was medically dispelled by the hospital surgeon who regrettably informed her he would die a slow and painful death. It is my understanding that there was an injury to the lung that was fatal.

Louisa was incredulous that such a vital man should die. Resolved to that sobering fact, Louisa sat and nursed John for three days until he passed. Her grief at his passing moved me and touched my heart, as she was holding onto John's hand for such a time after his death, that the Hospital physician came to remind Louisa "It is not good to mingle the living with the dead". She also mentions the imprint of John's grasping hand on hers long after he had passed, vivid and heartbreaking.

So in thinking of the beginnings of "My name is John Singer" Louisa's John and her description of what I could see was a very handsome man and her deep feelings of grief were at the root of this fictional account of John Wilkes Booth. I introduced the fictional Emma Dixon as a nurse working in an Alexandria VA hospital and introduce John Singer as the man hiding in plain sight as John Wilkes Booth.

But because of Louisa's inspiration, I reintroduced her into this story, only her beloved John is now named Jack who is a Virginia blacksmith from nearby Charlottesville VA. Her interaction with fictional Jack is a love story that was not meant to be, and the agonizing realization of love found and lost.

Louisa's presence in this fictional account has her returning to this hospital at the end of the Civil War to say goodbye to her former co-workers at the hospital and to visit Jack's grave to say farewell once more.

Her presence in the book is one of a kind and deeply compassionate person; it was for me a natural way to write about her based on that one sketch, that one interaction with a certain handsome vital Virginia blacksmith, with the bonny brown hair and eyes of a child.

Their images filled my heart with grief and sorrow yet burned into my thoughts to create such a scene as I brought them both forth to live once again.

Hospital Sketches by Louisa May Alcott (1832-1888). Boston: James Redpath, Publisher, 221 Washington Street, 1863.

Asia Booth Clarke

Asia Booth Clark was the older sister to John Wilkes Booth. History tells us she was about two years old before her parents Junius Brutus Booth, a famous actor and tragedian, and Mary Ann Holmes Booth decided on her name. It was her father Junius who initially thought Aisha after the Prophet Muhammed's favorite and youngest wife and her middle name as Frigga because she was born on a Friday. They eventually agreed on Asia Frigga Booth.

She was simply put, a sensitive young woman given to "sulks" yet by all accounts was a loving and devoted sibling and daughter. Her insights found in her book "The Unlocked Book, A Memoir of John Wilkes Booth" were laced with her memories and recollection of her life on the family farm at Tudor Hall in Bel Air, Maryland. Her description of her brother John, just two year younger were also invaluable insights into the young John Wilkes Booth. They were extraordinarily close and remained so even after they left the farm at Tudor Hall.

It was these vivid descriptions of her brother John on the farm when they were young that revealed to me a John Wilkes Booth I have never known.

History tells us of the heinous deed he committed when assassinated President Lincoln, yet that was all I knew of him. It was Asia and her writings that showed a unexplored side of John, the disconnect for me between him growing up as a loving son, sibling, friend and great actor to committing what could possibly be the most heinous act in American History, was one in which for me had no explanation. It still does not.

Because of Asia love of her brother John, in my fictional account, I have brought Asia into the story with her not wanting to believe her loving brother John could have committed such an act; even though all facts state he was murdered at Garrett's Farm.

The suffering I have brought forth in Asia is what I believe is the pain she actually went through after his horrendous deed. However, in my fictional account, I brought both brother and sister to meet once again with "John Singer" prevailing upon his sister Asia, that he was indeed alive and tried to explain to her the unexplainable.

In this adaptation, I have Asia as forgiving to her brother and his crime, working to find a way to help him leave the United States and live. Her great ability to forgive his deed, expose herself and family to treason, was in fact for me an adventure into that part of her. I believed she loved John above and beyond his crime.

But History tells us her grief was inconsolable. Asia left the United States in 1868 with her husband John Sleeper Clarke and her children, Asia, Edwin, Adrienne, Clarke, Lillian, Wilfred and Joan to reside in the English countryside.

Her children in my account are purely fictional.

Unfortunately her life there was not a happy one, isolated from her family in the United States and a growing isolation with her husband. She died at the age of fifty two in 1888.

Her last request to her children was to be buried in the United States at Greenmount cemetery in Baltimore Maryland, where the Booth family had their plot. Specific to her last request of being buried there, she was laid to rest next to her brother John who is buried there in the Booth plot in an unmarked grave.

Asia Frigga Clarke née Booth (November 19, 1835, Bel Air, Maryland – May 16, 1888, Bournemouth, England)

Clarke, Asia Booth. THE UNLOCKED BOOK: A MEMOIR OF JOHN WILKES BOOTH BY HIS SISTER…. New York: 1938. 1st ed., 205p., ft., plates. [M3611] Asia Booth Clarke's memoir of her brother John Wilkes Booth has been recognized as the single most important document available for understanding the personality of the assassin of Lincoln.

Walt Whitman

Walt Whitman presence in John Singer as himself, writer and sometimes nurse during the Civil War, was for me a journey brought forth from his interaction with President Lincoln.

Although history tells us he never met President Lincoln, he saw him some twenty or thirty times during his Presidency riding through Washington DC or to his summer retreat at the Soldier's Home.

His description of their meetings was summed up by Whitman stating "I see the President almost every day," he wrote in the summer of 1863. "We have got so that we exchange bows, and very cordial ones." Once Lincoln gave Whitman a long friendly stare. "He has a face like a Hoosier Michel Angelo," Whitman wrote, "so awful ugly it becomes beautiful, with its strange mouth, its deep cut, criss-cross lines, and its doughnut complexion."

There was, Whitman wrote, "a deep latent sadness in the expression." He was "very easy, flexible, tolerant, almost slouch, respecting the minor matters," but capable of "indomitable firmness (even obstinacy) on rare occasions, involving great points."

He was a family man but had an air of complete independence: "He went his own lonely road," Whitman said, "disregarding all the usual ways—refusing the guides, accepting no warnings—just keeping his appointment with himself every time." His "composure was marvelous" in the face of unpopularity and great difficulties during the war.

He had what Whitman saw as a profoundly religious quality. His "mystical foundations" were "mystical, abstract, moral and spiritual," and his "religious nature" was "of the amplest, deepest-rooted, loftiest kind." Summing Lincoln up, Whitman called him "the greatest, best, most characteristic, artistic, moral personality" in American life.

It was this admiration for the President and especially the line "a deep latent sadness in the expression", that was remarkable in its vivid imagery of Lincoln. So much so, that I brought forth Walt Whitman in my fictional account as to continue the sag of Mr. Whitman's' pain at the assassination of the President and to show his inconsolable grief.

In my fictional account, it was Mr. Whitman that initially believed that John Singer could be John Wilkes Booth.

Through his grief and defense of the President Mr. Whitman called out to John Singer his incredible resemblance to John Wilkes Booth. His moving poem recited to "John Singer," "Oh Captain! My Captain!" about the death of Lincoln was important. I again brought forth this historical writing as to strengthen his resolve to the loss of his friend as well as his grief over the loss of so many men.

Walt Whitman and his words and actions impacted me as I moved forward to create this story. His ability with his writing to make me see the pain he so eloquent describes in the President's eyes was for me too moving and heartbreaking not to once again try to bring back to life.

Walt Whitman- Occupation Journalist, Poet (May 31, 1819 - March 26, 1892)
David S. Reynolds, The Gilder Lehrman Institute of American History – Lincoln and Whitman

John Wilkes Booth

While History tells us that John Wilkes Booth acted alone (albeit in conjunction with several conspirators) to decapitate the Government at the end of the Civil War, in my fictional account I have placed the secret Confederate Society the Knights of the Golden Circle at the helm of this most horrifying deed. Also, in this fictional account Booth is repentant for the crime he committed, something of course History tells us not true.

Yet in all the research and reading I did preparing to write this story, a nagging feeling prevailed upon me, in such a way that the disconnect from John's youth to becoming a young actor was growing wider and wider as I read of how incensed he was of President Lincoln, the defeat of the south and the freeing of the slaves.

Yes he was a southern sympathizer most assuredly, yet the path travelled from a loving sibling, son, friend and highly regarded actor to moving forward to plan, conspire and follow through to assassinate the President was most assuredly a path of life choices that once again to me left me with more questions than answers.

The world will never know the truth.

History tells us John was the favorite of the Booth household, the ninth of ten children born to Junius and Mary Ann Booth. He was a lover of animals. As an adult it is written John watched in horror as a man in a wagon beat his horse while trying to move him from the mud. John saw this and punched the man for beating the animal.

Also one day, upon leaving Ford's Theater in costume on his way to the telegraph office, saw a small boy lost perhaps but plainly poor, John picked up the small child to him, hugged him, stood him up and gave him a few coins before running on his way.

Another story of his compassion for others is told in which an equally poor young boy selling programs at Ford's Theater was shivering in the cold. John came upon the boy and took him to the haberdasher's to fit in a proper news cap to keep the child warm.

And it is recorded that with sister's Asia' children, having placed a picture of himself above their beds and John reminded them to "Pray for me babies."

These and instances like these prevailed through my thoughts as I prepared to write his story.

There are still theories that believe he did escape the barn that another confederate sympathizer took his place, and there was a government cover-up to that effect.

Again, these are questions without any real answers.

In order for my story to work, I in turn used these theories, writing that John escaped the barn at Garrett's farm, and was hiding in plain sight in an Alexandria, VA hospital. Or was he?

In this adaptation, Booth is repentant for his crime, suffering silently in recounting the actions that led him to the hospital, asking God if it was by some trick of fate he was alive.

He does of course realize his fate to hide in plain sight. The uniform he stole from the dead confederate on his flight out to the barn will forever now cause him to be known as John Singer. His family is dead to him, all those who knew and loved him he would never see again. Lost forever for the crime he so boldly committed.

Yet the Booth I had read about from sister's Asia's recollections on their life at Tudor Hall, with his capacity for friendship and love, once again nagged at me to recreate this man and bring him back to life; all at once repentant and yearning to save his life from the burning desperation within his soul.

Be that as it may, I am not sure romancing the man known as John Wilkes Booth has ever been done, the fine line walked most certainly in romanticizing the man not his heinous crime, he was for me the most compelling of men in history.

In this fictional account, I believed there was but one thing that could save him, and that was love.

For in the end, isn't love all we really have?

John Wilkes Booth (May 10, 1838-April 26,1865)

About the Author

Lisa G. Samia

Lisa G. Samia is an Award Winning Author who loves American History. She devoted three years travelling, researching and writing the fictional novel based on John Wilkes Booth "*My Name is John Singer.*"

She graduated from the University of Massachusetts with a degree in English and has appeared on local television multiple times for her writing. A Boston native, she is happily married and lives in Avon, CT.

Lisa is also an accomplished poet. Her full-color book "*The Man with Ice Blue Eyes*" released July 2016, is a compelling collection of love poems and beautiful artwork that touch and pierce the heart. She is currently working on a sequel to "My Name is John Singer."

www.DestinyNovels.com
www.DestinyAuthor.us
www.LisaSamia.com

*This exterior photo was taken April 2016 by the author,
Lisa G. Samia on her tour of John Wilkes Booth's family home,
Tudor Hall located in Bel Air, MD*

ACCOMPLISHMENTS:

- Author of "*Don't Be Afraid of Fifty*," -- The Twelve Step Process to Turning Fifty.
- Appeared on CT-FOX 61 morning news program, WFSB Channel 3, Better CT and multiple times at WTNH Channel 8, Connecticut Style.
- Appeared on two Cable access channels; West Hartford, CT discussing "*Don't Be Afraid of Fifty*" and appeared in Guilford, CT discussing the award winning essay "*My Tiny Pieces of Wood*".
- Multiple book signings at Connecticut area Barnes and Noble's including Glastonbury, West Hartford and Canton and The Eastern States Exposition (The Big E) in Springfield, MA.
- Awards from the Connecticut Authors and Publishers Association Writing Contest 2013-2014 2nd place Essay and Honorable Mention Poetry; 2014-2015 1st place Poetry.

- Member of the following Historical Societies:
    - Ford's Theater, Washington, DC
    - Lincoln Cottage, Washington, DC
    - The Surratt Society, Clinton, MD
    - The Junius Brutus Booth Society (Tudor Hall), Bel Air, MD
- Graduate of University of Massachusetts Boston. Originally from Boston MA and currently resides in Avon, CT.

HISTORICAL PHOTO CREDITS

John Wilkes Booth –
Wikipedia / https://en.wikipedia.org/wiki/John_Wilkes_Booth
Wikimedia Commons
https://commons.wikimedia.org/wiki/Category:John_Wilkes_Booth
https://commons.wikimedia.org/wiki/Category:John_Wilkes_Booth#/media/File:
John_Wilkes_Booth_1865.jpg
https://commons.wikimedia.org/wiki/Category:John_Wilkes_Booth#/media/File:
John_Wilkes_Booth_cph.3a26098.jpg
https://commons.wikimedia.org/wiki/Category:John_Wilkes_Booth#/media/
File:John_Wilkes_Booth_CDV_by_Black_%26_Case.jpg
HistoryNet.com http://www.historynet.com/john-wilkes-booth

Asia Booth Clarke – Wikipedia / Wikimedia Commons
BoothieBarn https://boothiebarn.com/picture-galleries/booth-family/asia/

Walt Whitman –Wikipedia / Wikimedia Commons
https://commons.wikimedia.org/wiki/File:Whitman_at_about_fifty.jpg
https://commons.wikimedia.org/wiki/Walt_Whitman

Louisa May Alcott –Wikipedia / Wikimedia Commons
https://commons.wikimedia.org/wiki/Louisa_May_Alcott#/media/File:Louisa
_May_Alcott_headshot.jpg
Province Public Library -- http://www.provlib.org/news/coming-falllouisa-
may-alcott-woman-behind-little-women

CPSIA information can be obtained
at www.ICGtesting.com
Printed in the USA
FSOW03n1151240218
44661FS